Stripped of her family, her lover, her home and her title, Princess Anghara is condemned to wander the Earth. Her only name now is Indigo, and even in her deepest grief she may not rest, nor may she hope for death. Remorse is not enough: there can be no respite for her until the seven evils released by her hand are conquered and destroyed.

Now, in a land where sullen, volcanic fires simmer deep within the earth, Indigo must face an alien power that warps the minds and bodies of all who fall under its baleful spell.

Only by calling on a fire as dark yet more hideously ancient can she hope to eradicate its corruption. But fire burns. Can Indigo control the flames? Or will the wrath that blazes within her prove more deadly than the demon she is pledged to defeat?

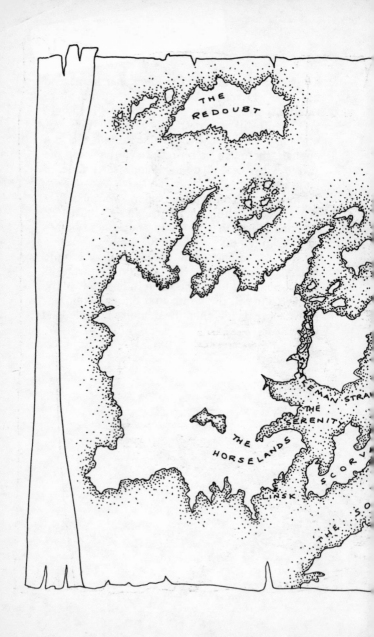

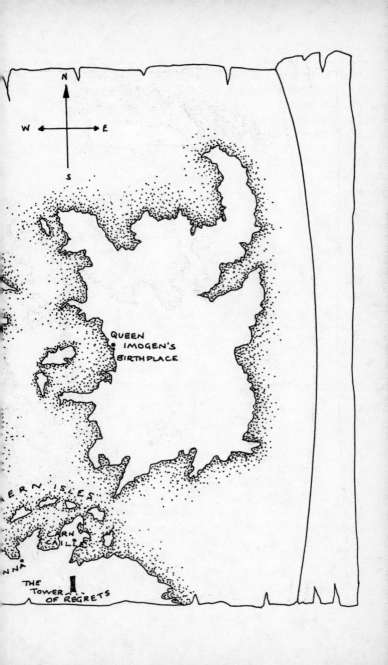

# INFERNO

## Book 2 of

## INDIGO

**LOUISE COOPER**

UNWIN
PAPERBACKS

LONDON SYDNEY WELLINGTON

First published in Great Britain by Unwin Paperbacks, an
imprint of Unwin Hyman Limited, in 1988

**UNWIN HYMAN LIMITED**
15–17 Broadwick Street, London W1V 1FP

Allen & Unwin Pty Ltd
8 Napier Street, North Sydney, NSW 2060, Australia

Allen & Unwin New Zealand Pty Ltd with the Port Nicholson Press
60 Cambridge Terrace, Wellington, New Zealand

**British Library Cataloguing in Publication Data**

Cooper, Louise, *1952–*
Inferno.
I. Title   II. Series
823′.914[F]
ISBN 0–04–440157–4

Set in 10 on 11 point Times by Input Typesetting, London
and printed in Great Britain by
Cox & Wyman Ltd, Reading.

We are dancing on a volcano.
Narcisse Achille Salvandy, 1795–1856


**For Gary**
who makes the dance worthwhile

# Prologue

*On a lonely and barren stretch of tundra, where the borders of a small kingdom meet the vast ice-ramparts of the southern glaciers, the ruins of a solitary tower cast their unnatural shadow across the plain. The Tower of Regrets – it has no other title – was the handiwork of a man whose name is now long forgotten; for, as the old bardic story goes, his was a time, a time and a time, before we who live now under the sun and the sky came to count time.*

*In those ancient days, mankind's foolishness and greed brought his world to the brink of ruin. At last Nature herself rose up against him, and the Earth Mother wrought her vengeance upon the children who had betrayed Her trust. But through the dark night of Her retribution, the tower remained unsullied. And when it was done, and a wiser mankind raised his head from the wreckage of his own folly to begin life afresh in a cleansed and untainted world, the tower became a symbol of hope, for within its walls the evils which man had made were at last confined.*

*For centuries, then, the Tower of Regrets stood alone upon the plain, and no man or woman dared turn their face towards it, for fear of the ancient curse that lay within. And so it might have remained – but for the recklessness of a king's foolish daughter.*

*Her title then was the Princess Anghara Kaligs-daughter; but now she has forfeited the right to name and heritage. For she broke the one law that had endured since her people's history began, when she* breached the sanctity of that aeon-old tower in a bid to learn its secret.

Oh, yes; the princess had her wish, and the secret was revealed to her. But as its chains were released, the Tower of Regrets sheared in two – and mankind's ancient curse came shrieking from darkness to fasten again upon the world, and upon the soul of Anghara Kaligsdaughter.

In the black night of the curse's reawakening Anghara lost hearth and home, liege and love, to that deadly power. And with the coming of the dawn she took upon her young shoulders a burden that now haunts her day and night, waking and sleeping. For the Earth Mother has decreed that she must make reparation for her crime, by seeking out and slaying the seven demons which came laughing into the world when the Tower of Regrets fell.

Seven demons; seven evils which, if not destroyed, will cast mankind back into the dark history of his own folly. Anghara is Anghara no longer. Her name now is Indigo – the colour of mourning – and her home is the world itself, for she has forfeited all claim to the hearth at which she was born.

Indigo cannot die. Nor will she age or change, for while her quest remains unfulfilled she is doomed to immortality. She has one friend, who is not human. And she has one enemy that will dog her footsteps wherever she may go, for it is a part of herself, created from the blackest depths of her own soul. The eighth demon – her Nemesis.

Five years have passed since Indigo looked for the last time on the mellow stones of Carn Caille, stronghold of the kings of the Southern Isles and her one-time home. A new liege rules there now, and the legend of the Tower of Regrets no longer exists; for the Earth Mother has decreed that all memory of the tower's fall, together with all knowledge of its true purpose, should be erased from the mind of man. Thus King Ryen instructs his bards to compose sad ballads of the fever

2

*that took the lives of Kalig's old dynasty. And he grieves for them as is right and proper, never suspecting that one of that old dynasty still lives.*

*But Carn Caille is barred to Indigo. Instead she has set her face northward into the hot heartlands of the great western continent, in search of the first of her demons; the first of her trials. Guided only by the lodestone which was the Earth Mother's gift to her, Indigo journeys and Indigo seeks.*

*And wherever her wanderings lead her, Nemesis is never far behind . . .*

# Chapter I

The arid heat of the night made sleep impossible for the she-wolf Grimya. She lay under the shelter of an overhanging rock, nose on front paws, tail occasionally twitching in discomfort, and gazed down the slope, past the clumps of stunted and ill-nourished bushes to the empty, dusty road and the slow river beyond. She had seen the moon rise, full and distorted to the shape and hue of a blood-orange in the shimmering air, and had watched it track across the sky among showers of alien stars until it hung, a glaring and hostile eye, above her. In stony crevices small reptiles stirred sluggishly and intermittently, as though the moon disturbed their dreams; Grimya was hungry, but lassitude overcame the hunting urge. She closed her eyes, trying to think of rain, of snow, of the green forests and cold, rushing streams of her homeland. But time and distance were coming between her and her memories: the forests of the Horselands were too far and too long away, lost in ever more dreamlike recollections of the distant south.

The bay pony tethered to a bush a few yards away swished its tail, one hoof scraping on stone, and the she-wolf opened her eyes again. Nothing to cause alarm; the pony dozed, head down, and the movement had been no more than a reflex. Grimya yawned cavernously. Then as though troubled by some deeper instinct she turned her head, looking back over her shoulder to the figure huddled on the worn blanket behind her.

The young woman slept with her head pillowed on the pony's saddle. Her long hair, which showed streaks of a warm auburn among the predominant grey, was brushed back from her face, and the uncertain moonlight gave her, momentarily, a peaceful look. Lines of strain were smoothed away, her mouth was relaxed, and echoes of a lost innocence and beauty seemed to shine through the contours of her cheeks and jaw. But the peacefulness was an illusion, and within moments the illusion shattered as the girl's lips trembled and the old shadow returned to her face. One hand clenched unconsciously into a fist, then opened again and reached out as though she sought to take and hold the fingers of an unseen companion. She found nothing, and as her hand fell back again she whimpered as though in distress.

Lost in another, crueller world, guarded under the hot moon by her only friend, Indigo dreamed.

*How long has it been, Indigo who was Anghara?*

'Five years . . .' The sigh took chilly wing and drifted away into emptiness.

*Five years, child. Five years since your crime brought this burden upon your shoulders. You have come a long way since those old, lost days.*

She saw the faces then as she had seen them so many times before, moving in slow procession past her inner eye. Kalig, king of the Southern Isles, her father; Imogen, his queen, her mother. Her brother Kirra, who would have been king in his time. Others: warriors, huntsmen, servants, all those who had died with their liege-lord at Carn Caille. A sad parade of ghosts.

And then, as she had known there must, came another, his dark eyes tormented, his black hair lank with sweat, the strength of his body broken and twisted by pain. She felt something within her constrict and tried to cry out against the vision and look away. But she couldn't. And involuntarily her lips formed a name.

'Fenran . . . ?'

Her lover looked into her eyes, once, and there was

6

such longing in his expression that Indigo felt her own eyes, in her dream, start with tears. Their marriage had been only a month away when she had lost him. They would have been long wed now, and happy, if only . . .

She reached out – as, in the physical world, one hand groped for a companion who was not there – and her fingers closed on empty air as Fenran faded and was gone.

'No.' She could barely articulate the word; though the nightmare was familiar, she could never inure herself to it. 'No, please . . .'

*It must be, child. Until the seven demons you released from the Tower of Regrets are destroyed, your love cannot be free. You know it is a part of your burden and your curse.*

She turned away, hating the voice that spoke to her, the voice of the Earth Mother's bright emissary; yet aware that no power in the world could deny the veracity of its words.

*When it is done, Indigo. When the demons are no more. Then you may know peace.*

She felt tears prick her eyes, her throat grow hot and stifling. 'How long? Great Mother, *how long?*'

*As long as it must be. Five years. Ten. A hundred. A thousand. Until it is done.*

In the sharp-edged twilight of her dreams the question and the answer were always the same. Time had no meaning, for she would not age. She was as she had been on that last day on the southern tundra beyond Carn Caille – the day when anger and recklessness and folly had conspired to lead her to the ancient tower, and to the wanton shattering of her world. She heard again the titanic voice of splintering stone as the Tower of Regrets cracked open; saw again the boiling, thundering cloud of blackness that was not smoke but something far, far worse erupting from the ruin's rocking chaos; felt again the insane goad of panic as she fled,

7

lashing her horse's neck, back towards the fortress, back towards her kin, back towards –

*the carnage and the horror as warped things that had no place in a sane world broke like a tidal wave over the walls of Carn Caille to rend and to tear and to burn. They were coming, the nightmares, the foul things; they were coming and there was nowhere to hide, nowhere to run, nowhere –*

She came out of the dream screaming, her body jack-knifed by a muscular spasm so that her back slammed painfully against the rock behind her. The world of the nightmare burst apart and, gasping, Indigo opened her eyes to the purple sky and the indifferent, unfamiliar constellations, and to the vast silence and the heat that crawled like something alive over her torso and across her thighs and into the webs between her fingers.

And met the lambent golden gaze of the she-wolf, who stood over her, quivering with unhappy concern.

'Grimya . . .' The relief of realising that the dream was broken was so strong that for a moment she felt giddy with it. She struggled into a sitting position, unpleasantly aware of her garments clinging, clammy with humidity, to her skin, and reached out to slide an arm over the wolf's shoulders.

Grimya's sides heaved. 'You w-were . . . *dreaming*?' The words that issued from her throat were stilted and guttural, but clearly recognisable; for Grimya had been born with the extraordinary ability to understand and speak human tongues. The mutation had made her a pariah among her own kind, but since her first meeting with Indigo – long ago, in a land that was now little more than a green and woody memory in the she-wolf's mind – the curse of it had become, instead, a blessing, for it had bonded her to the only true friend she had ever known in her life.

'Dreaming.' Indigo echoed Grimya's last word, pressing her face against the wolf's soft fur until the threat of a shaking fit subsided. 'Yes. It was the same dreams again, Grimya.'

'I . . . know.' Grimya licked her face. 'I w-watched you. I th . . . *ought* to wake you, but . . .' Her tongue lolled with painful effort as she tried to cope with syllables for which her larynx had not been designed. Indigo hugged her again.

'It's all right. They're gone now.' She suppressed a shiver that tried to assail her despite the oppressive heat, then looked about her, blinking against the gritty ache of tired eyes. To the east the stars were still bright; no sign yet of any paling in the sky's vast velvet backdrop.

'We should try to sleep for a while longer,' she said.

'But if the . . . dr-dreams should c . . . come back . . .'

'I don't think they will.' Now now; not now. She knew the pattern all too well, and in all this time of travelling it had not changed.

*But if . . .*

This time the shiver wouldn't be denied, and she dug the nails of one hand sharply into the back of the other, angry with herself for allowing the shadowy fear which lurked at the back of her mind to affect her again. As she had done often during the past few nights, Indigo looked northward to where the landscape was broken by the ragged silhouettes of mountain peaks in the distance. Beyond the first of those peaks, and etching them with phosphorescence, the sky was touched by a thin, eerie glow as though some vast but muffled light-source lurked just below the horizon. But no sun, moon or star had ever shone with such cold nacre: this pallid light looked treacherous, unnatural, an – the word came to Indigo's mind as it had done before, and no rationality could entirely banish it – an abomination.

Hardly aware of the gesture, she touched one hand to her throat and her fingers closed around a worn thong from which a small leather bag depended. Within the bag was a stone, apparently nothing more than a small brown pebble veined with traces of copper and pyrites. But within the stone's depths was something

9

else, something that manifested as a tiny pinpoint of gold light: something that was guiding her, inexorably, towards a goal from which she could not – *dared* not – turn aside. The stone was her most valued and most hated possession. And each day, as the sun slipped down the brass bowl of the sky, that tiny golden light began to agitate in its prison, calling her, urging her northward. Towards the mountains. Towards the nacreous light. Towards the abomination.

The pony stamped restively, and broke Indigo's uneasy trance. She snatched her hand away from the thong, feeling the bag with its precious contents tap against her breastbone, and tore her gaze from the distant mountains. Grimya was watching her, and as a new shudder racked Indigo's frame the she-wolf said anxiously: 'You are c-*cold*?'

She smiled, touched by her friend's simple concern. 'No. I was thinking about what may await us tomorrow.'

'Tomorrow is another day. Why thi . . . *ink* of it until we m-must?'

Despite her mood, Indigo laughed softly. 'I believe you're wiser than I am, Grimya.'

'N-no. But sometimes maybe I . . . see more clearly.' The she-wolf nudged her muzzle against the girl's cheek. 'You sh . . . should sleep now. I will watch.'

Feeling a little like a child shepherded by a fond nurse – and the sensation was comforting, even though it touched on old, raw memories – Indigo lay down once more. Grimya turned about; she heard claws scrabble lightly on the rock, felt the wolf's moon-shadow settle over her, and scents of dry stone and dusty fur and her own heat-prickled skin mingled in her nostrils. Another dawn, another day. Don't think about it until you must . . .

Her fingers clenched, relaxed, and the arid world faded as she closed her eyes and slipped away into a dreamless sleep.

By mid-morning, the stillness that lay over the land was absolute. For a while a small, capricious breeze had raised the dust a little, but now even that was defeated by the vast heat, and the sun, an angry eye in a sky the colour of molten iron, glared down through air that was stifled and motionless.

Indigo knew that they must stop soon and find a place to shelter from the burning midday temperatures; but she was reluctant to leave the road until she must. From the carved stones set at intervals along the way she guessed that they had little more than five miles to travel before reaching the town ahead, and she was anxious not to prolong this wearying journey. She longed for shade, for something other than sere rock on which to rest – and above all, she longed for cool, clean water to wash away the sweat and dust which felt ingrained in every pore of her skin.

Six days had passed now since they had set out on the northern road from the province city of Agia, and their route had taken them through the most barren landscape that Indigo had ever seen. At her homeland far away in the south they would be celebrating Hawthorn-Month, the time of new leaves, fresh grass, the birth and growth of young animals; but in this country such a concept had little meaning. For some miles beyond Agia's walls brave efforts had been made to cultivate and irrigate the thin, red-brown soil; there were terraces of grapevines, stands of sturdy, dark-leaved fruit trees, patches of crimson or vivid green where vegetable crops defied the searing heat. But soon even these lost their hold, giving way to rock, dust and scrub that stretched away to the distant foothills of the mountains. And once the last few fields had fallen behind and vanished in the heat haze, there was nothing to be seen but unending barrenness.

The rhythm of her pony's slow but steady gait was hypnotic, and several times in the last few minutes Indigo had had to shake herself out of a heavy, heat-induced stupor. In an attempt to keep the weariness at

11

bay she changed her position on her mount's back, then looked at the river flowing no more than twenty yards away beside the track. Yesterday, when the paths of road and river had first converged, she had wanted to climb down the rocky bank and bathe in the water; but Grimya's urgent warning had held her back. *Unclean*, the she-wolf had said. *It is dead water – it will do you harm!* And, looking now at the brown, churning rush of the current, Indigo realised how right she had been. Unnatural colours moved in the water's depths, effluvium from the vast mineral mines that lay among the volcanic mountains brooding in the distance, from whence the river flowed. Nothing could live in that polluted current: the only life that the river carried now was the human crews of the big, slow barges that brought their loads of smelted ore out of the mining region.

One such convoy had passed them the previous day; four massive, grimy vessels roped one behind another, the leading barge guided by eight taciturn oarsmen who sculled their craft skilfully in the centre of the current. They had spared no more than a single disinterested glance for the solitary rider on the road: dressed in the loose, belted robe that was the everyday garb of men, women and children alike in these hot lands, her hair hidden under a broad-brimmed hat draped with white linen to shield her from the sun, Indigo might have been any good citizen of Agia journeying to a market, a fair, a family wedding or funeral. And the grey and shaggy creature loping in her pony's shadow was nothing more than an unusually large dog, a guardian that might accompany any wise traveller to protect them from thieves or vagabonds.

Now, however, the river and the road were empty of all traffic, and the quiet as the day grew on was intense. No birds sang; not even a lizard moved among the rocky scree that flanked the track. Sunlight reflected dazzlingly from the river's sliding surface and

Indigo turned her gaze away from the water, her eyes aching from the glare.

*We should halt soon.* The heat had made Grimya too breathless to speak aloud; instead she resorted to the telepathic link they shared. Her mental voice intruded on the girl's sleepy mind and she realised that she had been on the verge of dozing in the saddle again. *The pony is tired. And the sun is beginning to affect you, too.*

Indigo looked down at the she-wolf, and nodded. 'You're right, Grimya. I'm sorry: I'd hoped to reach the town without resting again, but it was a foolish idea.' Groping behind her, she laid a hand on the comforting shape of her waterskin. 'We'll find a little shade, and sit out the worst of the heat.'

*Beyond that overhang there may be some trees,* Grimya said. *They offer better shelter than rocks. I am hungry. I think when I have rested I shall* – and she stopped.

'Grimya?' Indigo reined the pony in as she saw that her friend had stopped and was staring intently at the empty road ahead. 'What is it? What's wrong?'

Grimya's ears were pricked forward: she showed her teeth in an uncertain gesture. *Someone comes.* Her nostrils flared. *I smell them. And I hear them. This is something I do not like!*

The girl's pulse quickened arhythmically and she glanced quickly about her. Prudence urged her to find a hiding place, but there was nowhere among the rocks where even Grimya could be concealed, let alone a horse. Whatever approached, they must meet it.

She looked at the wolf again and saw that her hackles had risen. Slowly, forcing herself to stay quite calm, she reached behind her and unlooped the crossbow that hung on her back, bringing it round to lie across her lap. The metal of the bolts in her quiver was almost too hot to touch, but she managed to fit one into the bow, and drew back the string. The heavy click as she set the bolt was comforting, but she hoped she wouldn't have occasion to use it. So far, her journey had been peaceful; to run into trouble so close to her destination would be painfully ironic. Then, cautiously, she urged the pony on.

She heard the newcomers, as Grimya had already done, before she saw them. The first intimation of their approach came with snatches of a peculiar, ululating chant that rose and fell in chaotic discords, as though some bizarre choir were trying to sing a song that was unfamiliar to them. Then, where the road bent abruptly to follow the river around a shallow escarpment, a thin cloud of red dust began to billow and churn in the shimmering air: and moments later the oncoming party appeared.

There were some ten or twelve of them, men, women and children, and Indigo's first thought was that they must be a band of travelling players, for they were dressed in an extraordinary motley of garments and they seemed to be dancing a bizarre and unco-ordinated jig, jumping and skipping, arms waving wildly and supplicating to the sky. Then as they drew closer and she was able to see a little better through the dust kicked up by their prancing feet, she realised with a shock that these were no players of a kind that she had ever seen.

Mendicants – religiouses – fakirs – the concepts tumbled through her mind, but even as she struggled to assimilate the possibilities her eyes told her other-wise, and the sweat on her skin seemed to change into a million cold, crawling spiders of ice. Beside her she heard Grimya snarl, and the sound crystallised and dragged together the chaotic images in her brain as she stared, appalled, at the approaching group.

The motley garments that the prancing travellers wore were nothing but a crude collection of rags – and every one of the dancers was hideously afflicted in some way. The two men at the head of the group both had skin the colour of dead fish; one was utterly hairless, the other covered with running sores. Behind

14

them came a woman whose nose appeared to have caved in and whose eyes were blank and white with cataracts; her mouth sagged open like an idiot's. Another's skin bore huge blue-grey patches, like fresh bruises, over large areas of his body; another sported limbs as distorted as the branches of an ancient blackthorn. Even the children – Indigo counted three – were not free from disfigurement; one was white-skinned and hairless like the leader, one limped with a sideways, crablike gait forced on him by the fact that one of his legs was half again as long as the other; the third seemed to have been born without eyes.

'Eyes of the Mother, close on me!' The Southern Isles oath caught in Indigo's throat and mingled with bile, nearly choking her as she jerked the pony's head around and dragged it to a halt. In her mind she heard Grimya's wordless cry of shock and distress, and she tried to avert her head from the sight.

But she couldn't. An awful fascination had hold of her, and she *had* to look, *had* to see. The group came on, prancing towards her with a horrible inexorability that made her heart crawl under her ribs; and she saw now that as they chanted and screeched they were scourging themselves and each other with lashes whose vicious tips seemed to glow nacreously, unnatural bluegreen fireflies in the dazzling sunlight.

The pony snorted, sidestepping, and she felt a charge of fear in the muscles under its smooth coat. She snatched at the reins, striving to get the animal under control without losing hold of her crossbow, and pulled it as far off the road as the encroaching scree would allow. A sick spasm clutched at her stomach as her tumbling mind made out words amid the chanting babble; words in the sing-song tongue of this land which she had learned to speak tolerably well during her stay in Agia – *glory – grace – the blessed, the blessed* – and another word, one she did not know – *Charchad! Charchad!*

For a moment she thought that they might pass her

15

by, too engrossed in their own private madness to pay heed to her. But the hope was short-lived; for even as she at last managed to calm the pony, one of the men at the head of the grotesque procession raised a hand, palm outwards, and shrieked as though in triumph. Behind him his companions ground to a chaotic halt, the blind stumbling over the lame, one of the children falling, cries of confusion and chagrin replacing the ululating chant. A monstrous inner shudder racked Indigo and she hauled the reins in tightly, staring in appalled revulsion as the group's leader, the hairless man with the dead-fish skin, raised his head, looked directly at her, and grinned a wide grin that revealed a split black tongue, like a snake's, lolling over his lower lip.

'Sister!' The deformed tongue made his speech grotesque. 'Blessed art thou whose path has crossed that of the humble servants of Charchad!' The grin widened still further – impossibly, hideously further – and suddenly the man broke from the group and scuttled towards her like some huge, deformed insect. Indigo uttered an inarticulate noise and hefted the crossbow; the man stopped, bobbed his head at her and made an obsequious bowing gesture.

'Have faith, sister! Blessed are the faithful! Blessed are the chosen of Charchad!' Seeing that her grip on the bow didn't slacken, he backed off a pace. 'We greet you and we urge you to be enlightened, fortunate sister! Will you take of our blessing?' And he unfolded his hands, revealing something that had been concealed in one palm. A piece of stone – but it glowed, like the tips of their scourges, with the same ghastly radiance that lit the northern sky when the sun relinquished its grip.

Grimya's mind was frozen with shock; Indigo couldn't reach her, couldn't communicate. She could only pray that the wolf wouldn't panic and attack the man, for an instinct as sure as anything she had ever

16

known told her that to do so could be more dangerous than either of them yet knew.

'The sign, sister!' The madman feinted with the hand that held the stone – amulet, sigil, whatever it might be – then when he saw Indigo flinch he cackled. 'Ah, the sign! The eternal light of Charchad! See the light, sister, and in giving of reverence you, too, may be blest! See, and give!'

She could kill two, perhaps three, before the rest would be on her . . . but Indigo forced down the panic, knowing that such an action would be utter folly. She believed she knew what the grotesque man wanted: his words were a threat couched as a plea for alms. She had food, some coin; a gift in apparent good faith might persuade them to go their way and leave her unmolested.

Biting back the sour taste of sickness in her throat she nodded, and reached to her saddlebag. 'I . . . thank you – brother, for your goodness . . .' Her voice wasn't steady. 'And I – will consider it a privilege if you will permit me to . . . make an offering . . .' Her fingers fumbled, hardly knowing what they were about; a corner of her mind registered the items on which her hand closed. A small loaf of unleavened bread, a honeycomb, one of three small coin-bags: she didn't know how much it contained and didn't care.

'Sister, thou art thrice blessed of Charchad!' He darted forward and snatched the items from her almost before she could display them; the stench of a charnel-house assailed Indigo's nostrils and she gagged as the pony stamped in fear and Grimya whimpered. The man backed away, still grinning his ghastly grin; behind him his followers stood motionless, staring at the girl on the horse. 'Blessed!' the man repeated. 'Blessed by the light of Charchad. The light, sister – the light!' And with a high-pitched yell he turned, flinging both arms heavenward and displaying his prizes to the rest of the group, who began to murmur, then to babble, then to chant as they had chanted before.

'Charchad! Charchad!'

Indigo could bear it no longer. Wise or foolish, she had to get away, and she drove her heels hard into the pony's flanks, so that the animal took off at a standing gallop with Grimya at its heels. Only when they reached the buttress where road and river turned did she slither to a halt, heart pounding suffocatingly, and look back.

Dust rolled in her wake, and the road was obscured. But through the red cloud she could just make out the figures, thankfully no more than dim shapes now, of the human wrecks as, shuffling, hopping, chanting, they shambled on their way.

Later, neither Indigo nor Grimya could bring themselves to discuss the bizarre encounter. Beyond the outcrop, as Grimya had hoped, a small stand of trees straggled against the heat, and there they stopped and took shelter until the sun began to decline. Conversation between them was conspicuous by its absence; Indigo couldn't banish the after-images of the group of religious cultists from her mind, and in particular that of the white-skinned madman with the split black tongue. The memory made the water she drank taste foul in her throat, and Grimya, despite her earlier claims to hunger, had lost her urge to hunt and simply sprawled on the hot ground, ears drooping and eyes glinting redly, as though she looked into another world and did not like what she saw.

Now and again as they rested Indigo drew the lodestone from its pouch and studied it afresh. The tiny golden eye buried within it was quieter now than it had been for some days, only moving, when she turned the stone, to point northward. The mountains beyond the town ahead were now hidden by the trees' dusty, leathery foliage, but she was nonetheless aware of their pervasive presence on the horizon – and of the strange, cold glow that, when night fell again, would tint the sky with its dangerous phosphorescence.

18

And she couldn't rid herself of the feeling that the talisman carried by the fork-tongued madman on the road shared a common source with that unearthly light.

Time passed; the moment came when shadows began perceptibly to lengthen, and Indigo got to her feet and slung the blanket over the pony's back once more. Grimya stirred from a doze, licked her chops, rose and shook herself.

*I slept.* There was no satisfaction in her statement, an underlying implication that she would have preferred to stay wakeful. *Did you?*

'No.' Indigo shook her head.

The she-wolf blinked. *Perhaps that's just as well.*

It was the only reference, however oblique, that either of them made to the earlier encounter before they set off on the road once more. And an hour later, as the sun began to slip down the brassy sky, they reached the first outposts of the mining town of Vesinum.

Indigo reined the pony in and turned her head so that her hat-brim masked the westering sun. From a distance the town appeared to consist of little more than a ramshackle collection of low buildings scattered at random and bisected by the dusty road; beyond these sprawling outskirts, however, she could make out the more substantial outlines of warehouses flanking the river, although detail was obscured by a haze as dust mingled with the lowering shafts of light. Sounds that were too distant to identify drifted faintly to her ears; she looked down at Grimya, who sat at the pony's side gazing at the scene ahead with interest.

'Our journey's end.' She felt less relief that she might have done earlier in the day. 'We'll find accommodation for the night, then see what's to be done in the morning.'

Grimya's jaws opened in a cavernous grin. *I will be glad of the chance to rest properly*, she communicated. *Can we go on now?*

Indigo clicked her tongue, and the pony started

forward again. She was so intent on watching the town ahead that she failed to notice the small wooden structure by the side of the road until they were almost upon it; when finally it registered at the periphery of her vision she jerked on the reins so abruptly that her mount snorted a protest.

'In-digo?' Startled by her friend's untoward action, Grimya gave voice to a guttural growl. 'Wh . . . *at* is wr-wrong?'

Indigo didn't answer her. She was staring at the splintered and broken pieces of what had once been a little, roofed platform, standing on a wooden pole between the road and the river. To anyone unfamiliar with the religious practices of this region its purpose would have been a mystery; but, despite the fact that it had been smashed almost to matchwood, she knew what it was – or rather what it had been. And a scrap of torn red fabric protruding from between two broken spars confirmed it.

'Indigo?' Grimya said again. 'What – '

'It's a shrine.' Indigo's mouth was suddenly very dry. 'To Ranaya. You remember, the festival we attended in the city? Ranaya is the name these people give to the Earth Mother . . .'

Understanding dawned, and Grimya stared at the ruined structure. 'But . . .' Her tongue lapped uneasily at her own muzzle. 'It is br-*ok*en. S-soiled: I – do not know the right word – '

'Desecrated.' And a name, *Charchad*, echoed afresh in Indigo's memory. Quickly she looked over her shoulder, as though expecting to see the group of crazed and deformed celebrants dancing down the road towards them once more.

Grimya's eyes were orange with an anger which she couldn't articulate. '*Why?*' she snarled.

'I don't know. But it's a bad augury, Grimya.' Indigo touched the lodestone with a light finger, and shivered inwardly. 'If these people have abandoned worship of the Earth Mother, then who knows what kind of power must be abroad?'

'How c-can any . . . one turn away from the Earth?' A sad confusion crept into Grimya's tone now. 'The Earth is l . . . l . . . *life*.' She licked her chops again, uneasily. 'I d-do not understand humans. I th . . . ink I never shall.'

Indigo began to dismount. 'I must make some reparation,' she said harshly. 'I can't leave a holy place defiled like this – '

'What is the use?'

'What?' She paused.

The wolf shook her head in distress. 'I said, wh-*at* is the use, Indigo? Done is done. You c . . . cannot change it.' And abruptly her inner thoughts focused clearly in the girl's mind. *Do you think that by saying words, or scattering salt or water or gold coins, you will make it right again? That may ease your conscience, but it will achieve nothing else. The sickness that made this happen needs much greater healing.*

Indigo met her friend's eyes for a moment, then cast her gaze down. 'You shame me, Grimya.'

*I do not mean to. I only tell you what I think is the truth.*

'And you're right.' She looked again at the desecrated shrine; realised there was nothing more she could say. 'Come.' She turned the pony's head about. 'We'd best be on our way.'

As they left the small, sad ruin behind, she did not look back.

# Chapter II

It seemed that Vesinum did little to live up to its reputation and position as a centre of prosperous activity. Passing through the first ugly sprawl they had come upon the docks, where great stone jetties jutted out into the slick flow of the river and warehouses built without a moment's aesthetic thought rose to challenge the hot sky. Here, though there was enough noise and bustle to satisfy the hardest taskmaster, Indigo sensed a subdued air. Men hurried about their business with heads down and shoulders hunched, averting their eyes from any unnecessary contact with their fellows'; foremen shouted orders in clipped, terse voices; and there was no sign of the idlers, gawpers, hucksters and dockside whores who almost always haunted any busy water-thoroughfare.

Disturbed by the atmosphere, Indigo turned aside and rode into the town's centre. The buildings here were easier on the eye; merchants' houses jostled for position in the wide streets with inns, small storehouses, slate-roofed arcades where sellers of food and clothing and saddlery and utensils displayed their wares on woven mats. But the prevailing mood was the same. An uneasiness, an uncertainty, a sense that neighbour mistrusted neighbour. No children played in the streets, no laughter rang in the arcades, and no one showed any trace of what would have been natural curiosity towards a stranger in their midst. It was as if – though Indigo couldn't define what prompted her to choose such a word – the whole town was afraid.

She halted the pony at the edge of a broad square

dominated by a bizarre central sculpture made of many different metals. On the far side, a hostelry – only the second she had seen – declared itself as the House of Copper and Iron. It was low-built in the severe, angular style of the region, its façade broken by a series of arches edged with a neglected mosaic but otherwise undecorated. Indigo slid from the pony's back, flexing stiff leg-muscles, and looked at Grimya.

*It will do as well as anything else here, I suspect.* She projected her thought rather than speaking aloud; despite their seeming indifference, the townspeople might not react kindly to a stranger apparently talking to herself.

Grimya's tail was between her legs; she whined softly. *I don't like this place.*

*No more do I. But we've been led here for a reason, Grimya.* She touched the thong at her neck, feeling the familiar mingling of reassurance and resentment that the lodestone always provoked in her. *We can't turn back now.*

Grimya sniffed the atmosphere cautiously. *The air smells of bad things.*

*It's the mining; the dust is—*

*No,* the she-wolf interrupted emphatically. *Not that. I know such scents, and though I don't like them I have learned to accept them. This is something else. Something . . .* Briefly she struggled to find the right word, then added with emphasis: *Corrupt.*

Corrupt. Indigo's unease abruptly crystallised and she realised that Grimya's interpretation of their shared feeling was all too apt. The town's subdued atmosphere, the pervading sense of fear, the desecrated shrine, the mad celebrants on the road . . . something was very wrong in Vesinum.

She laid a hand on the she-wolf's head, hoping to reassure by her touch. 'Come on. We'll eat and we'll rest, then we'll see what more we can learn.'

They started towards the House of Copper and Iron, and were half way across the square when they were startled by a chiming sound, as though a dozen tiny bells were striking discordantly together. Grimya's hackles rose, and Indigo realised that the noise came from the bizarre sculpture in the centre of the square. On the sculpture's north face two brass weights moved slowly, one upward, the other downward, on hanging chains; while at its crown a series of small, metallic discs had begun slowly to spin. Ranks of tiny hammers on short levers were striking the discs as they turned, and the thin, erratic sound of their chiming echoed across the square.

*What is it?* Grimya backed away from the sculpture, teeth bared, and Indigo laughed.

'It's some kind of timepiece.' Relief coloured her voice after the momentary shock; the whole structure, she could see now, was an intricate clockwork mechanism, the work of a skilled and inventive craftsman. 'It can't harm you, Grimya. It's nothing more than a plaything.'

The she-wolf was unconvinced. *Play is running, or chasing leaves in autumn, or pretending to fight. What games are to be had from such a thing as that?*

Gently amused by her friend's simplicity, Indigo opened her mouth to explain as best she could; but paused as she heard the sounds of many shuffling footsteps. She turned, and was in time to see a group of men emerge into the square and hasten towards a street that led northward out of the town. From their shabby clothes and underfed faces she surmised that they must be miners, doubtless on their way to a shift in the mountains. And with a cold inner shock she realised that almost every one of them bore some sign of disease or deformity. Their afflictions weren't of the hideous order sported by the Charchad celebrants, but the signs were clear enough none the less: falling hair, filmy eyes, skin disfigurements that looked like huge, ugly birthmarks but weren't. And the timepiece, like some cold metal overseer, had summoned them.

Involuntarily she backed away as the miners sham-

24

bled across the square, passing no more than a few feet from them. Not one man raised his eyes to look at them, and they stared silently after the departing group.

'Charchad . . .' Indigo said at last, softly.

*Charchad?* Grimya forgot her mistrust of the sculpture.

She shook her head, negating the thought before it could take hold, and aware of a sense of unfocused anger igniting somewhere deep within her mind. 'No matter. No matter . . .'


The House of Copper and Iron, it seemed, had few guests. Despite the lack of trade, however, the thin and obsequious landlord was still inclined to put up some initial argument concerning Grimya – 'It is not our practice,' he said, twisting his hands together as though washing them, 'to allow beasts within the walls,' – but, hearing the hot spark of anger underlying his customer's suggestion that she might take her patronage elsewhere, he relented with as good a grace as he could muster. They were shown to a small but tolerably comfortable room with a shuttered window that overlooked the square, and while Indigo washed and changed her clothing, Grimya, who had never been able to overcome her natural antipathy to being within the walls of any building, paced the floor, disliking the confinement and the heat which the room's shadows made stifling.

The house's kitchen opened at sunset, the landlord had said; and chimes would be rung to announce the serving of meals. Feeling cleaner but not entirely refreshed, Indigo sat on the low, straw-stuffed couch that served as a bed, and brought out the lodestone to look at it once more. In the room's fading light the tiny pinpoint within the stone seemed unnaturally brilliant; as she held it in her palm she saw that the spark was agitating wildly, as though some living entity were trapped within the stone and trying to break out. And still the light was pointing northward.

From the window, Grimya said: *There is much activity in the square. Men carrying wood. Torches being set. I think they are preparing for some celebration.*

The idea of the folk of Vesinum wishing to celebrate any event seemed unlikely, but Indigo rose and crossed the room to crouch beside the wolf, resting her arms on the sill. The sun was now no more than an angry glare beyond darkening rooftops; the arcades seemed to have closed, and the square was steeped in heavy shadow unrelieved by any lamps. Hampered by eyesight far less acute than Grimya's, all Indigo could make out were a few indistinct human figures moving in the gloom below, although her ears caught the occasional murmur of voices or thump of something heavy being shifted.

A rattle of harsh-voiced little bells sounded suddenly from below, and she turned at the signal, relieved as she acknowledged how hungry she was. A traveller's diet of dried fruit and strips of heavily-salted meat – anything else turned rancid within a day in the blistering heat, and Grimya had only been able to hunt enough game to feed herself on the road – might be nourishing, but it palled quickly; even the most mediocre of fresh food would be a welcome change.

Grimya turned from the window as Indigo prepared to leave. 'Sh-all I . . . stay here?'

'No. You, too, need to eat; I'll see to it that they feed us both.'

'I can hh . . . hunt. Later, when it is quiet.'

Indigo smiled. 'Why should you, when there's no need? Besides, I think we should stay together.' She eyed the door. 'I, for one, would feel easier for not being alone.'

Indigo was surprised to find that she was by no means the only diner in the hostelry's taproom. Nearly half of the arched alcoves that bordered the room were already occupied, and a group of merchants were being served with flagons of wine or ale at one of the scrubbed central tables. A thin young girl with tired, wary eyes bowed and asked Indigo her pleasure; she stared down any objections the child might have raised, on her master's behalf, to Grimya's presence, and was led to an alcove separated from its neighbours by a filigree copper screen.

Though it might have little else to recommend it, the House of Copper and Iron at least offered its guests good food. Indigo chose a dish of spiced meat cooked with preserved olives and apricots, and – her purse was long enough, she decided, to allow for such a luxury – ordered a side dish of fresh legumes brought from the artificially irrigated fields of Agia, and a great rarity. Savouring the meal, with Grimya contentedly devouring a plate of mixed meats at her feet, she began to relax a little for the first time in many days. The room's atmosphere was soporific, the conversation of the taproom's other occupants a muted background hum; her plate cleared, she began to drift into a comfortable reverie . . .

'Blessings to you, sister, on this auspicious evening.'

Indigo started, and looked up to see three men and a woman blocking the entrance to her alcove. They were soberly dressed, and – like the celebrants, like the miners in the square – each was afflicted in some way, though their defects were less shocking than those she had seen before. Hanging from their belts were amulets similar to the strange, glowing talisman that the madman on the road had carried; in the taproom's lamplight their phosphorescence was subdued and sickly.

Indigo felt Grimya's fur brush against her legs as the she-wolf rose, bristling. She slipped one hand under the table to quiet her friend, mentally projecting a warning to silence and caution, and nodded to the group. 'Good evening to you.'

27

'You are a visitor to Vesinum?' The tallest of the three men – whose skin appeared to be flaking – smiled, but the smile didn't extend as far as his eyes, which were steady and unpleasantly cold.

'Indeed.' Indigo felt her mental hackles rise as the spark of formless anger made itself felt once more.

'Then we welcome you as a stranger, and as a seeker of enlightenment.' The smile faded and the man's face became sly. 'You are not of Charchad, sister?'

That word again. Indigo quelled an icy frisson. 'I'm sorry,' she said calmly. 'I have no knowledge of the Charchad, whoever or whatever it might be.'

The woman hissed as though Indigo had uttered some blasphemy, and her interrogator's expression hardened. 'Sister, I counsel you to observe the proper respect! The name of Charchad is not to be spoken lightly, and I exhort you to retraction of your error!'

Indigo looked wildly about her, seeking to call the landlord and demand that these interlopers be turned out. But when she found him his face was turned away, and she realised that he had no intention of intervening.

One of the other men spoke up. His mouth was badly distorted, giving him a speech impediment that made his words all but unintelligible.

'Our hhister errs . . . hhh . . . only by omihhion. Hhhe may hhtill hhee the light of tru'h, and be blehhed.'

Indigo felt Grimya tense, and the she-wolf hissed silently: *Danger!*

*Wait.* Indigo's fingers closed on her shoulder. *Do nothing yet.*

Her interrogator's face relaxed once more into a chilly smile. 'Indeed, brother, indeed. The light of truth! Sister, you are fortunate in that we of Charchad are endowed with a degree of mercy and justice lacking in the uninitiated.' The smile widened, leaving Indigo with the impression of the treacherous grin of a reptile. 'It would seem that your arrival is timely; for we are

28

able to offer you an unparalleled opportunity to rise from the darkness in which you flounder, and take your first steps upon the only true path.'

Grimya shifted again, muscles bunching. *I do not like this! The man speaks threat–*

*Hush.* Indigo touched her again, aware that her own heart was beginning to beat too rapidly – not from fear, but from the formless anger, which at last was beginning to focus. She met the gaze of the Charchad spokesman with steady eyes, and said with icy formality:

'Sir, I have no doubt that you mean well, and are sincere in your beliefs. But I do not take kindly to such exhortations being forced on me when I wish for privacy, and I do not respond kindly to veiled threats.' The anger glittered with sudden heat in her eyes. 'I will therefore bid you good evening.'

The woman hissed again – Indigo wondered fleetingly if she was capable of speech – and the show of friendliness abruptly dropped from the leader's manner.

'Sister, your discourtesy will cost you dearly!' He stepped forward, his companions shuffling behind him until the exit from the alcove was completely blocked. Indigo started to her feet, reaching quickly for the knife at her belt –

'Cenato!'

The new voice carried sharp authority, and the four Charchad spun round as though they had been physically struck. A tall, swarthy man was making his way across the room towards them; he pushed the woman roughly aside, shoved one of the men in her wake, and glared at the group's faltering leader.

'Leave the lady in peace, Cenato. How many times must I warn you about this kind of conduct?'

Cenato's mouth worked. 'I – we were – '

'You were making a damned nuisance of yourself! What impression do you think that will give of us to a stranger?' He pointed towards the door. 'Out. And don't let me see your faces in here again.'

Their gazes dropped; they murmured, shuffled, drew away. The newcomer stared after them as they moved towards the door, and only when they were gone did he turn back to Indigo.

'*Saia.*' He made a short bow, putting one palm to his shoulder in the manner of the region. 'My name is Quinas, and I am at your service. I apologise to you for the conduct of Cenato and his friends – they are good and pious people, but their approach to newcomers is sometimes a little over-zealous.'

Indigo had subsided back on to her seat, her knife still sheathed, but as she stared at her rescuer she saw that he, too, wore an oddly glowing amulet at his belt. Another of them . . . relief and gratitude shrivelled within her, and when she replied, her voice was hostile.

' "Good and pious" are not qualities I would have attributed to your friends, sir, if their manner is anything to go by.'

He made a helpless gesture. 'I'm afraid that's often the way with those who have but recently seen the light of Charchad. Their enthusiasm makes for an approach that can alarm the uninitiated; they need time and guidance to learn to temper their enthusiasm with consideration for others. Please, accept my assurance that they won't trouble you again.'

'I trust not, sir. I'm not accustomed to such treatment, and I don't find it amusing.'

'Naturally not.' He looked up, snapped his fingers at one of the landlord's serving-girls. 'You – a flask of the five-year vintage, now!' And, turning back to Indigo, he added, 'It's small recompense, *saia*, but the very least I can do.'

He was doing his best to conciliate, and although Indigo had taken an instant dislike to him, she couldn't maintain her hostility without being churlish. 'Thank you, sir. I appreciate your kindness.' She hesitated, then realised that from common courtesy she had little choice but to add: 'Will you join me?'

'For a few moments only.' He smiled. 'I have no wish to intrude on your privacy any further.'

The serving-girl hastened to the alcove with a brimming jug, and as she set it down Indigo saw naked fear in her expression. Quinas, whoever he might be, clearly had influence in more quarters than one. The girl was sent for another cup, and while she fetched it, Quinas took the seat opposite Indigo.

'To your continuing health and prosperity.' He poured for them both, and they drank. Grimya had quieted – Indigo could feel the she-wolf's body against her legs as she lay down under the table – but her thoughts were still uneasy, and Indigo took a moment to assess her companion. He was, she guessed, in his middle or late thirties, and he had the black hair and olive skin typical of people born and bred in the region. He was too well-dressed and clearly too educated to be a miner or a boatman, although his hands looked hardened to manual work and the skin of his face was browned by sun and wind. Quite a handsome man, in his way – until, for the first time as the lamplight exposed his face more clearly, she saw his eyes. They were oddly hooded, and when he blinked – at first she couldn't be certain, but the second time confirmed it – a crimson film came briefly down, like a bizarre second lens, to cover them.

Another deformity . . . Indigo controlled a desire to shrink back in revulsion, and hastily looked down at her cup. When Quinas spoke to her, she had to suppress a shudder.

'May I ask your name?'

She made herself look up again. 'My name is Indigo.'

'Indigo . . . very unusual. You are not, I presume, from this area?'

'No.'

'Might I inquire what brings you here?' He saw her expression grow wary, and smiled self-deprecatingly.

'Please forgive my curiosity. I ask simply because I have the privilege to be overseer at the North Scar mine; in the course of my duties I often conduct visiting merchants to view our operations. If you have business at the mines, I will be happy to offer my services.'

Indigo relaxed a little. 'I see. Thank you, Quinas, but I'm not concerned with the mineral trade. Vesinum is simply a stop on my route.'

'A pity.' Like Cenato, his smile didn't reach his eyes. 'None the less, your arrival is fortuitous. Has anyone told you of our festival?'

'Festival?'

'In the town square: you may well have seen the preparations. Tonight, we of Charchad celebrate, and the town celebrates with us. It is a time of cleansing, of renewal and re-affirmation.' A new note crept into Quinas's voice, and Indigo caught a sharp and unpleasant echo of the fanaticism of the mad celebrant, and of the group who had accosted her in the taproom. 'It is also, I think, a part of the reason why Cenato was so insistent in his approach towards you.' He looked up, and his face was so guileless that she was thrown mentally off balance. 'The festivities are due to begin at midnight. I hope you will do us the honour of attending, so that we may correct the bad first impression you have of us?'

She might do well to attend, Indigo thought, if it helped her to learn more of the Charchad. She nodded. 'Thank you. I will be glad to.'

Quinas drained his cup, and rose. 'Then I'll take my leave and allow you to finish your meal uninterrupted.' He stepped out of the alcove and bowed to her. 'I am happy to have made your acquaintance, Indigo. And I trust that I may yet play some small part in aiding you towards understanding and enlightenment. Good night.' And he turned and walked away across the room, to the door.

Indigo stared after him, trying to assimilate the extra-ordinary mixture of feelings that he had evoked within her. Surprise, chagrin, an element of confusion – but overriding them all was a powerful and near-violent sense of dislike. As yet she would put it no more strongly than that; but it was enough to make her skin prickle, and to add kindling to the smouldering anger deep within her.

Under the table Grimya moved restlessly, and she heard the wolf's thoughts. *I do not like that man.*

'No.' Indigo spoke softly. 'Neither do I.'

*Everyone else is afraid of him. That is not good.*

Grimya's finer senses had picked up what her own could not, she realised; that it was not merely Cenato and his henchman who feared Quinas's influence. The serving-girl's attitude, the looks on the faces of her fellow diners as he strode from the taproom . . . For a mine overseer, he wielded a disproportionate power.

She looked at the flask, which was still half full, and moved to pour herself another cup of wine. Before she could touch the flask, however, the serving-girl appeared.

'Beg pardon, *saia*, but the landlord tells me to say that there'll be no charge for your food and drink tonight. Thank you, *saia*.'

Indigo stared, nonplussed, at the girl's departing back, then beyond her to the landlord, who caught her eye and bowed respectfully. Quinas's doing; or an attempt to please Quinas . . . Suddenly she didn't want the wine, wished she hadn't eaten the meal. She wanted only to get away from the taproom and from the invisible but all-pervading influence of her self-appointed champion.

She leaned down, slipping a hand under the table to touch Grimya's head lightly. *Let's leave*, she projected silently.

*Now? Gladly! What do you wish to do?*

Indigo smiled with faint cynicism as she realised that the true answer to the she-wolf's question was: get away; get drunk; forget the existence of Vesinum. *I'm tired*, she said. *If we're to attend the festival at midnight, I'd like to rest for a while.*

*I don't think I could rest. This room smells of fear; it disturbs me.* Grimya wriggled. *I would like to go out for a while, in the open air. But I don't want to leave you alone.*

Indigo smiled, remembering her friend's hatred of confinement. She looked about the room. The landlord was deep in conversation with an obviously favoured customer. The serving-girls scurried with laden trays between the tables. And the influence of Quinas, who had favoured her with his patronage, still hung, an invisible but emphatic presence, in the air.

*I'll be in no danger,* she told Grimya. *Not yet, at least.*

Heads turned surreptitiously as they crossed the room, and one or two murmured asides were exchanged. Indigo ignored the looks, the whispers; ignored the landlord as he tried to catch her eye ingratiatingly: she watched Grimya slip through the decorated door that opened directly on to the square, and for a moment breathed in the hot but still relatively fresh air of the night. Then as the she-wolf vanished into the darkness she turned and walked out of the taproom towards the stairs.

# Chapter III

Indigo had left a lamp burning in her room, but its light was eclipsed by the strange, pervasive glow from the northern sky, a ghostly reflection shining in at the window. She slammed the inner shutters; the presence of the light made her feel tainted and she couldn't be easy until it was shut out, no matter how stifling the room might become.

The quiet and the airlessness were soporific, and Indigo soon fell asleep, though her rest was light and punctuated with odd dreams that seemed unrelated to past or present. She finally woke at the sound of her door creaking, and opened her eyes to see Grimya padding across the floor towards her.

The she-wolf flopped down beside the bed. *Hot*, she projected, her tongue lolling. *It disturbs me. I can find no relief from it.*

Indigo sat up and reached for her water-bottle to give Grimya a drink. 'Did you discover anything?'

*Nothing significant.* Gratefully Grimya lapped from the dish which Indigo had set before her. *I kept to the side streets, to the shadows; I didn't want to be seen.* She paused to lick her chops. *That is good. Did you know that the river here glows at night, like the sky?*

'No.' The thought was unpleasant, suggesting that the source of the light was palpably closer, and perhaps more physical than she had surmised. 'And what of the square? The festival?'

Grimya finished drinking and shook her head, drops of water flying from her muzzle. *I think they must have completed their preparations. There is no one about.*

*Just some piles of wood: I don't know what their purpose could be.*

'It must be close to midnight.' Indigo opened the shutter a crack. A breath of faintly cooler air slunk in, and with it the dim, unnatural reflection from the sky. The square below was, as Grimya had said, empty, the shadows too deep to make detail visible. She looked up, peering towards the jumble of rooftops on the far side of the paved arena. No lamps burned in houses or arcades, and the only sound was the faint murmur of voices from the taproom beneath them. All activity seemed to be in abeyance, as though the entire town were holding its breath in anticipation.

Or trepidation . . .

A faint whirring broke the quiet then, and suddenly the timepiece in the centre of the square began to chime as it had done earlier in the day. Indigo could see the discs spinning, catching the cold light from the sky like winking, lambent eyes, and as the bell-like discords rang out, a torch sprang to life in the dark maw of one of the side streets. Then another, and another; catching and flaming as they were ignited and hurling grotesque shadows over walls and paving. In a window a candle was lit; in another house a door opened, spilling lantern-light into the square –

A furtive rapping came at Indigo's door and she whirled round, pulse quickening. 'Yes? What is it?'

A girl's voice, mumbling; she caught only the word *saia*, and laid a restraining hand on Grimya. 'Enter.'

The door opened and she saw the wide-eyed child who had served her in the taproom. The girl bowed nervously.

'If you please, *saia*, the festival is beginning. We must all attend, so the taproom is to be closed. The master said to tell you.'

She was frightened, Indigo saw; and the emotion went far deeper than fear of a harsh employer.

'Thank you.' She got to her feet, and remembered

36

the terms in which Quinas's invitation had been couched. A courtesy? she asked herself. Or a threat?

Anger stirred afresh, and the air tasted suddenly sour and rotten in her throat. She looked at the girl again, and forced herself to smile. 'If you'll be so kind as to leave a candle lit on the stairs, I shall find my way well enough.'

'Yes, *saia*.' The child vanished; hasty footsteps clattered on the steps, and Indigo looked at Grimya.

'Are you ready?'

Grimya's nostrils flared and she said aloud: 'Rr-*eady*.' The word was a guttural challenge to the outside world. The wolf slipped through the door, her shadow rearing huge and distorted across the landing to the stairwell beyond. Indigo paused a moment, considering – then picked up the knife in its sheath, which she had discarded while she slept. Looping the sheath into her belt, she covered it with a fold of her outer robe, then followed Grimya down the stairs.

They heard music in the square as they emerged from the hostelry. Cushmagar, the old Southern Isles bard who had been Indigo's tutor, would have covered his ears in horror at the discordant racket; cymbals clanging, pipes screeching and shrilling, a dozen different kinds of percussion rattling with seemingly no thought for time or rhythm. To the girl's ears it sounded like the din made by farm boys set to the task of scaring crows and pigeons from their masters' fields; as her eyes grew accustomed to the play of brightness and shadow she sought the source of the noise, but in the space of a few minutes the square had become so crowded that she could see nothing through the press of bodies.

'Keep to the wall,' she said to Grimya, bending to enable the she-wolf to hear her over the rising tide of sound. 'We'll try to find a less obstructed view.' They began to thread their way along the narrow aisle between the buildings and the jostling throng, but progress was slow, for more and more people were converging on the square from every direction. Some-where towards the square's centre light danced brilli-antly, and occasionally Indigo glimpsed the flickering, fiery crown of a flamboy raised above the heads of the crowd. Some folk, too, were reacting to the discordant music, beginning to shuffle in an odd, sidestepping dance that carried them slowly anti-clockwise around the square. Many of the dancers, Indigo saw, wore the glowing amulets that seemed to be a badge of the Charchad cult, and she couldn't shake off the uneasy feeling that these symbols had united their wearers in some indefinable way into one mass entity with a single, mindless purpose.

Suddenly the music stopped. The tide of dancers broke into a hundred small eddies as they shambled to a halt, and for a moment the silence was absolute. Then torchlight flared anew, the crowd pulled back and a low but intense murmur rippled through the square. Indigo stood on tiptoe but still could see nothing; frustrated, she looked about her for some vantage point and glimpsed a wall topped with an ornate iron balustrade a few paces on from where she stood. Pointing to indicate to Grimya what she meant to do, she elbowed her way through, hitched up her robe and scrambled on to the wall. The stonework was crumbling but the balustrade seemed sound enough; taking a grip she hauled herself upright and at last was able to see the square in its entirety.

The bizarre timepiece glowed as though red-hot in the light of the dozen huge flamboys that surrounded it. Each torch was held by a robed and hooded figure standing stiffly at attention, and each figure bore an amulet that proclaimed his allegiance to Charchad. Beyond the group of sentinels Indigo saw for the first time the 'piles of wood' that Grimya had described; unless the celebrants planned to highlight their festival with bonfires, she too could see no purpose for them.

She was about to climb down and describe the scene to Grimya when a section of the crowd parted to admit a newcomer to the middle of the square. By his height and his dress Indigo identified him immediately: Quinas. He strode towards the torch-bearers, who drew back respectfully, and surveyed the crowd with an air of authoritative satisfaction. Then he began to speak.

At first his speech was what might have been expected of any dignitary at such a celebration: he extolled the town's prosperity, the virtues of honest labour and the rewards of diligence – but after a few minutes the tone of the oration began to change. The word *Charchad* grew more prevalent: Charchad was to be thanked, to be praised, to be honoured. And to be obeyed. Those who did not obey were misguided, and until such misguided souls saw and admitted their error they must be led on the proper path by those who had achieved enlightenment. Indigo felt the food she had eaten curdle in her stomach; this was merely a repetition of the fanatical homily with which the cultists had assailed her in the taproom. But as she listened she realised suddenly that there was a far more dangerous undercurrent to Quinas's speech: and a chill crawled through her veins as she heard him speak the word *heresy*.

Heresy. She recalled the dread in the eyes of her fellow-diners when Quinas walked into the House of Copper and Iron, as though he were some avenging angel who might without warning turn and point the finger of fate at them; and she realised with a shock that that assessment was perilously close to the truth. A heretic, in Quinas's terms and as he was now forcefully outlining, was one who refused to acknowledge and accept the authority of Charchad. And heretics who would not recant and repent of their wrongdoing must be punished.

'Brothers and sisters, we of Charchad have been patient.' Quinas would, Indigo thought with a chilly shiver, have made a persuasive bard; his voice had a fine, carrying timbre and he had taken good care to judge the mood of his audience and play upon it. 'But our patience is not infinite, and Charchad demands its rightful due.' He surveyed the throng, his eyes glittering. 'The time has come, my brothers and my sisters, to prove our loyalty and our fealty. The time has come to renew our faith. And for those who have not seen the light of Charchad,' – now he raised an arm, fist clenched, and his words rang across the square – 'the time has come to *repent!*'

So suddenly that Indigo was almost startled into falling from her precarious perch, the cacophonous music burst out again, and at its signal the torch-bearers surrounding Quinas spread out and began to move in pairs towards the throng. From the far side of the square Indigo heard a shriek, then a ragged figure burst from the crowd and ran to the central tableau. The man – she thought it was a man, but the creature was such a raddled scarecrow that it was impossible to be sure – was waving his arms wildly, and his face, under a wild scum of greying hair, was distorted with an ecstatic, dervishistic mania. On his scrawny chest a glowing amulet bounced at the end of a long chain.

*'Charchad!'* the creature screamed. *'Charchad save me. Charchad bless me!'* And he hurled himself to the flagstones, where he lay twitching and convulsing at Quinas's feet.

The overseer flung both his arms skyward, his own face almost as twisted as that of the gibbering celebrant on the ground. 'See how our brother is uplifted!' he roared. 'Witness the glory of his unwavering faith – and look into your own hearts! Are you wanting? Who among you will *dare* to fail the Charchad?'

Another figure, a woman this time, stumbled from the crowd to throw herself to the ground, tearing at her own hair. Then another, another, more and more fighting their way through the press of people, screeching and jostling and fighting in their efforts to outvie one another in displaying their faith. Quinas watched the growing chaos with a faintly supercilious smile on his face. From time to time he inclined his head in recognition of one worshipper, occasionally he would deign to make a sign of blessing towards another, while his acolytes stalked among the crowd exhorting people to new heights of adulation. And all the while, whipped up by the music's frenzied discords, lit by the guttering flamboys, the scene grew more and more like something from an unhuman hell. In the sky overhead the eerie light from the north glared down, adding its own terrible dimension to the shadows, to the wild faces, and to the flamelit figure of Quinas, who orchestrated the mayhem like a demon king presiding over his court.

Horrified, Indigo began to scramble down from the wall to join Grimya, who was snarling, hackles raised and eyes red with fear. The she-wolf couldn't see what was happening, but had heard Quinas's exhortations among the furore, and she felt the psychic shock-wave erupting in the square. But as the girl prepared to jump to the ground she was almost knocked off balance by the hunched figure of a woman who scuttled out of the press of bodies and darted past her towards one of the dark side streets. Indigo had only one glimpse of her face, but it was enough to tell her that the woman was terrified. And from somewhere nearer the centre of the crowd came a scream; not of ecstasy this time, but of stark fear.

Quickly she swung herself upright again, gesturing to Grimya to wait, and peered over the sea of bobbing heads. Torchlight illuminated a section of the crowd, and she saw two of Quinas's acolytes wrestling with a young man who fought them with all his strength. People jostled to get out of the way, and the captive was dragged into the central circle, where his hands and feet were bound and he was forced to kneel. No one in the throng made the smallest move to protest, and now Indigo saw that there were other such skirmishes taking place, other victims, chosen seemingly at random, hauled from the anonymity of the crush to sprawl shivering on the flagstones.

41

But the choice was not as arbitrary as it at first seemed. Quinas still stood like an evil demi-god in the square: he watched the crowd intently, then called out and pointed. At his signal two more acolytes darted into the press, and another struggling figure was brought forward. Nine, ten, a dozen – and not one of the captives, Indigo saw, wore a Charchad amulet.

At last it seemed that Quinas was satisfied with his cull. At another signal the acolytes began to pull the bound figures to their feet, and as they were manhandled towards the woodpiles behind the central timepiece, Indigo realised with a sudden, nauseous shock what their fate was to be – for one of the torch-bearers had stepped forward, and was touching his brand to the first of the pyres.

*'Mother of all life blind me!'* She gripped the iron balustrade, frozen by an inability to believe that anyone was capable of such mad barbarity. One of the prisoners started to scream, a mindless, repetitive wail that his captors ignored. Tongues of yellow flame were catching in the wood of the pyre, brightening the scene; and Quinas, who had been watching with satisfaction, turned to the throng again.

'Thus do we prosecute the just retribution of Charchad against the unbeliever!' The prisoner's screams faded to a series of unsteady whimpers. 'I call upon you now, brothers and sisters – open your hearts and look to your own salvation, lest you lose your last hope of grace and blessing, and share the doom of the irredeemably damned! I exhort you; look to your souls! *Who else among you will dare to turn their face from the all-seeing Charchad?'*

Someone in the crowd screeched: *'Charchad!'* and several others took up the cry with a kind of desperate urgency. A few people close to Indigo began to jump and wave their arms, calling out and striving to attract attention to themselves, as though they feared the consequences of failing to draw Quinas's approving

42

eye. But for the most part, the crowd merely stood and watched in silence.

Wildly, Indigo looked at the faces around her. Apathy – tightly-controlled fear – careful indifference – not one person would protest against this madness, not one would move to stop it, despite the fact that Quinas and his henchmen were vastly outnumbered. And suddenly her control snapped.

'*Do something!*' Heads turned, expressions registering blank surprise, and she realised that in her agitation she had screamed at them in her own tongue. She sprang down from the wall and ran for the person nearest to her, a burly man.

'You've got to stop this!' She switched to his language, grabbing him by the arm. 'You can't let them do it – it's murder, it's *insanity* – '

The man threw her off with a convulsive movement, as though he'd been touched by something unclean. For a moment she saw naked terror in his eyes: then his look hardened.

'Foreigner!' he spat. 'What do you know of anything? Look to your own affairs!'

A woman beside him shook her first in Indigo's face. 'Get away from us! Heretic! Heretic!'

Infuriated, Grimya snarled and crouched to spring at the woman, but Indigo cried out, 'Grimya, no!' She held out a hand to ward off the she-wolf, at the same time backing away from the couple. *They don't understand, Grimya. They're too frightened.*

The wolf's snarls dropped to a threatening growl, but she held back. Indigo looked at the man again, but before she could speak there was a sudden gasp from the front of the crowd, and an unhuman screech of agony. Light flared up in the centre of the square, and even over the cries Indigo heard the eager crackling of fire –

'Please!' She held out both hands in supplication, her voice choked with emotion. 'You can't want to see innocent people die in such a way! You could stop it, all of you, if you'd only – '

The woman interrupted her shrilly. 'Leave us alone, outlander! Get back to where you came from, and leave us be!'

It was hopeless. Indigo swung round, blocking her ears against the screams of Quinas's burning victims, and with Grimya at her heels plunged away through the crowd, fighting to get back to the House of Copper and Iron. She couldn't think, couldn't stop to consider; all she felt was an overpowering, inchoate need to flee the scene of the carnage and shut herself away before she, too, was tainted by the madness of Charchad.

Close to the hostelry the crowd was denser as the main press of people in the square met and merged with latecomers trying to jostle in from a side street. Indigo fought her way through, Grimya snapping at recalcitrant ankles, and at last they were past the worst of the congestion and the door of the inn lay only a few yards away. Indigo started to run towards sanctuary – but as she reached clear space the throng before her suddenly parted, forming an aisle from the middle of the square. Torchlight bobbed and flared, and a small procession came striding from the direction of the pyres, with Quinas at its head.

The look of fanatical self-satisfaction on the over-seer's face stopped Indigo in her tracks. She stared at him, feeling a tide of fury swelling within her – then suddenly her attention was snatched by a scuffle at the edge of the crowd. A woman in worn and stained garments, her black hair tied in a single, heavy braid, rushed from the mill of people and threw herself in Quinas's path, snatching at his garments and forcing him to halt.

'Please!' The woman's voice was shrilly hysterical. 'Sir, take pity! Don't turn me away again; hear me, I *beg* you – '

'Out of my way, woman!' Quinas tried to brush her

aside but she clung on, heedless of the fact that he was dragging her painfully along the ground.

'No! Hear me, you *must* hear me! Sir, my – '

She got no further, for Quinas turned and with the flat of his hand struck her full across the face. She lost her grip on him, tumbling back with a cry of pain, and one of the acolytes who had been following Quinas kicked her viciously in the small of the back.

Indigo didn't pause to think rationally. Her rage needed an outlet and she ran forward, drawing her knife.

'*You!*' She barred Quinas's way, eyes ablaze, feeling that at the smallest provocation she'd plunge the knife into his stomach. 'Is this your idea of mercy and justice, you abomination?'

'*Saia* Indigo.' Quinas regarded her calmly. 'Well, well. Do I detect a change in your manner from our first meeting?'

'Indeed you do! You gave me the impression that you were a civilised man. I see now that you're no better than a maggot!' She pointed to the woman, who still lay on the ground and was weeping quietly. 'Help her to her feet. I believe she has something to say to you.'

A cool smile made Quinas's mouth twitch. 'For your own sake, *saia*, I would strongly recommend that you stop attempting to interfere in the business of others. In fact, I must insist on it.' He reached forward to take hold of her arm and push her out of his path, and she brought the knife flashing up to hover before his face.

'Touch me and I'll cut your entrails out!'

Quinas stayed his hand, but his face grew dangerous. He blinked; again, the crimson lenses came down briefly over his eyes, and the renewed shock of his deformity momentarily threw Indigo's concentration. The knife wavered – and three of the Charchad acolytes pounced on her. She yelled in surprise, then the yell cut off in a whoop of expelled breath as a fist drove into her stomach. Another pulled her hair, jerking her head round, and she lost her footing, falling to the ground under a rain of kicks and blows.

*Indigo!* Grimya howled and leaped at her friend's assailants, only to be kicked back to roll yelping on the flags. Through eyes that watered with pain Indigo saw the she-wolf crouch for the kill, saw a blade in the hand of one of the acolytes –

'No, Grimya! *Stay!*'

Grimya whimpered, frustrated but instinctively bound to obey, and hands hauled Indigo roughly to her feet. She doubled over, struggling not to complete her humiliation by vomiting in full view of the crowd, and saw Quinas's feet planted squarely before her.

'Very prudent, *saia*; and as well for you that your dog is obedient.' He looked up, nodded to his followers. 'Release her. I don't think she's in a condition to cause any further trouble.'

The hands fell away, one giving Indigo a last, painful pinch, and she slumped to her knees, too sick and dizzy to stand upright unaided.

'She is a foreigner,' Quinas said with withering contempt, 'and as such, her ignorance is to be pitied rather than punished. But she will learn the folly of her ways, brothers and sisters. Charchad will see to that.'

She might have blacked out for a moment; Indigo couldn't later be sure. When she opened her eyes again she was no longer surrounded, and Grimya was at her side, anxiously trying to lick her face.

*Indigo! I should have stopped them, I should have torn out their throats! I failed you!*

'No . . . no.' She started to shake her head but thought better of it. One kick must have connected directly with the back of her skull . . . Her knife lay on the flags before her; shakily she retrieved it, then pushed a begrimed strand of hair from her eyes and looked up.

Quinas and his companions were gone. People in the crowd were staring at her; as she met their gazes they turned their backs, shuffling away to give her a wide berth, and any thought she had of asking someone to help her to her feet died. As with Quinas's earlier victims, they would do nothing to aid her.

The raucous music had stopped. The flames of the pyres still stained the scene but there was no more screaming now: the fires had done their work and the festival of Charchad was over. Indigo looked about her for the woman she had attempted to champion, but she was nowhere to be seen, and after a few moments more she risked struggling to her feet. The ground seemed to dip and sway beneath her, but with an effort she managed to stumble the few steps to the hostelry door and make her way inside. The taproom was, thankfully, empty, and with Grimya an anxious shadow at her heels she climbed slowly and painfully up to her room. The worst of her nausea was passing, but when she gingerly fingered her skin she found several shallow grazes, and there were painful patches on her cheek and jaw which would form livid bruises by morning.

She eased herself on to her bed and lay down. Grimya paced the room, tail and ears twitching, still distressed. *I wish I had killed them!* the she-wolf said. *They have hurt you –*

'No, Grimya; they haven't really hurt me. They could have done far worse, and there were too many of them for you to fight alone. Besides, it doesn't matter. Those poor people – what Quinas did, it was *monstrous!*'

*That one called Quinas is a madman – I could smell his sickness. Indigo, is he the source of the evil here? Is he the demon?*

Indigo hadn't once considered the possibility that the evil force she sought might be embodied in a single human being, but Grimya's suggestion had an ugly logic. She put her hand to the bag around her neck and drew the lodestone out to look at it.

'It's quiescent.' Chagrin coloured her voice. 'But it still points northward.'

*When the man Quinas went away, he went south from here. I was wrong: it cannot be him.*

'Perhaps not . . . but he's part of it, Grimya.' Unwanted images of the pyres and their struggling victims rose in Indigo's mind and she focused desperately on her own hands in an effort to blot the memory out. 'The heart of the Charchad – whatever it is – lies in the north. And Quinas holds a key to it, though maybe not the only key.' She shivered, glanced at the window then away again. 'I will have revenge on that man. Not only for myself, but for the ones who died tonight.'

Grimya started to reply, but suddenly stopped, looked towards the door and uttered a soft growl. *Someone comes.*

A heavy footfall sounded on the landing. Indigo tensed, then started up as without any preamble the door opened and the landlord of the House of Copper and Iron walked into the room.

Hot colour rose to Indigo's cheeks. 'How dare you intrude on me without so much as knocking! What do you think you're about?'

'Save your fine indignation, *saia*' The landlord's obsequiousness was gone, and he uttered the courtesy title with heavy irony. 'I won't waste words. You're no longer welcome under my roof, and you'll oblige by leaving as soon as daylight comes.'

'What?'

'You heard me well enough. We're a peaceable town, and we don't take kindly to outsiders coming here and trying to make trouble.'

'*Trouble?*' Indigo echoed, incredulous. 'You witnessed *murder* in that square outside, and now you have the audacity to accuse *me* of making trouble?' She stood up, her whole body shaking with fury and frustration. 'What's the matter with you people? Are you so afraid of that piece of offal who calls himself mine overseer that – '

'And I'll have no besmirching of our good brother

48

Quinas!' The landlord shouted to drown her words, and she saw beads of sweat on his forehead. 'You're not welcome here, d'you understand? Take your dirty outland ways and your dirty outland animal, and be gone from my house by morning!' His voice dropped and he took several deep breaths, chest heaving. He would not, Indigo noted bitterly, meet her gaze directly. 'Go, woman. Or you'll be given more cause for repentance than you've had tonight!'

On the brink of a furious retort, Indigo paused. There was no point in arguing with the man; she could gain nothing from it. Whether he was motivated by fear or by genuine loyalty to the Charchad made no difference; his was only one voice among many. She couldn't oppose the entire town.

She turned away, and spoke with cold disdain. 'Very well.' Her purse clinked, and she threw two gold coins on to the floor. 'That, I think, will cover my indebtedness for your hospitality.'

'I want none of your money.'

'Then you may leave it to rot where it lies, for I'll be under no obligation to the house of a craven coward.'

There was a sharp silence. Then the landlord said: 'Your pony will be saddled and ready at dawn,' and the uneven floor shook as he slammed the door behind him.

# Chapter IV

By mid-morning, Indigo and Grimya were far enough from Vesinum for the physical, if not the psychic, stench of the Charchad festival to be gone from their nostrils. They had left under a paling dawn that hadn't yet entirely banished the nightglow from the sky, and had taken the northward road out of the town.

There had been few eyes to see them on their way. Indigo was aware of the landlord watching from an upper window of the House of Copper and Iron as she mounted the pony, but there was no one abroad in the streets, and the clatter of hooves as they moved off had been the only sound to break the early quiet. The square, too, was deserted; she had turned her face from the charred and grisly legacy of the festival and ridden away without a backward glance. Now, as the sun climbed and the heat increased to the steady intensity of a furnace, she hurried the pony on as fast as common-sense allowed, anxious to put as much distance between herself and the town's unpleasant memories as possible.

She and Grimya had said little to each other about their experience. Words seemed inadequate; though Indigo knew nothing of the victims who had died on the Charchad's pyres she none the less grieved for them. And her simmering rage still showed no sign of abating. Her mind was quieter now, but she knew herself well enough to acknowledge that it would take little to provoke her into a fit of furious railing against the Charchad and all it stood for.

She reflected, however, that as yet she still had no

clear idea of what the Charchad *did* stand for. All she knew was the little she had seen in Vesinum, and though the events had shocked and sickened her they had revealed nothing of the cult's origins, or of its ultimate purpose. But whatever the nature of Charchad, she had seen more than enough to convince her beyond all doubt that the cult had a direct and inextricable link with the demon she was seeking.

A huge, low wagon laden with timber and drawn by four straining oxen came rumbling towards her, and she drew the pony to the side of the dusty road to let the convoy pass. The driver gruffly thanked her, one of the two mounted outriders saluted and smiled, and while she waited for the dust-cloud of their passage to clear Indigo took a few moments to assess the way ahead.

She was still on the main trade route that ran alongside the river, but from her maps she knew that two or three miles on, the road met the barrier of the volcanic mountains and there turned abruptly eastward. The red-brown peaks dominated the skyline now, sere and sunbaked and indefinably threatening; and the sky beyond the first ramparts was tinged with the sulphurous yellow pollution of the mining and smelting operations in the heart of the range. Grimya had already complained of the foul smells assailing her nostrils, and even Indigo, with her far less acute human senses, was unpleasantly aware of the taint.

She took out the lodestone and regarded it again. The tiny gold spark at its heart still pointed unwaveringly northward, and she gathered up the reins in preparation to move on. Grimya, who had flopped down in a patch of dry, withered grass, rose reluctantly to her feet. Her tongue lolled and she said tentatively, *I would like to rest soon . . .*

'It isn't far now to the mountains.' Indigo looked down at her friend and smiled. 'We'll find shade as soon as we can.'

During the next mile, traffic on the road increased

51

until there was a steady flow moving past them from the north. Trade caravans, supply wagons, small groups of horsemen, even a few dusty walkers. No one spared more than a glance for Indigo and Grimya, and at last they reached the first foothills and with them the junction where the road turned to cross the river and carry its traffic away into the east. A huge and ugly iron toll-bridge spanned the river, flanked by rough sheds, and on both banks a number of opportunistic tinkers and small-traders had set up stalls and were loudly proclaiming their wares to travellers.

Indigo reined in and looked at the scene. Her direction lay north, not east; yet it seemed that she had little choice but to follow the road, for the only way northward was by a broad, rutted track that followed the river where it vanished into the mountains – and the track was barred by tall and heavily-guarded gates.

She spoke quietly to Grimya. 'That must be the entrance to the mines. Without the proper documents, those guards won't let us pass. I have the impression they don't encourage casual visitors.'

Grimya's nose wrinkled and she sniffed at the heavy air. *I cannot believe that anyone would want to go there without good reason.*

'Nor I. But we can't dispute what the lodestone tells us.' She scanned the slopes ahead of her, but saw nothing to lift her spirits. The mountains looked impassable; to either side of the mine track the volcanic rock rose in near-vertical folds where, long ago, a huge fault had developed in the land. No one in their right mind would even attempt to climb such a cliff, let alone hope to succeed. And yet if she continued on the trade road she would have little hope of finding a way into the range further on, for beyond the river the road veered further and further away from the mountains, separated from them by a pitted lava plain that no horse could traverse.

Two well-dressed riders clattered past, pushing their horses faster than any man with a spark of kindness would have done in such heat, and turned off the road to approach the mine gates. A guard intercepted them, and Indigo saw one rider wave a small metal token under the man's nose before the gates were opened and the pair spurred their horses through. She touched her tongue to lips that were dry and sore from the sun, and realised that she couldn't sit indecisively here for much longer. It was only just past noon; they needed shelter of some form, and a chance to rest until the day became a little cooler. Turning her gaze from the mine track, she surveyed the landscape again – and suddenly saw something that in the sun's dazzle she had missed. Another path, so old and abandoned that it was barely discernible, which branched from the main road and meandered away westward. At first glance it appeared to end where it met the volcanic wall; but, looking harder, Indigo thought she saw a fissure in the massive folds of rock, into which the track vanished.

An old miners' road, fallen into disuse? It was possible: and it was their only chance.

She looked down at Grimya and projected a thought. *Grimya – do you see that path, leading westward?*

The she-wolf looked. *I see it.* She sensed Indigo's eagerness. *Do you think it may lead to where we wish to go?*

*I don't know. But I have a feeling; an instinct . . .* Unconsciously she fingered the lodestone, and Grimya opened her jaws in a lupine grin, licking the air.

*If nothing else, it may bring us to some shade!*

Indigo laughed. 'Grimya, you're single-minded!' she said aloud. 'Come, then – let's investigate, before we broil in the sun!'

She had wondered, with some trepidation, if the mine guards might challenge or impede them before they could reach the track, but it seemed that the sentries' interest extended only to anyone who set foot on the mine road itself. And the heat was taking its toll of them, too; of the four men on duty only one now braved the day while his fellows sheltered in a ramshackle hut to one side of the gates, and as Indigo and Grimya passed by the entrance he didn't so much as look in their direction.

They turned on to the disused path, and as the cliff rose beside them Indigo felt as though she had ridden into a furnace. The sun beat against the rock face and shimmered back in stifling waves, burning all traces of moisture from the air and making the mere act of breathing a torment. The pony's head hung and it refused to move at more than a shambling walk; Grimya panted at its heels, trying to stay within its shadow, and Indigo prayed silently that she hadn't been mistaken about the path. She could bear no more than a few minutes of this.

Suddenly the she-wolf stopped and yipped a warning. Turning, Indigo saw her looking back, ears pricked.

'Grimya? What's amiss?'

*Something behind us – a disturbance –*

Were the guards alerted, and coming after them? Indigo looked for her knife, winced as her hand touched the metal of the hilt which was hot enough to burn. But Grimya was trotting back the way they had come, and after a few moments she called back aloud, 'In-digo! They are h . . . *urting* her!'

She frowned, not comprehending. Then Grimya called again more urgently and, realising that something was amiss, Indigo dismounted and ran back along the path.

From Grimya's vantage point the mine entrance was just visible – and by the gates a skirmish had broken out. A woman, screaming and pleading, was struggling to break free from the grip of two guards, while a third jabbed viciously at her with a metal stave. Shocked, Indigo recognised her as the same woman whose part she had tried to take the previous night; the one who had sought to petition Quinas.

With a jerk that must have nearly wrenched her arm

54

from its socket the woman broke free; but only for a moment before one of the sentries snatched a handful of her clothing – Indigo heard the worn fabric rip – and his companion swung the heavy stave against her shoulder with stunning force. She reeled, staggered, fell; the guards caught her under the arms and dragged her clear of the gates before throwing her down in the dust at the side of the road.

Indigo stared after the three grinning men as they swaggered back to their posts. Bile rose in her throat, but she forced herself not to give way to the furious instinct that urged her to storm after them and claim retribution on the woman's behalf. She had made that mistake once before, and the odds against her were no more favourable now.

The woman, meanwhile, had tried to get to her feet, failed, and was crawling slowly and painfully towards the rock face where the abandoned path began. She reached the cliff, then collapsed against the wall, doubled over and began to retch dryly. Indigo swore softly and, motioning to Grimya to stay back, ran towards her. As she bent to help her up the woman started and tried to shield her face with one arm, crying out incoherently.

'It's all right.' Indigo caught her shoulders, steadying her. 'I won't hurt you – I'm a friend. Come; can you stand, if I help you?'

Wide, terrified eyes in a pinched face stared back at her, and the woman's lip quivered. 'I . . . I'm all right . . .' She tried to shake Indigo's hands away, but the effort was weak. 'You shouldn't touch me; I'm – '

'Hush.' Indigo spoke gently but firmly. 'You need to get out of the sun. Come with me.' And she called over her shoulder, 'Grimya, fetch the pony! I don't think she can walk more than a few steps.'

Grimya hurried away, and returned a few moments later with the pony's reins gripped in her teeth and the animal plodding reluctantly behind her. The sight raised a faint, dazed smile from the woman, and she didn't protest as Indigo helped her into the saddle.

Grimya said to Indigo: *I will go on ahead and see if the path leads to shade.* She paused, then added: *She is very sick, I think.*

*She'll recover when she has shelter, and water and food.*

*I'm not so sure. There is something else . . . ah, no matter.* The she-wolf shook her head, and before Indigo could question her turned and ran away along the path.


To Indigo's intense relief the path did not, as she had feared, end at a blank rock face. Instead, it snaked into a fissure in the cliff where two great folds of petrified lava met, and as they entered the gap the sun, blessedly, was hidden by the rising wall.

Grimya, who had explored some way into the fissure, reported that the track seemed to follow a huge fault that skirted the outer faces of the mountains; she had found no means of penetrating further into the range, but neither did the path show any sign of petering out. The canyon was also wide enough to allow them to rest in relative comfort, and Indigo spread a blanket out on the rough, pitted floor before lifting the woman down from the pony's back. Water was the most vital consideration, and she saw to it that both Grimya and the pony had their fill from her supply before she held the bottle to the woman's lips. She drank, but seemed to have difficulty in swallowing; watching her as she struggled Indigo realised with a shock that she was far younger than at first she'd thought; barely out of her teens, in fact, though hardship had aged her prematurely. Also, her skin in places was blotched an unsightly red, and there were sores on her neck and the inner flesh of her arms; recalling Grimya's cryptic observation Indigo wondered if the girl might have a fever to add to her troubles. But when at last she finished drinking and looked up, there was no sign of delirium in her eyes.

She laid a hand on Indigo's arm and whispered: 'Th-thank you, *saia*.'

Indigo smiled a little grimly. 'I hope I've made amends for my failure to help you last night.'

She was momentarily puzzled: but then her face cleared. 'Of course . . . you were in the square – you tried to stop them from hurting me – '

'And failed, I'm afraid.'

'No – you were so kind, so good – and now – ' The woman coughed, and spittle ran down her chin. 'I owe you so much, *saia*, and I can't repay you . . .' She twisted her hands, which were thin and work-roughened, in a strand of her own hair, and began to cry in painful, gulping sobs. There was an appalling hopelessness in the sound, and Indigo was horribly moved. She brushed quickly at her own eyes and said,

'I need no payment. Please, don't weep. Tell me your name, and why the mine guards were abusing you.'

She couldn't answer at first, only shook her head and continued to cry. But Indigo persisted, and at last she calmed a little. Her name, she said, was Chrysiva, and she was wife to a miner – but she got no further before a fresh bout of sobbing overtook her, and amid her gasping efforts to continue Indigo caught only one word.

*Charchad.*

A cold worm moved within her, and she caught hold of Chrysiva's shoulders. 'What has the Charchad to do with your trouble?' she asked urgently. 'What have they done to you?'

Chrysiva drew a deep, shuddering breath and looked up, red-eyed and blinded by her tears. 'They took him away . . .'

'Your husband?'

She nodded, and bit hard on her lower lip until a bead of blood welled. 'They – they said he had insulted

57

an overseer. It was a lie, he was *innocent* – but they wouldn't listen; they wouldn't even let him speak! Th-they said he must be punished, and . . . and they sent him to Charchad!'

'Sent him to Charchad? Chrysiva, what does that mean?'

She didn't heed the question. 'I have pleaded with them, I have begged them; I have tried *everything*, but they won't set him free!'

'Chrysiva – '

'Two months since they took him . . . *two months* and still they have no mercy! He won't live through it, I *know* he won't!'

'Chrysiva, please listen to me – '

*It is no use*, Grimya said sadly. *She is too distressed to answer your questions. All she can think of is her sorrow.*

With a sigh Indigo sat back on her heels. Grimya was right; they'd learn nothing more from Chrysiva until she had expunged the worst of her grief and was calmer. And she herself felt the need to rest; although they were out of the sun's reach the canyon was still breathlessly hot, and they would be well advised to sleep for a few hours until the day became cooler.

Chrysiva had huddled down on the blanket, face buried in the crook of one arm. The pony was already dozing; Indigo unsaddled it, then made herself as comfortable as she could and, with Grimya beside her, settled down to sleep.

She did sleep; but dreams came to haunt her, interlaced with a dim and feverish awareness of the heat and the hard discomfort of the rock on which she lay. In the dreams she saw Fenran again, but his face was disfigured by terrible scars, skin seared and burned by a disease that raged within him and would not be checked. Indigo knew that without swift and skilled attention her lover would die, and in her nightmare she cried out for Imyssa, the wise old witch who had nursed her in childhood. But her cry only echoed uselessly through the empty halls of Carn Caille, and Imyssa did not answer. And when she turned and reached out for the jars of potions and simples that stood on a shelf beside her, they yielded only a foul black dust that vanished to nothing in her hands. And Fenran was calling her name from the bed of twisted thorn-branches where he lay, and he was fading, and she couldn't help him, and he was dying–

She woke with a cry that echoed in the canyon and made Grimya spring to her feet, hackles raised in alarm. Then came the familiar realisation that it had been no more than a dream, and the clamminess of sweat drying on her body; then at last the reassuring touch of the she-wolf's fur as she tried to give her friend some comfort.

*Another of the nightmares?* Grimya's question was filled with sympathy.

She nodded, then looked over her shoulder at Chrysiva. The girl still seemed to be sleeping; her face was turned away. Indigo sighed.

'I dreamed of Fenran again, Grimya. But this time he was dying of a fever.'

Grimya whined softly in her throat. *It was the story this woman told that put you in mind of such things. She, too, has lost her mate and pines for him.* She hesitated. *I have never had a mate. But I have a friend, and I think I understand.*

There *were* parallels between Chrysiva's tragedy and her own, Indigo thought with wry bitterness, and it deepened her sense of fellow-feeling for the girl. She stared down at her tightly-clasped hands and said: 'I only hope she has a greater chance of finding her love than I have of finding mine.'

*You shouldn't say such things*, Grimya chided anxiously. *While we live, there is hope.*

'Hope?' Indigo's face was suddenly haggard, then her expression tightened into a mask. 'Yes; there's hope.' Abruptly she turned away and got to her feet, brushing herself down with unnecessary energy. 'It's cooler now. The worst of the day's over – we should move on.'

Grimya made no further comment, but as Indigo went to saddle the pony – refusing to meet the she-wolf's gaze – she padded to where Chrysiva lay and nudged gently at her to rouse her.

'In-digo . . .'

Her tone carried an undercurrent of alarm. Indigo rubbed quickly at her eyes and looked back. 'What is it?'

'She . . . will not s-stir. I th-*ink* she is s . . . sick.'

Swiftly Indigo came to join her, and turned Chrysiva over. There was dried spittle on the girl's lips; she moaned and mumbled something unintelligible, but either would not or could not open her eyes. And her skin was hotter than was natural even in such a climate.

'She has a fever.' Silently Indigo cursed herself for the shortcomings in her own medical skills. She had a small collection of herbs in her saddlebag, but her knowledge extended little further than an ability to staunch bleeding or splint a bone or relieve pain. To give the wrong potion to the sick girl, or even the wrong dosage of the right potion, could do more harm than good.

If only she had attended more closely to Imyssa's teachings . . . the thought was bitterly ironic, and angrily she thrust it away, straightening and staring at the volcanic peaks piling into the sky above and before them.

'She needs better care than I can give her,' she said harshly. 'We have two choices, Grimya. Either we take her back to the town, or we go on as we planned, and hope that the fever will burn itself out.'

'We cannot . . . go back.'

'I know. But if we don't – '

'She may d-*die*.' Grimya moved closer to Chrysiva and sniffed at her face. 'But there is s-something . . .' She raised her head in puzzlement. 'This sickness. It is not . . . *usual*.'

'What do you mean?'

'It is . . . ah, I don't have the w-*words* . . .' The wolf grimaced with frustration, then gave up her panting efforts to speak aloud. Her thoughts touched Indigo's mind. *The thing that ails her is something that no man-healer could cure.*

Indigo dropped to a crouch and studied Chrysiva more intently. The blotches, the sores . . . she recalled the disfigurements sported by so many of the Charchad faithful, and the miners in the square with their dreadful afflictions, and felt suddenly cold.

'We must go on,' she said. 'You're right; there's no other choice.'

'And the w-woman?'

She didn't fear fever or sickness. That, too, was part of her curse. 'Hope and pray for her,' she said with quiet bitterness. 'We can do no more than that.'

By the time the sun began to set they had found no path to lead them deeper into the mountains, and Indigo's early hope had dulled to leaden pessimism. The track through the rock fault continued to rise perceptibly but otherwise showed no signs of changing, and when the last light failed they stopped by the side of the path and made a makeshift camp.

Indigo sat on the ground, clasping her own knees and peering into the darkness ahead, not wanting to share her gloomy thoughts even with Grimya. Behind her, Chrysiva was propped against the rock wall: during the past hour she had rallied a little and was now conscious, though too weak and disorientated to be coherent.

A faint whine from Grimya alerted her and she looked over her shoulder. The she-wolf lay sprawled a few paces away, and in the dimness Indigo could just make out the flickering red of her tongue as she stretched her head back, one paw twitching. Grimya was almost asleep, the sound nothing more than an expression of her lupine dreams, and the girl smiled faintly. She, too, should be trying to rest, but she could no more sleep than grow wings and fly. The night was hot, the canyon preternaturally quiet, and she couldn't still the restiveness within her, the frustrated urge to be doing something more positive than simply awaiting the dawn.

She looked up at the narrow band of visible sky above the canyon. The light of the moon was eclipsed by the cold, unnatural glow that from this vantage point dominated the upper atmosphere and cast peculiar, dimensionless shadows on the peaks. From here she might have expected to feel some vibration from the massive, day-and-night mining operations which could be no more than a mere two or three miles away; but there was nothing. Only the stillness, and the silence.

She touched a hand to the lodestone, but didn't take it out to examine it. To do so seemed futile; she knew well enough what it would tell her. *But how?* she asked herself – or perhaps asked the stone – wordlessly. *How are we to find our way into the mountains, when there's no path, no track, nothing but this endless canyon?*

Something flickered momentarily at the periphery of her vision; a firefly perhaps, darting in the air and glinting red-gold. Indigo rubbed her eyes, which prickled with heat and dust, then shook her head to clear it as the firefly's after-image danced on her retinae. She stretched her arms, flexed her fingers to ease cramp – then stopped, and stared along the path.

There were more tiny sparks hovering in the canyon; but they weren't fireflies. Their formation was too contrived, too regular: as she stared harder she realised that they made an unevenly flickering pattern. Almost a crude representation of a human outline . . .

Slowly, cautiously, Indigo began to lever herself to her feet. Another glance over her shoulder showed Grimya now apparently sound asleep, and Chrysiva's face was turned away, her shoulders apathetically slumped. Indigo fingered her knife, then on impulse crept to where her saddlebag lay and loosed her crossbow from the thongs that secured it. She set a bolt into the bow, thrust three more into her belt, then looked along the canyon again.

The dancing image was less clear now, but still visible. Grimya's tail twitched and she made an odd, throaty noise, but she didn't wake, and Chrysiva paid no heed as Indigo stepped quietly on to the path and moved towards the peculiar lights. Her eyes were as adjusted to the dark as they would ever be, and she judged that the sparks were perhaps fifteen or twenty yards away, neither approaching nor receding. Closer, and for a moment the humanlike pattern seemed to glow brighter as though on the verge of taking three-dimensional form – then suddenly, as she prepared herself for a swift rush towards it, it vanished.

Startled, Indigo couldn't stop the reflex that had already begun to propel her forward, and she swore under her breath as one foot stubbed painfully against a low rock projection. Firefly ghosts echoed in her vision, confusing her; she reached out to the cliff to steady herself and regain her balance –

And sprawled full-length into a gap in the rock wall.

Indigo sat up, spitting dust and nursing a grazed hand. For a few moments she couldn't assimilate what had happened; but then realisation dawned, and with it came a sharp stab of excitement.

There was a break in the cliff. It was barely wide enough to accommodate a broad-shouldered man, but, against unimaginable odds, she had stumbled into it. Heart thumping, Indigo scrambled to her feet and turned around, stretching her hands out before her into the gap. She anticipated the disappointment of meeting a solid barrier, of finding that the flaw was no more than two or three feet deep; but the disappointment didn't come. And when, cautiously, she moved forward, groping ahead, still there was no barrier, and the ground beneath her feet began suddenly and sharply to rise.

A gully into the mountains. And no more than thirty

steps from where they had abandoned their search. Indigo's excitement caught stiflingly in her throat, and she forced herself to take several deep breaths to calm her thoughts. If – *if*, she stressed to herself – the gully led anywhere, then it would be a hard route for the pony, especially with the added burden of Chrysiva. The gap between the walls was barely wide enough now for the animal to squeeze through; any narrower and it would become impassable. When daylight came she and Grimya would be well advised to explore further before committing them all to a trek that might prove fruitless.

When daylight came . . . Indigo looked back along the track, then into the gully again. Impatience gnawed at her; she didn't relish the prospect of lying wakeful and restless, counting the minutes until dawn. She wouldn't sleep, not with this discovery so close yet so frustratingly out of reach. And she didn't want to wait for morning.

She could, surely, explore a little way into the gully at least? The going would be slow and tricky, but the eerie glow in the sky did a little to alleviate the darkness, and if she took care she should come to no harm. Grimya would disapprove, but with luck Grimya would sleep on until her return and be none the wiser. Just a short way, she thought. To be certain.

She looked back once more, but her companions weren't visible, and her eagerness was urging her on. Shouldering her crossbow and keeping one hand pressed to the rock wall beside her as a sure guide, Indigo moved on and up into the gully.

She had resolved to count no more than fifty paces before turning back. But after fifty paces the gully was still rising quite steeply, and had widened a little, making the going easier than she had feared. So fifty became a hundred, and then another twenty, and another, until she told herself that if she pressed on just a little further she might emerge above the lower volcanic slopes, where the light in the sky would be sufficient to show the way ahead far more clearly.

She paused at a place where the gully curved, to resettle her crossbow which had been slipping and threatening to unbalance her. She was sweating, and the night air tasted faintly metallic; from the pumice-like feel of the rock beneath her fingers she hazarded that the path was winding through the petrified course of an ancient lava flow. Indigo knew little about geology, but it seemed logical to surmise that the flow must have originated in the mountains' heart, and could therefore be her one chance of finding a way into the depths of the range.

Just a few more steps, and she would turn back. The return journey would be easier; she could reach the camp in a matter of minutes. And then she would have a tale to tell when Grimya woke –

Indigo yelled in shock as, from nowhere and with no warning, searing red light suddenly blasted through the gully. A wave of intense heat erupted from the ground, snatching her breath away; the gully floor lurched and she spun off balance, stumbling against the wall and falling to hands and knees. She started to get up: then froze as, through eyes nearly blinded by the brilliance, her stunned senses registered a mad image of some-thing vast, heaving, boiling, blazing red-hot, rolling down from the surrounding peaks towards her. *Lava* – molten lava, burning and hissing and crowned with roaring flames, belching out of the night in a monstrous, slow-moving river.

All coherent thought collapsed into chaos, and Indigo's entire body turned slick with the sweat of terror. It was *impossible* – these volcanoes had been extinct for centuries; their lava flows were fossilised, petrified. *This could not be happening!*

The crackling roar of fire dinned in her ears, counter-pointed by a massive, thundering vibration, and the heat of the oncoming molten river beat against her skin like great breakers. Impossible or not, the lava flow was real – and it was searing through the gully, straight into her path!

She turned, slithering on shale and loose pumice, struggling to hold back the panic that threatened to overwhelm her. She *had* to keep her wits, or –

Horror hit her like a physical punch to the stomach as she saw the blazing orange tributary that had diverged from the main flow and curved around behind her to burn a swathe through the cliffs at her back. Already rocks within the gully were melting, losing shape and solidity, glowing crimson, then scarlet, then gold. In seconds, her retreat would be cut off.

Indigo ran. A sane part of her mind screamed that it was hopeless, that she couldn't hope to reach safety before the lava came boiling across her path; but desperation made her hurl the knowledge aside as she plunged down the slope. Underfoot the ground was blisteringly hot, already burning through the soles of her shoes; she ran faster, and her skirt, which she'd hitched about her thighs as she climbed, suddenly came loose in a tangle of fabric that caught about one foot and tripped her. She hit hard rock, rolled, felt heat blast her as yellow brilliance erupted in her path – then as her eyes refocused, she screamed.

A huge, phantasmic creature reared on the path before her, reptilian forelegs flailing, forked tail lashing, vast, membranous wings beating the air towards her in suffocating waves. A corona of fire blazed about it and it roared, the sound breaching dimensions from reality to nightmare.

*Dragon!* her mind shrieked. But it was a myth, a legend, an impossibility – there were no such things as dragons! And suddenly through the cacophony of panic Indigo knew with a sure and terrible instinct what was afoot. *Sorcery* – and she had walked blindly into its trap!

She rolled again, springing to her feet in the same movement, and spun round to race back up the gully, away from the rearing, bellowing phantom.

66

She had taken three strides before the scene in front of her exploded. A wall of sound, thunder and earth-quake and tornado together, smashed down from the mountain peaks to hit her full on, and with it came a wave of furnace-hot power that buffeted her off her feet and sent her tumbling back down the defile like a leaf in a gale. She heard the dragon scream a furious challenge, and as the world fragmented around her she had a mad, momentary glimpse of a human figure, arms raised, wreathed in white flames that silhouetted him against the burning sky.

*Heat – a new onslaught of power – agony –* Indigo's consciousness raced head-on into darkness, and smashed through it into nothing.

# Chapter V

She tried to move her arms, to ease the pressure against the small of her back; but they refused to respond. Someone's fingers were clasped on her wrists, pinning them . . . she writhed, attempting to pull herself free, but only succeeded in losing her balance and sliding like a child's rag doll to lie helplessly on her side.

Not fingers. Her mind was unclear still; but they were not fingers holding her. Not hands: rope. It chafed, and when she tried again to move her arms she felt the rough bite of its strands against her blistered skin.

*Hot.* She could feel sweat trickling between her breasts and down her spine, and her hair was plastered clammily to her cheeks and forehead. The air was hot; the floor on which she lay was hot. And she couldn't quite make herself remember where she was, or how she had come to be here.

Indigo opened her eyes, blinking in an effort to clear them. There was light, and though it wasn't intolerably bright, she couldn't focus at first on anything in her field of view. Then after a few seconds her vision cleared a little. And she found herself staring directly at a small shrine. Different coloured stones had been set carefully before it, forming a neat semi-circle, and at the shrine's centre, lit by a smoking votive lamp, was a figure the size of a man's hand, hewn from what looked like basalt. Agates glittered in its eye-sockets, and the tongue that protruded from its open mouth was carved into the likeness of a flame. Its hair, too, was fashioned to resemble flames; a halo of fire like a stylised solar corona, and in between its outstretched hands it held a frozen bolt of lightning. The figure was naked, female, and with a twinge of shock Indigo recognised a skilled craftsman's representation of the fire-goddess Ranaya.

And with a second shock, the fierce image pulled together the tangled threads of her memory.

'Grimya – ' In her sudden alarm Indigo forgot the bindings on her wrists and tried to get up, only to fall awkwardly back again. Nearby, something hissed angrily – she froze; then slowly turned her head.

Two feet away, something that she had thought existed only in legend crouched on the uneven rock floor, staring at her with alien yellow eyes. A salamander. Its body was, perhaps, as long as her arm, and made of green flame so translucent that she could see tiny arteries of scarlet fire pulsing beneath its burning skin. Golden claws scraped the rock, and where its body touched the floor, the floor smoked and sizzled.

Indigo gasped and shrank back. The salamander opened its fiery mouth and hissed again, adopting a hostile stance as though to lunge at her – then from somewhere beyond Indigo's head a voice that carried dangerous undercurrents of both fury and loathing grated:

'If you so much as move again without my permission, my servant will burn your heart from your body!'

A shadow fell across her, and she looked up to see her captor standing over her.

He was tall, and his height was emphasised by the fact that undernourishment had reduced his frame to a bony gauntness under his old and tattered clothing. Hair that in his youth had been black but was now greying – in places almost white – tumbled in a wild mass over his shoulders and half-way down his back; the overall impression was made doubly bizarre by the fact that the tangle was overlaid by clusters of intricate braids, and something about the peculiar style rang a bell in Indigo's mind. But she had no time to search her memory, for the stranger was leaning over her, shoulders and chest heaving with quick, angry breaths. Crazed green-brown eyes stared into hers from a face that was lined by unnatural strain, and he hissed, 'Do you understand me? *Do you?*'

Indigo got a grip on her pounding heart and quelled her own rising anger, aware that any attempt to argue could be very dangerous. 'Yes. I understand.'

The salamander settled on to its haunches; she could feel the heat emanating from it, as though she were lying too close to a fire . . .

'Then understand, too, that I shall have answers.' The man began to turn away, then spun back to face her, pointing a threatening finger. '*Answers!* And if you *dare* to lie, you will *burn!*'

Indigo twisted uncomfortably in her bonds. Although she was prudent enough to realise that at the smallest provocation he both could and would hurt her, she couldn't crush her anger. It was there, and it was growing stronger.

Teeth clenched against her natural instinct to give vent to a furious tirade, she snapped, 'I've already said I understand you! Ask your damned questions, and have done!'

He continued to stare at her for a few moments more. Then, so quickly that she was caught unawares, he snatched a handful of her hair and yanked on it, lifting her and slamming her back against the cave wall. Indigo's skull cracked against rock, and giddy nausea made her gasp; when her senses stopped spinning and she was able to open her eyes again, and he was crouched in front of her, staring madly at her as though he sought to see into her soul.

'Why did you come here?' His voice was husky with suppressed rage. 'What devious motive brought you creeping along my paths like a snake in the gutter?' A hand shot out and gripped her jaw, squeezing painfully. *'How did you know where to find my sanctum?'*

'*Damn* you!' Indigo wrenched her jaw free, breathing hard. 'What in the name of all that's sacred makes you think I was looking for your sanctum? I don't even know who you are!'

'Liar!' He drew back his hand as if to strike her, then paused. 'There's no other living soul in these slopes, and you know it! You knew I was here! You were *searching for me*!'

'I was not!' Indigo fired back.

'No?' He rose, flexing his hands. 'We shall see, *saia*. We shall see.' A crooked smile distorted his face, and his eyes took on an odd, distant look. 'You're no ordinary intruder, that much I can judge well enough. You have a little power of your own. Haven't you?'

Indigo looked away.

'Yes,' he continued thoughtfully. 'A little power. But not enough.' The smile widened. 'No match for my illusions. My rivers of lava. My dragons. My pets.'

The salamander rose to its hind legs, and a shrill, unearthly sound vibrated in its throat.

'Wait, little one. In time; in time.' He saw Indigo's gaze slide unwillingly to the elemental, and chuckled softly. 'When they are called, they must be fed before they can be banished again. And when they feed, they char both flesh and bone. It isn't a quick process. But it is, I understand, very painful.' He paced slowly away from her, paused, turned, came back. 'So. The truth. How did you find me? And why did you come?'

Indigo's gaze slid surreptitiously past him as she attempted to take in her surroundings. They were, it appeared, in a large cave, modestly but adequately lit by candles set in rough alcoves about the walls. On the far side the mouth of a tunnel gaped, but she could see nothing in the darkness beyond, and certainly there was no obvious way of escape, even if she could have loosed her hands or evaded the salamander.

She looked at her interrogator again, and realised that he wasn't sane. The anger that burned in him, whatever its cause, was looking for an outlet: he *wanted*

71

to hurt her, and was only waiting for her to give him justification. Her gaze flicked to the little statue of Ranaya again, and it gave her a glimmering of hope where otherwise there would be nothing. Whatever else he might be, this man was clearly no devotee of the Charchad. He had power; he had proved that shockingly with the illusions by which he had trapped her in the gully. But his goddess was an avatar of the Earth Mother, so the power on which he called was a *clean* power.

He said: 'I await your answer.'

She had to tell him the truth. She had nothing to lose.

'My business in these mountains has no connection with you,' she said, her throat dry. 'I knew nothing of your existence until you used your sorcery to capture me, and I had no intention of trespassing on your sanctum or anyone else's. The plain truth is that I was trying to find a way of reaching the mines without alerting those who work there to my presence.' She blinked, licked her lips. 'That's the long and the short of it, and you may believe me or not as you please.'

Silence followed her statement. Whether or not the man was considering her words seriously she couldn't tell; his expression was unreadable. The only sound in the cave was a faint crackling from the salamander, which was growing ever more restive.

At last her captor spoke. 'A way of reaching the mines.' One bony finger rested lightly on his chin, then suddenly his gaze snapped to her, manic. 'Why? What business have you there that must be conducted in secret?'

*Earth Mother*, she thought, *aid me now, if you can* . . . And aloud she said: 'I am searching for the source of the Charchad.'

The salamander whistled shrilly, and white fire flared from its nostrils. Its fury was reflected in the eyes of the sorcerer, which seemed suddenly to catch light with a surge of insane rage. For an instant only he was

72

motionless, rigid; then he swooped down on her and dragged her to her feet, shaking her as a blood-maddened shark might frenziedly shake its prey.

'What have you to do with that filth?' His voice was a screech, echoing horribly in the cave, and he slammed Indigo again and again against the wall. 'Answer me! *Tell* me, before I tear you apart with my bare hands! You serpent, you miserable, squalling abortion – what are those demons to you?'

Indigo cried out, the sounds torn involuntarily from her throat as, with a strength that belied his build and gauntness, he flung her to the floor. The elemental sprang at her head, eyes burning white-hot, mouth agape, but he commanded harshly, '*No!*' and the creature fell back. Indigo lay retching, every nerve aflame with pain, and from a vast, whirling distance she heard his voice grating close to her ear as he dropped to a crouch beside her.

'Tell me the truth! That poor woman in your charge – where were you taking her? What have you done to her?'

'*Uhhh* . . .' She couldn't articulate, couldn't think; her senses were red, burning. 'Chrys . . . iva. She . . . oh, Great Goddess, help me!' And through the daze she felt it coming, rising. The anger. The fury. The hatred and the loathing that had lurked like a disease in her heart and in her stomach since she had first heard the name of Charchad. There was bile in her throat; she choked it back and the hatred found a focus in her tormentor, in the man who had hurt her, ruined her plan, threatened her friends – '

'Let me alone, you stinking piece of offal!' Her voice rose shrilly, close to hysteria, as any consideration for her own safety shattered and the rage came roaring through. 'How *dare* you accuse me of such blasphemy! The Earth Mother curse you, and shrivel your soul! Untie me! *Untie* me, you coward, you cur, you – '

A hand cracked across her right temple and she rocked back, biting her tongue as her tirade broke off

73

in mid-flow. As she struggled to right herself, head reeling, she saw that a rope had appeared in her tormentor's hands; a rope made of blue flames that flickered and shivered yet did not seem to burn him.

'Oh, it is easy for the scum of Charchad to swear by the Great Goddess.' His voice was soft, deadly. 'But we will see, *saia*, how your righteous protestations fare in the face of trial!' He tautened the fire-rope between his fingers. 'Stand up.'

Indigo's shoulders heaved with the effort to suck air into her lungs. 'I will not!'

He smiled. 'Then die in pain, here, at the behest of my little servant, and prove yourself afraid of the truth.'

*Truth?* Indigo thought dizzily. But it was enough to goad her.

'No.' Trying to maintain some semblance of dignity, she struggled to her feet and stood facing him. 'Your pet may wait. Try me, if that's what pleases your warped mind. And *truth* is what you will have!'

He stared at her for a few moments; then a small, sour smile deepened the lines on his face.

'That way.' He indicated the dark tunnel she had seen earlier. 'The salamander will be at your heels; if you hesitate or run, you will feel its breath. Do I make myself clear?'

'You do.' She gave him a withering look, and turned towards the tunnel mouth.

The tunnel was unlit, but the flickering green glow of the salamander was enough to illuminate their way. Indigo felt the heat increasing as she walked, until, when she was finally told to halt, she felt as though she stood on the brink of an open furnace. Choked by the stifling air, she turned to look at her captor.

'What now?' Her voice echoed horribly: she tried to inject a note of defiance into her tone, but it was a poor attempt; she felt claustrophobic, and her earlier fury had ebbed, leaving her vulnerable and fearful.

74

'Be silent.' He brushed past her, the salamander skittering at his heels, and by the light emanating from the elemental's body she saw that the tunnel ended a short way ahead, seemingly at the lip of a deep well that dropped away into darkness. Sulphurous smoke rose in dense, lazy coils from the darkness, and she realised that the well was a fumarole from one of the ancient volcanoes.

But surely the volcanoes were dead . . .

'Sit.' A hand pushed her back; she stumbled and dropped to her knees. From somewhere in the depths of the fumarole light flickered suddenly, painting the tunnel walls a fiery red; against the glow her captor was a skeletal silhouette as he turned towards her and held out the burning rope. He uttered five harsh, foreign syllables – and the rope came alive, snapping from his hands to snake like a whiplash towards Indigo. Involuntarily she jerked back, but her reactions were too slow; the flaming cord coiled around her and she felt as though something huge and hot had breathed out in a great, gusting sigh. Warmth that was all-embracing yet stopped short of the threshold of pain enfolded her. The rope didn't burn. But as it settled about her body she realised that she was held fast, could neither move nor – and the second realisation came much in the way that she sometimes knew she was slipping from wakefulness into dreaming – think clearly. Consciousness was fading in and out, rising and falling as though to the rhythm of a slow, inexorable heartbeat. Her captor – tormentor, sorcerer, nemesis *(that concept had a crucial meaning. But what? What? She couldn't remember)* – was a black silhouette before her, an outline etched in sparks. He was speaking, but the words made no sense.

'You see the power of the cord of fire, that binds death to life, sleep to wakefulness, reality to illusion. And truth to falsehood. Now we shall learn the truth, *saia*. Now we shall learn.'

Smoke rolled from the fumarole, and she could smell

sulphur again and feel the heat of the crackling rocks around her. But there was more than sulphur and heat. There was a sound in her head, like the chiming of a strange, mechanical timepiece. There was the murmuring hiss of flames. There was the softer murmur of a river current, flowing sluggishly into the baked southlands. And further. There was the sea, forever breathing with a cool, slow rhythm against tall cliffs. There were ships and there was the sharp bite of cold salt spray. There was a shore, and woods, and plains, and –

And the old terrors of her homeland superstitions, when a warm, living creature who was lonely and outcast cried in the night for a friend and said *wolf* in her drowsy mind . . .

And there was Carn Caille. Old, beloved Carn Caille, fortress of the Southern Isles where the summer sun never set and the winter snow swirled through the day-long dark from the ramparts of the glaciers. And there was King Kalig, whose nine-times-great grand-father had wrested power and founded a dynasty within Carn Caille's worn and mellowed walls. And Kalig's queen, and his children; Kirra, who would be king in his own time, and –

And –

'*Nnnh* . . .' The word wouldn't come; her lips were frozen and she couldn't speak it. But the denial was in her mind, the fear, the terror, as Fenran's dying face screamed to her from the carnage of battle, as the Tower of Regrets crumbled on the tundra, as horrors that shouldn't have walked the earth vomited from the ruins to bear down on home and life and love, and tear her world apart –

*And Fenran wasn't dead, but in limbo, in a demon world where thorns tore his flesh and nightmares stalked his endless waking hours. And she alone could save him. But only when her quest was finally over, if it took ten years or a thousand –*

'*No!*' The chains that held Indigo's mind heaved and

76

broke, and she screamed like a banshee, thrashing on
the floor of the tunnel. The salamander screeched, its
form burning brighter until it rivalled the brilliance of
the light spilling from the fumarole. Smoke belched
upward to form a black cloud over her head; she tried
to fight the hands that gripped her, pulled her back,
glimpsed a face white with shock that swam before her
like a demented vision, and –

And –

Someone was holding a cup to her lips. The water was
warm and a little brackish but she drank gratefully,
feeling it ease the strangling constriction in her throat.
Some caught in her windpipe and made her cough;
reflexively she raised one hand to cover her mouth,
and only then, remembering, did she realise that her
bonds had been cut.

Her wrists felt sore, but otherwise she seemed to be
unharmed. Again the water was held out to her; she
drank more and her mind abruptly began to clear,
focusing recollection of the last few hours. She had
expected to die or for the torment to continue: instead
it seemed that someone or something had intervened
to rescue her.

Confused and not knowing what to anticipate, Indigo
opened her eyes.

She was back in the cave. The candlelight still flickered, but the salamander had gone. And a voice said
quietly:

'*Saia* Indigo. Can you ever forgive me?'

He was kneeling at her side, the cup held in a hand
that shook perceptibly. Some of the plaits in his hair
had come unfastened, making him look more than ever
like a crazed scarecrow, and his face was streaked with
soot. But the dementia in his eyes had gone, and in its
place were fear and shame.

He extended the cup again and involuntarily Indigo
drew back, breath catching sharply in her throat.
'Don't touch me!'

Chagrined, he set the cup down, and she saw that several plates of food – some cooked meat, a melange of rapidly wilting vegetables, a small cake with a crust of dried fruits – had been placed in a semi-circle before her, much as a petitioner might lay an offering before a temple shrine. She looked at him again, suspicion tensing every muscle.

'What game are you playing with me now?'

He shook his head emphatically. 'No game, *saia*. An attempt – pitiful I know, but an attempt – to make reparation to you.' His gaze met hers, painfully candid. 'If such a thing is possible.'

Warily, Indigo watched his face as she tried to gauge how far she could trust this apparent change of heart. If the man was as mad as he'd seemed earlier, he might simply be trying to lull her as a prelude to some devious new assault.

Then in the distance, and muffled by a vast density of rock between them, she heard the chilling howl of an angry wolf.

'Grimya!' She started to scramble to her feet, then realised that she couldn't judge the direction from which the sound had come. She whirled on the man. 'Where is she? What have you done to her?'

'Please.' He held up both hands in a pacifying gesture. 'The animal is unharmed. She has food and water, and she is perfectly safe.' He smiled wryly. 'I had no choice but to use my sorcerous skills to confine her in another cave, or she would have torn my throat out. But I swear to you, she has suffered no hurt.'

Quickly, Indigo focused her mental energy on the direction from which the howl had come, and immediately felt the red-heat of Grimya's inchoate anger. The she-wolf's mind was in too much turmoil for her to be able to make telepathic contact, but her captor had spoken the truth: Grimya was unharmed.

She looked at the sorcerer again. 'And what of Chrysiva?' she demanded.

'Chrysiva?'

'The girl who was with us. She's sick, and if you – '

'She too is safe, *saia*. Please – ' tentatively he extended a hand and, although Indigo still refused to unbend, this time she didn't shrink away. He clenched his fingers. 'I must explain my actions to you; why I reacted so violently to your arrival. You may think me mad, *saia*, but I beg you to believe that I am not.' He paused, and his face muscles worked into a peculiar expression that she couldn't begin to interpret. 'Tormented, yes; and *angry*; so angry . . . But not mad.'

Reserving judgement, Indigo said: 'And do anger and torment alone justify your behaviour towards strangers?'

'Under normal circumstances, no.' He acknowledged the point with a wry glance. 'But circumstances here are not normal, *saia*; nor have they been for the past five years. When I was first alerted to your presence in the mountains, I thought you must be one of them, searching for me – '

'Them?' Indigo interrupted.

'The followers of the filthy abomination that has blasphemed against Ranaya, and taken all that was good and strong and . . .' The furious words tailed off abruptly and he got a grip on himself. 'Let us say that I have learned through bitter experience that any stranger is more likely than not to be an enemy.'

Indigo began to understand, and she said softly, 'The Charchad?'

He nodded, his face tight. 'I can hardly bear to hear the name spoken aloud, even now. And when you told me that you were here to seek them out, I – ' He expelled a harsh breath. 'I didn't stop to consider what your motives might be; the rage in me was too strong and I wanted only to exact vengeance on you. It was only when I used the cord of fire and saw what was in your heart that I realised the mistake I had made.'

A cold, dead hand clutched at Indigo's stomach as she saw suddenly what he implied, and she remembered the nightmare experience she had undergone by the fumarole in the tunnel. A sorcerer of such power – and he was powerful; she had seen more than enough to convince her of that – could look into the depths of another mind, draw out all that was there and see the naked soul beyond.

She met his gaze and her fears were instantly and horribly confirmed by the underlying pity she saw in his eyes. He knew what she was. Unwittingly, unwillingly, she had shown him everything: her past, her crime, the curse that the Earth Mother had laid upon her. He *knew*.

She turned away as a sick wave of misery and shame washed over her, and put a fist to her mouth, biting the knuckles. 'I – '

'Please, *saia*.' He touched her arm with a gentleness that surprised her. 'What's done is done and neither of us can change it. I don't pretend to understand what lies behind your quest, and I don't mean to try. Let no more be said of it, if it's what you will. But don't you see that we're two of a kind?'

She lowered her fist and looked at him uncertainly. 'Are we?'

'Yes! I know what you've lost. And I know the grief that such a loss brings, for I have suffered in the same way. We share a goal, *saia* Indigo, and I believe that the quirk of fate that brought us together is nothing less than the deed of Ranaya herself!'

His eyes were beginning to light again with the unmistakable glow of fanaticism, and Indigo felt herself overwhelmed by his eagerness – though not altogether unwillingly, for suddenly he had struck an answering chord within her.

She said: 'I'm not sure that I see – '

'You *must* see! It's so clear! The Goddess meant us to meet, for She has a task for us. Your quest and mine are one and the same – and where alone our powers are limited, together we can work to do Her will and we can succeed!'

A tight, uneasy knot of excitement grew abruptly in Indigo. 'The Charchad?'

'Yes!' He caught hold of her hands, gripping them so tightly that she winced. 'Ranaya has answered my prayers, and you are Her instrument. Together, Indigo, we can face the Charchad – and we can destroy it!'

# Chapter VI

Indigo said: 'Jasker, I'm sorry. I grieve for you.' She raised her head and met the unquiet, green-brown eyes of the man sitting opposite her. 'Truly, I grieve for you.'

At her side Grimya shifted restively and added her own sympathetic agreement in a soft whine. The sorcerer glanced at the she-wolf, then smiled sadly and cast his gaze down.

'Your friend has more forgiveness and kindness in her heart than I have any right to expect,' he said.

'Grimya isn't hampered by human weaknesses. But her feelings are as strong as any man's or woman's.' Indigo looked at the rough-cut stone platter before her, then slowly pushed it away. Jasker's story had diminished her appetite to the point where thought of food made her stomach queasy; instead she picked up the water-skin he had set beside the plate, and refilled his cup and her own.

Jasker – he had, she gathered, no family name; they were not customary in these parts – had done all he could to make amends both to her and to Grimya for the ordeal of their first encounter. When the truth came out Indigo herself was willing enough to forgive and forget; however, calming Grimya sufficiently to make her understand that the man need no longer be regarded as a threat hadn't been easy. Indigo had finally managed to make telepathic contact with her, and patiently persuaded her not to launch herself at Jasker's throat the moment he released the sorcerous barrier that held her trapped in a smaller cave. When she finally emerged Grimya had been crimson-eyed and bristling with angry suspicion; but Indigo's reassurances and a dish of fresh meat had mollified her at last, and she agreed to join them in the main cave to hear Jasker's story.

That story, as the sorcerer had now told it, did not make pleasant hearing. With a quiet, grim determination that couldn't mask the pain evoked by his memories, Jasker explained that he was – or, more accurately, had been – a member of the respected sorcerer-priesthood of the Fire-Goddess Ranaya, avatar of the Earth Mother who had been worshipped in the region for generations. But with the arrival of the Charchad had come violent and hideous change. The cult – and as yet Jasker had told Indigo nothing of its origins – had grown with chilling rapidity, until its officers felt themselves powerful enough to challenge the reign of Ranaya through the deposing of her priesthood.

Perhaps, Jasker said bitterly, he and his fellow priests had been fools to resist. Perhaps they should have realised before it was too late that a direct confrontation with the Charchad would bring only disaster; for its devotees had used fear and torment to spread their influence through the mining lands and no ordinary man or woman dared raise a voice, let alone a hand, against them. But they had resisted; and their fervent hope that the people for whom they had interceded with Ranaya for so long would rise with them proved false. Jasker's friends, his dearest companions, were slaughtered. They tried to use their sorcery, but Charchad had powers of its own that they could neither comprehend nor combat. And when the torture and the killing were done, Jasker's own wife, whom he adored, was among the torn and broken corpses that the Charchad left behind.

The icy detachment with which the sorcerer related the manner of his wife's death shocked Indigo to the core, for she could sense the titanic strain that the retelling put upon him. One momentary lapse, one small hint of emotion, and Jasker would have broken down uncontrollably. His wife – he would not tell Indigo her name; by his tradition it was a discourtesy to speak the names of the dead aloud – had been tortured for the duration of an entire night. He didn't reveal the details of her torture, and Indigo did not ask. But he described how he, stripped of his power and beyond all ability to help her, had been forced to watch her slow and agonising journey towards death.

Jasker's own end would have come on the evening of the following day; the Charchad, it seemed, wanted to preserve a few victims to provide a public example for doubters and unbelievers, and so they had imprisoned him, with two barely conscious comrades, in his own temple. How he had escaped was something he couldn't now remember; his only recollection was of being overcome suddenly by a rage the like of which he had never known before, a berserker fury that wiped out all reason and all fear. He had broken from his prison and had killed two men, perhaps three; from then his mind was blank until the moment when he came to his senses to find himself in the volcanic mountains with the sun setting in an angry crimson blaze at his back.

That slaughter had taken place two years ago, and since then Jasker had lived here alone, an outcast and a fugitive. The old mountains were riddled with caves, tunnels, wells, all carved out by molten lava in the days when volcanic activity was at its height. There had been no eruptions now for more than three generations, and so the network of passages and caverns made an ideal and near-impregnable refuge. However, Jasker told Indigo, the volcanoes were by no means extinct. There was life in the deepest shafts of the fire-mountains – shafts such as the fumarole she had seen – but it was dormant, he said with an odd smile. Not dead; dormant. As though it waited for something to break its long quiescence.

Whether the Charchad leaders were aware of Jasker's presence he didn't know. Throughout his exile only four strangers before Indigo had strayed into the area of his stronghold, and none of them had lived long enough for Jasker to establish whether their presence was mere accident or something more sinister. She had asked him why he stayed in the mountains rather than seeking out a new life elsewhere, and his answering smile turned her cold.

'For vengeance.' His eyes glittered in the cave's gloom and she saw a sudden resurgence of the old mania. 'The world has nothing to offer me, Indigo, for nothing could replace what I once had and lost. So I have dedicated my life to one purpose and one alone: retribution.' A fist clenched unconsciously and his knuckles whitened. 'I can't begin to explain the true meaning of wrath to one who hasn't experienced its greatest heights. But I have schooled myself and driven myself and steeled myself, to the point where I am a living weapon; I eat and drink and breathe vengeance, and vengeance is incarnated in my flesh, my bones, my soul. I *am* vengeance.' He drew in a sharp, quick breath and looked towards the shrine, adding in a soft undertone: 'Ranaya has granted me that gift, and I will not fail her!'

Indigo had looked down at her own clasped hands, aware of Grimya's uneasy thoughts and, too, of an answering frisson within herself that responded involuntarily to Jasker's words. She had tasted wrath, had felt its hot fires in her veins; and the atrocities that had set light to it were such that it would take little to trigger it anew. She *shared* Jasker's wrath – and that was a dangerous contagion; for despite the change in his manner she was well aware that Jasker wasn't sane. Intelligent and lucid he might be, but his insatiable rage against the Charchad had unhinged him, and now fuelled and fed his already considerable sorcerous skills. It would be all too easy to succumb to the same tide of emotions that drove him, to abandon caution and reason and hurl herself headlong at their common cause. That, Indigo knew, could be a fatal mistake, for of one thing she was now certain: Jasker's hated Charchad and the demon she sought to destroy were one and the same entity.

Some minutes had passed now since either of them had spoken. In this cave it was impossible to judge the hour; outside Indigo surmised that dawn must be breaking, but here day and night were one, and the sense of timelessness was dreamlike and a little eerie. Grimya had fallen into an uneasy doze; the she-wolf was still suspicious of Jasker and every so often her amber eyes opened and she regarded him mistrustfully before lapsing back to sleep. Chrysiva, too, slept, on the sack of coarse linen stuffed with dry leaves and twigs that served Jasker as a bed. Earlier the sorcerer had studied the contents of Indigo's medicinal pouch and selected two herbs from which to make a draught for the girl which he said would ease her fever. The decoction seemed to have soothed her and her sleep was more natural than it had been. But Indigo was still deeply troubled about Chrysiva, and now she turned to look at her. Her skin was deadly pale, almost the colour of a dead fish. And the marks on her arms and face, the blotches, the sores, seemed if anything to be worsening.

'She'll sleep for a good few hours yet,' Jasker said quietly.

'I know.' Indigo turned back. 'But those scars she bears . . . they're showing no signs of healing.'

'No.' He paused, regarding her intently, then added: 'They won't heal. Not now. If I'd found her two days earlier there might have been hope, but it's too late.'

Indigo stared at him, feeling as if worms moved in her stomach. 'Too late?'

'She didn't tell you what was done to her?'

'No . . . all I know is that her husband has been "sent to Charchad" – whatever that means – and that she'd been to the mines to plead for him when I found her.'

'Ah.' Jasker clasped his hands together, stared at them. 'There is a great deal more I must relate to you, Indigo, and this poor woman's story is only a small part of it.' He looked up at her again and his eyes glittered like cold crystal. 'Before you regained consciousness, I spoke with Chrysiva and learned the part of her tale which, it seems, she has not told you.' He poured himself another cup of water and sipped at it as though it might drown an ugly taste in his mouth. ' "Sent to Charchad" . . . *ach!* They haven't even the courage or honesty to call it what it is – *slaughter!*'

'What – ' Indigo began to say, but before she could get any further Jasker reached out and snatched hold of her wrist, gripping it so tightly that her fingers were numbed. He leaned forward and the glitter in his eyes caught fire as shadow gave way to candlelight. 'Do you know what afflicts that woman? *Do* you?'

'No – '

With his free hand Jasker pointed at Chrysiva, and his entire arm began to tremble with rage that he could barely control. 'She has been granted the honour and the glory of achieving a state of grace!' He pulled on Indigo's wrist, almost dragging her off balance. 'A *Charchad* state of grace! Do you know what that means? No, you don't; you're a stranger, a foreigner; you've been spared the blessings of that knowledge, haven't you? Pray to Ranaya that you never find out at first hand!'

His furious voice roused Grimya, who raised her head in alarm. Seeing what was afoot she sprang to her feet, snarling, but Indigo pulled her wrist free from Jasker's grip and made a pacifying gesture. 'No, Grimya; it's all right.' Her gaze didn't leave the sorcerer's face. 'What do you mean, Jasker? What did they do to her?'

He subsided, but it took a great effort and for a few moments he had to struggle before getting his breathing under control. At last he said: 'You've seen them. If you spent a single night in that filthy town, you *must* have seen them. The exalted ones; the favoured of Charchad. The scarred, festering, mutated *monsters!*'

The celebrants on the road; the creatures who had assailed her in the House of Copper and Iron – appalled, Indigo looked wildly at Chrysiva. 'But she isn't – '

'One of them? Oh, she is, Indigo; she is. But she had no choice in the matter!' Jasker shut his eyes tightly and ran both hands ferociously through his hair; his shadow jerked crazily on the cave wall. Indigo heard him suck air into his lungs, then his shoulders slumped.

'There is a substance,' he said, straining to contain his fury. 'Metal or stone, I don't know its nature. But it glows.'

Grimya growled softly and Indigo put an arm about her furred shoulder. 'We've seen it.'

'Then you doubtless know that it's a symbol of power to those Charchad demons.'

'Their amulets?'

'Yes, their amulets. A badge of rank, of favour. And it *kills*, Indigo. Slowly, and as surely as the course of the sun in the sky, that unearthly abomination warps and erodes the bodies of all who come into contact with it, until there is nothing left for them but death!'

Indigo hugged Grimya more tightly. 'Then the disfigurements we saw, the mutations . . . they were caused by this – this stone, this ore?'

'You saw the least of it. You saw the ones who can walk, the ones who can still speak, the ones whose mouths haven't yet rotted away so that they starve even before the last stages of the sickness can claim them. You did *not* see the horrors of those final stages, the agony, the threshing, dying, screaming *hell* of it . . . ah, *Ranaya!*' He covered his face with his hands.

'Jasker.' Indigo moved towards him, laying a hand on his shoulder and feeling helpless in the face of his torment. 'Jasker, please – '

He shook her off, but gently, implying no hostility. 'Forgive me, *saia*,' he said with tight formality. 'Sometimes it is hard not to remember.'

'Remember?'

He shook his head, not in denial but to clear his thoughts. The fury and the emotion were under control again, at least for the moment.

'This child's husband was punished for a supposed crime,' he continued. 'But the crime was an excuse, an invention. In truth, he was punished for refusing to give fealty to the Charchad. There are still some who resist the cult, though their numbers must be very few now.'

Indigo remembered the 'festival' in the town square, the frightened faces, the closed minds. 'Yes,' she said soberly. 'Very few.'

'Then this woman and her husband have been more courageous than most. They should have known better. The man was chosen as a scapegoat, an example to strike fear into the hearts of any who might have considered following his example; but his suffering wasn't enough for those serpents. They deemed that his wife should be made to share his state of grace. And so they forced her . . .' His voice wavered, almost broke; then he got a grip on himself again. 'They forced her to eat a piece of that cursed stone, to infect her with the sickness that is, to them, a sign of the Charchad's blessing.'

'Sacred Earth . . .' Indigo looked quickly over her shoulder at Chrysiva. 'Then – she will die?'

'Yes. The fever, the disfigurements; they're just the beginning, but once they have a hold there's no hope. Chrysiva will die, Indigo. They have murdered her.' He paused. 'Just as they murdered my own wife.'

Her head snapped round and she stared at him. '*That* is how they killed her?'

Jasker nodded. 'It can be done in the space of a few hours,' he said, and the terrible, detached chill was back in his voice. 'If they have enough of the stone, and the victim is forced to – ' He shook his head violently, unable to say more.

Indigo stared at the floor with unfocused eyes as she felt the hot, bitter vibrations of anger stir within her again. The thought that any living creature could be capable of such atrocities, could revel in their execution, made her sick to the core of her soul. And all for what? *Power.* Power, and insanity of an order that made Jasker's mad lust for revenge pale to a dim candle by comparison.

She felt a gentle touch in her mind, and heard Grimya's silent thought. *It is not truly men who do these things, Indigo. It is the demon. Men are only its . . . instruments.*

That was true. But . . . *They are willing instruments, Grimya. That's what is so hard to comprehend or accept.*

*I know. But I believe the demon has corrupted them. Without its influence, such things as have happened here could never exist.* Grimya paused, then: *You and I know how strong such corruption can be. Do you not remember the child with the silver eyes?*

'Nemesis – ' A cold, inner stab made Indigo forget caution, and she spoke the name aloud without realising it. Jasker's head came up.

'What?'

'I – nothing.' Indigo's face had paled. 'A word only; I – I merely thought aloud for a moment . . .'

'You said – '

'Please.' She held up her hands, palms outward. 'It was of no consequence.'

He looked at her speculatively, then shrugged. 'As you wish, *saia.*'

Indigo and Grimya exchanged a private look, and each knew without the need for words what the other was thinking. Nemesis. It was the ever-present threat, the worm in the bud of Indigo's own soul. She had faced it twice, and on the second occasion only Grimya's intervention had saved her from a folly that would have turned all hope to dust. But on the first occasion there had been no Grimya. And Indigo had fallen to the pride, the arrogance and the hunger within her that had brought the world to the brink of damnation.

But for the warping influence of the Charchad, the atrocities rife in this land would not exist. Yet had it not been for her, the Charchad itself would not exist; for the seven demons that were humanity's creation would still lie bound, as they had lain for so many centuries, in the ruined Tower of Regrets. Seven demons, of which this warped horror was but the first. And hers was the hand that had released them . . .

'Indigo?'

She looked up and saw that Jasker was still watching her. His eyes were quieter now and he said, 'You're distressed. Can you not confide in me?'

Mad though he might be, she thought, he was a good man. And although she couldn't tell him all her story, their goals were one and the same.

She said: 'I can't confide in you, Jasker; not in the way that you mean. But I have my own reasons for sharing your need for retribution.' Unconsciously her fists clenched and she leaned towards him. 'Tell me of the Charchad. Tell me all you know of them, all you know of the power that they wield. I want to *destroy* them, Jasker. I want to see them wiped from the face of the world!'

A slow smile touched the edges of Jasker's mouth, and he nodded. 'I believe I understand you, *saia*. Perhaps inasmuch as Ranaya sent you to aid my cause, she has also charged me to aid yours.' He hesitated, then got to his feet. 'You want me to tell you all I know of the Charchad. I'll do better than that; I will *show* you. From here, there are a number of ways into the heart of the mountains where the mines are sited. And there's something else; something you should see with your own eyes.' His face became grim. 'It will tell you more of the Charchad than words could ever do.'

She started to rise. 'Then let's waste no time. I want – '

'Not yet.' He held up a hand. 'We dare not risk being seen; we must wait until the sun westers and the light begins to fade.' He smiled with a faint trace of ironic humour. 'Besides, it's an arduous climb for one who isn't accustomed to it, and not advisable in the heat of the day. I don't intend to lose my only ally to the perils of sunstroke! No; we'd be best advised to sleep for a few hours, and renew our energies.'

Grimya's voice in Indigo's head joined the argument. *He is right*, the she-wolf said emphatically. *We have hardly slept since leaving Vesinum. I am tired. You are tired. What the man wants to show us will not run away while we rest.*

Indigo wanted to argue, but realised that both Jasker and Grimya counselled good sense. And so, after checking on the pony which was tethered in the relative cool of an outer passage, she settled down on her folded blanket with Grimya at her side. Jasker, with a propriety that touched her, insisted that he would fare well enough in another cave, and left with a promise to wake Indigo as soon as the time was right for them to leave.

When he had gone Indigo snuffed out all but one of the candles, and the cave sank into deep gloom. She lay back, not sure that she would be able to sleep but determined to try, and Grimya settled with her muzzle resting on her front paws. For a few minutes there was silence; then Grimya projected a thought.

*I still don't trust him.*

Indigo raised her head. 'Who? Jasker?'

*Yes. There's something wrong. I can smell it, but I can't yet see it.*

'You're still angry with him because you think he meant us harm, that's all. He was only defending his territory, Grimya, as any wolf might do.'

*It isn't just that. It's something else.* Grimya's tail twitched. *He is mad. I saw colours in his mind that should not have been there; bad colours.* She looked up unhappily. *Be careful, Indigo. There is great danger here, and it does not lie where we might expect to find it.*

'Oh, Grimya . . .' Indigo leaned across and stroked the wolf's coat, trying to reassure her. 'Yes, Jasker *is* mad, in a way; but he has suffered a great deal. What matters is that he can help us to find and destroy the demon.' She buried her fingers deeper in Grimya's fur. 'Alone, I don't think we could hope to be strong enough. We *need* him. Just as he needs us.'

*I know. But still . . . you must be careful.*

'I will.'

*Promise me.*

'I promise. Go to sleep, now.'

Grimya wriggled, then laid her head back on her paws. Indigo's breathing soon grew shallower and slower as she drifted into sleep, but for some time the she-wolf lay wakeful, thinking her own thoughts and watching her friend with unquiet eyes.

Grimya's was not the only restless mind in the mountain network. A short distance away in a small, bare cave lit by a single candle Jasker leaned against the rock wall, idly cleaning the curved blade of an old scimitar. It was the only weapon he possessed, although during his exile it had seen service only as a hewing and honing tool. Jasker wasn't a skilled swordsman, preferring to fight with spells rather than steel; none the less he found a certain satisfaction in keeping the scimitar oiled and polished, and the mechanical nature of the task helped him when he needed, as now, to think.

The images that had come storming from Indigo's subconscious mind during the truth-ordeal by the fumarole had both shocked and horrified him. And Jasker was honest enough to admit to himself that mingled with his respect and fellow-feeling for her was a good measure of fear: for he had seen clearly the hand of the Earth Mother upon her, and yet sensed that the great goddess's visitation was a punishment rather than a boon. What Indigo had done to earn the burden she carried was not Jasker's concern, and to probe further than he'd already done would be little short of sacrilegious. But there were, nevertheless, questions in his mind to which he would have given much to know the answers.

A word that Indigo had uttered was preying on his mind. Nemesis. Whether it had any parallels in his own language Jasker didn't know, but clearly its significance went far deeper than the girl had been willing to admit. He had glimpsed that same word as a fragmented image in the darkness which surrounded her innermost being, and with it had come a fleeting impression of an evil face which was and yet was not Indigo herself. That, and a sense of *silver*.

Silver. It made no sense. Yet in some indefinable way it was Indigo's eternal and dreadful link with the ghosts of friends loved and lost – and with one love in particular. Jasker had heard his name as an agonised scream in the girl's mind, and it had sent an answering knife of pain through his own soul. He too had known the torture of watching his lover die; but in the soul of this girl of the southlands with her prematurely greyed hair and her old, old eyes there lurked something that went far beyond grief and guilt and bitterness, a suffering that he could never comprehend.

Jasker realised suddenly that he was in danger of breaking his own taboo, and with a gesture so swift and familiar that he was hardly aware of it he brushed the palm of one hand across the newly-polished scimitar blade. Blood welled from a long, shallow cut and the pain brought him sharply back to earth. He clenched his fist, and his hand stung as a few drops of blood dripped on to the rock floor. *Better*. To look more deeply into Indigo's life than he had already done was a breach of his own discipline, and he must permit no more such lapses lest he give offence to the goddess.

He laid the scimitar down and leaned back against the wall. A travelling outlander, and a wolf which obviously understood human speech and – he couldn't be certain, but he strongly suspected it – which was capable of telepathic communication. Strange allies in his cause; but it was not for him to question the ways of Ranaya. Jasker looked again at his cut hand, and smiled thinly.

'Mysterious art thou, O Ranaya, Lady of Fire,' he said, his voice soft with love and reverence. From somewhere deeper in the volcanic network he heard a faint rumble, as though the old, molten rocks that slept far down in the earth had heard and answered him. The sound faded back into silence, and Jasker let his head fall back against the warm cave wall as he closed his eyes to sleep.

# Chapter VII

The sun was a vicious red eye staring through a haze that dulled perspective and made distances unreal as Indigo and Jasker, with Grimya a short way behind them, emerged from a narrow defile and on to the open slopes near the summit of Old Maia. Old Maia, Jasker had explained, was the southernmost of the three giant craters known as Ranaya's Daughters that dominated the volcanic region, and from its massive shoulder it was possible to see the entire spread of the mining valley in the centre of the mountains.

At this height the air was relatively clear, and a hot, arid wind blew from the south. Jasker sat down in the lee of an outcropping of petrified magma which the wind had scoured into a fantastic sculpture, and indicated that Indigo and Grimya should do the same.

'A few minutes' rest will stand us in good stead now,' he said. 'And I'd prefer to let the sun fall a little lower before we go on to the north face.'

Grimya flopped down immediately, but Indigo stood for a few moments surveying her surroundings. The sky to all horizons was sulphur-tinted and disturbingly featureless, and the haze had contracted the setting sun to a blurred, distorted fireball. Closer to, there was nothing to be seen but the naked mountains, an unearthly landscape of harsh edges and hot colours and sharp-edged shadows. Not a blade of grass, not a leaf, not a sign of movement. Just the bare bones of a dead land.

She hunched her shoulders against a shiver and said: 'There aren't even any birds . . . .'

Jasker looked up. 'Birds?' He laughed, a short, bitter bark. 'No, there aren't any birds now. The few that did once scratch an existence here – birds of prey mostly, or scavengers – died out because being hatched with no eyes or no feathers or no wings doesn't make for good flying. And those that might have come in from outside soon learned better.'

Indigo glanced at Grimya, who was listening intently to Jasker's words. 'And animals?' she asked.

He shrugged. 'There are still a few, though I doubt if you'd recognise many of them. And some vegetation, though not on the higher slopes. Most of the things that grow or run here can still be eaten, if you take certain precautions and aren't overly fussy.'

Grimya said silently to Indigo: *I saw something, as we climbed through the defile. I thought at first it was a goat, but it was very small and it had only one horn and no hair on its head.* She paused. *It was not a pleasant thing to see, and I would not have wanted to eat it.*

Indigo didn't reply, but the she-wolf's comment struck home. Mutation, poisoning, death . . . she looked at the sky again and saw that the sun was now barely visible above the far side of the mountains. Perspectives were changing as the light began to fade; and now, rivalling the setting sun, she could see the first traces of a colder luminescence in the north, an unnatural glow reflecting from the sky and slowly gathering strength.

Jasker saw her eyes narrow as she stared at the eerie, faraway reflection. 'Ah, yes,' he said softly. 'Our nightly visitation. The power and the glory of Charchad.' He rose, staring out across the darkening slopes. 'Time, I think, for us to complete our journey, Indigo. And when we reach our final vantage point, you will see for yourself what the Charchad truly is.'

Indigo got to her feet. Overhead now the cold glow was spreading, and even as she glanced westward the last fiery edge of the sun vanished below the ragged peaks. Shadows around them merged and flowed into a uniform soft, grey gloom, and as her eyes adjusted to the new darkness she saw that the air was tinged with a faint phosphorescence that hovered on the border of the visible spectrum. And suddenly, despite the dusty heat, she felt cold.

The slopes that brought them to the summit of Old Maia were gentle enough to present no real danger even with only the tricky glow from the northern sky to light their way. And when at last she emerged in Jasker's wake to stand on the narrow spine of the volcano's highest ridge, Indigo could only stare in stunned silence at the scene which was revealed.

Immediately below them, Old Maia's north face fell away in a sweep of bare rock pitted with the crazed patterns burned centuries ago by molten rivers of magma. The crater, some way to the right, formed a huge and grotesque scar a third of the way down the mountainside, a vertiginous throat that culminated in a massive, sagging and threatening black mouth over-hanging the valley.

But it was the valley itself that transfixed Indigo's attention and utterly eclipsed the crater's drama: for as she stared down into the vast vale, she could easily have believed that she was witnessing a scene from a demoniacally-inspired hell.

There was light below: the yellow, sulphurous light of torches set high on iron poles, a hundred or more burning beacons. And they illuminated a smoking, boiling chaos of smog and steam and toiling activity. Huge, unnatural shapes loomed out of the miasma; massive networks of struts and girders, great iron booms that reared skywards like unearthly monsters, moving platforms, supported on titanic wheels, that called up images of nightmare prehistoric creations. And, dimly visible through the pall, gangs of human figures laboured in the filthy, eerily glowing smog like the mindless denizens of some vast anthill.

The rock beneath Indigo was vibrating. She hadn't been consciously aware of it before but now she could feel it, a huge, subterranean pulse below the threshold of hearing that beat through the mountains like a ghostly and irregular heart. They were upwind of the valley and the noise of the mines was being carried away from them; but that muted underground thunder told her that from close quarters the chaos of sound would be earth-shaking.

She felt Jasker's hand on her shoulder and realised that she had started to shiver uncontrollably. She took a grip on herself, then stared beyond the smoke and the machines and the tiny, toiling figures towards the valley's further reaches. Here there were more engines, alien silhouettes which belched and snorted clouds of boiling steam shot through with nauseating colours. Beyond them, the roaring white heat of three gigantic furnaces stained the night, reflecting fierily in the glowing waters of the river as it flowed through the vale on its southward journey.

And beyond the furnaces and the engines and the river, behind the towering far wall of the great volcanic valley, shone the grim and ghastly radiance of the eerie northern light.

Indigo gripped Jasker's fingers tightly. 'The source . . .'

'Yes. It lies immediately beyond that far ridge – in the Charchad Vale.'

She turned away from the turbulent scene below. Grimya was still staring down at the mines and her ears were flat to her head, her eyes red with reflected light. No coherent thoughts came from the she-wolf's mind, only a mute sense of distress, and Indigo felt a wave of bitter remorse as again her own accusation ran through her head: *if it hadn't been for me . . .*

'Tell me about it, Jasker.' Her voice was hoarse with suppressed anger. 'Tell me what that thing is, and how it came into existence.'

Jasker was gazing down into the valley once more.

Then he nodded, and lowered himself on to a lava ledge that jutted out from the slope. Indigo followed his example, and he began his story.

'Five years ago, there was a landslip in one of the further valleys, beyond that distant wall. The valley was known as Charchad; several promising copper lodes had recently been found there, and there were a lot of men – tribute miners, mostly, although some of the bigger consortia were starting to take an interest – prospecting to see how far the lodes went. Anyway, the valley caved in, and a vast pit opened up at the bottom.' He glanced obliquely at her. 'The pit glowed. Not like a fire or even a furnace, but with a blinding green radiance. I talked to some of those who went to look at the pit during the first days after its appearance, and they told me it was as if the sun itself had fallen to Earth; they couldn't look at it directly.' He paused, touched his tongue to dry lips. 'Some of them tried, and went blind as a result.'

'And the men who were working in the valley?' Indigo asked.

'At first it was believed that no one had survived the catastrophe. They called on us – the priests – to pray for the souls of the dead, speed them on their way to Ranaya's breast.' Jasker shuddered. 'So much grief, so much bereavement: I thought at that time that I could never see such misery again. If I had only known what was to follow . . .' Jasker sighed, then his expression hardened. 'But there was one survivor: a man named Aszareel. He emerged from the valley on the day after the disaster, and he was carrying a wand made of a substance that no one had ever seen before. A shining mineral, a cold, green, glowing thing. He was unscathed. And whatever had happened to him, whatever he might have experienced in that place, I for one believe that he was no longer human.

'Aszareel proclaimed that he had had a revelation. The pit, he said, was the source of a great new power in the land – the power of Charchad – and he was its

100

chosen avatar. His miraculous survival was proof of Charchad's intent, and Charchad had bidden him to return and demand that all should give fealty. Those who did not, Aszareel said, would be damned forever.'

Indigo stared at him. 'And people *believed* him?'

Jasker smiled humourlessly. 'Whatever it was that changed Aszareel had also given him a charisma that was nothing short of incredible. I saw the man on several occasions: he was like a vortex, Indigo; a vortex of intense energy that drew the eyes and the minds, even perhaps the souls, of all who crossed his path. Almost like a living volcano. If every man, woman and child in Vesinum had thrown themselves at his feet I wouldn't have wondered at it.

'But it wasn't like that. Charisma or no, it needed more than Aszareel alone to turn the miners and their families from Ranaya. There were some, of course, who caught his fervour from the beginning, but their numbers were small . . . until the sickness and the dying began.'

Indigo looked over the valley again. Full darkness had fallen now, though the landscape was stained with the guttering flare of the torches, the brilliance of the smelting furnaces – and the sickly shimmer emanating from the distant Charchad vale.

'It started with the men who were working the adits in the northernmost slopes,' Jasker continued. 'Their bodies warped, their skin peeled away, their eyes rotted in their sockets. No healer could help them. Then those who laboured in the furnaces began to succumb. Birds and insects disappeared; animals died or started to mutate. Grass refused to grow. And people panicked. Miners and smelters refused to work in the mountains, and for a while it seemed that the entire operation would have to close for lack of willing men.

'But then Aszareel started to preach in Vesinum. He declared that the sickness wasn't a plague but a blessing; that those who fell prey to it were favoured of Charchad, because they had had the faith and the courage to brave the valleys where their cowardly fellows had failed. He started to demonstrate powers – they were conjuror's tricks, barely worthy of a neophyte, but to the ignorant and superstitious and frightened they were impressive enough – which he said were Charchad's gift to the favoured. And he exhorted the miners to return to the mountains, to offer their minds and their bodies to the glories of the new power, and be saved.' He paused, then turned and spat very deliberately on the rock a few feet away.

'What choice did those men have? Without the mines, without the ore to smelt and sell, their only prospect was starvation. Yet if they returned, if they exposed themselves to what lay in the Charchad vale, they, too, would sicken or mutate. So they began to believe what Aszareel told them; that the sickness was a sign of blessing, that through suffering they would be elevated, transformed. *Saved.* They *made* themselves believe him, for it was their only hope.'

Indigo nodded. She was still staring into the valley, but her eyes were unfocused. 'So the cult grew,' she said quietly.

'It didn't merely grow; it erupted. The miners returned to the valley, and they fed their families; and when the sickness visited them and their children were born mutated, they listened to Aszareel and his acolytes who told them that they were the chosen. Those who dissented were shouted down; and before long the cult grew strong enough to start *demanding* allegiance.' Jasker's lip twitched. 'There are always opportunists; men who will grasp at a chance of gaining power over their fellows for their own aggrandisement. Aszareel had no shortage of lieutenants to pursue his cause with the most fervent zeal.'

With a stab of loathing Indigo recalled the overseer, Quinas. She started to say, 'There was a man I encountered – ' but broke off in mid-sentence as a beam of vivid light suddenly lit the face of Old Maia immediately below them. Grimya yipped in alarm and Indigo swore aloud, involuntarily jerking back as the light skimmed past them and on across the volcano's upper slopes. For a moment the crater gaped like an awakened monster in the beam: then the light vanished.

'Ranaya incinerate their bones; they're sweeping!' Jasker scrambled backwards, throwing himself flat; as Indigo seemed about to stand up he grabbed her arm, pulling hard. 'Get down, woman! D'you want to be seen?'

A second beam stabbed the night, higher this time. She saw it coming, ducked her head just before it blazed across the spot where she had been standing. Grimya snarled, her hackles rising defensively, and Indigo looked at Jasker.

'What in the Mother's name was that?'

'They're directing light beams on the mountains, to search for anyone on the slopes.'

'Light beams?' Indigo was incredulous. 'But how can that be done?' A new shaft of brilliance cut the darkness and instinctively she ducked; but this time the beam swept eastwards, missing their vantage point.

'Look carefully at the outer ring of torches,' Jasker told her. 'Beside each one you'll see a huge metal disc – there!' as yet another beam appeared and began its wavering search. 'See? They're made of highly polished copper, and they use them to reflect the light on to the rocks.'

She was just in time to glimpse a momentary, blinding refraction as torchlight fell on a gigantic sheet of metal far below. The disc was turning – it was just possible to make out tiny, straining figures labouring over a great capstan – and she realised that the scale of the things must be enormous if they could cast the light so brightly and so far.

'But it makes no sense,' she said. 'Even if the beams were to reveal anyone in the mountains, they couldn't hope to see them from such a distance!'

'Oh, they could. With the great glass.' And, seeing her blank expression, he shifted his position, fumbling at his waist, and unhooked what looked like a small, brass cylinder. Indigo had noticed it hanging from his belt when they left the cave but had thought little of it, assuming it to be some priestly symbol; a staff of office perhaps. Now, though, she looked at it more closely, and started with surprise when Jasker twisted one end of the cylinder and drew out an inner barrel that doubled the instrument's length.

'A spyglass,' he said. 'Surely you've seen one before? Hold it to your eye, and it enables you to see objects from far away.'

A very old memory stirred: and suddenly Indigo remembered a curio that her father had once received as a gift from her mother's people in the east. A tiny tube of silver, encrusted with filigree and jewels . . . they had called it by a different name, but the principle was the same. King Kalig had considered it nothing more than an elaborate toy with no practical value; by the time one had fiddled with it, focused it and found what one was looking for, he'd said, the quarry would probably have run a mile or more out of bowshot. He had kept it, not wishing to be discourteous to his wife's relatives, but he had never used it; nor had he permitted his children to play with it lest it might damage their eyesight.

She said: 'I've seen one, yes.'

'Well, imagine the same thing on a greatly increased scale. A tube as long as a man is tall, mounted on a table that can be turned.' He grimaced. 'They could see a fly on the face of Old Maia with that, if there were any flies left to be seen.'

She still didn't fully understand. 'But why should they want to scan the slopes? I know that outsiders aren't encouraged, but – '

'Outsiders have nothing to do with it. It's their own men they're watching for. Miners who might try to escape.'

'Escape?'

Jasker's face was grim. 'I told you that the Charchad are now strong enough to gain converts by force where persuasion fails. There are still those who love Ranaya and refuse to give fealty to the monstrosity in that valley – men like Chrysiva's husband – but now that all pretence of free will has been abandoned, such "unbelievers" are obliged to toil with their fellows whether they will it or no. A few have the courage to try to escape. None, to my knowledge, has yet succeeded.'

Indigo was silent. Beside her, Grimya lay with her muzzle on her paws. She seemed to be staring into the darkness, but Indigo had the feeling that the she-wolf saw nothing, that her mind was not fully on Jasker's words. Tentatively, she projected a gentle query.

*Grimya? What troubles you?*

The she-wolf blinked and although her head didn't move her gaze fastened on Indigo's face. *Why do they do such things? Men sending other men to their deaths. Men rejoicing in sickness. Why, Indigo? What power can it be that wants such things to happen? I would ask the man, but I cannot; he doesn't know that I can speak to humans. Ask him for me. I want to try to understand.*

*I will.* It was the very question she herself had wanted to ask, but Grimya had articulated it more simply than she could have hoped to do. She looked at the sorcerer.

'What *is* the Charchad, Jasker?' With one hand she indicated the grim vista spread out below them. 'They have a stranglehold; they force men to work against their wills; they punish supposed wrongdoers by consigning them to that demoniac valley. But *why*? What do they seek to gain by it?'

Jasker shook his head. 'I don't know. Power? Dominion? Who can say what moves such depraved minds?' He fingered the spyglass. 'As well ask the true nature of what lies in the valley itself.'

She felt her throat constrict; the answer was plain,

though she didn't want to acknowledge it. 'Then you've not seen it for yourself?'

'No. A glowing pit; that's all I know of it. But there's something evil there, something blacker than I can comprehend, and it's powerful.' Jasker's eyes lit harshly. 'You might call it a demon.'

A demon. Jasker was more right than he knew . . . recent memories stirred sharply in Indigo, and she turned back towards the sorcerer, speaking more curtly than she had intended.

'Your device – the spyglass. Let me look through it, Jasker. Let me see what it can do.'

He made an acquiescent gesture and held the brass tube out to her. 'As you will. But it has nothing like the power of the great glasses they use below.'

'No matter.' She took the instrument, raised it to her right eye. 'Tell me what to do.'

His hand closed over hers. 'Train it, like so, on the area you want to survey. When you have a picture of sorts, twist the outer barrel until the image comes into focus.'

Grimya queried: *Indigo, what is it? Why such haste?*; but she couldn't answer. She was lost in the intricacies of the spyglass, fascinated and not a little awed by the intensified vista she saw through its lens. She trained the glass on the distant smelting furnaces, and forced herself not to recoil as it focused suddenly on the slick surface of the river, brilliantly reflecting the furnace fires as though the very water were alive. Further – she was shuffling forward on her elbows, oblivious to the rock grazing her skin – and she saw the valley's north wall, cracked and pitted, an unhealthy, greenish radiance spilling down the slopes. She raised the glass a fraction, then swore as the picture was swallowed by a nacreous shimmer that filled her field of vision and blotted out all detail. The radiance from the Charchad vale. But she couldn't see what lay beyond its borders, couldn't glimpse even the smallest clue as to the nature of her demon.

'Indigo.' Jasker's restraining hand shook her out of her preoccupation. 'Have a care. Even the light from Charchad is dangerous.'

She wanted to say bitterly: *not to one who cannot die*, but bit the retort away, and let the glass sweep back past the river, past the infernally glowing furnaces, into the main mining area once more. A torch flared briefly in one corner of the lens, making her wince; she steadied her hand, pulled back further –

And stopped.

Men, moving among the litter and debris of one of the lower slopes. Magnified now to human proportions, they were slump-shouldered, shuffling to form a long, ragged line like reluctant warriors mustering before battle. She shifted the spyglass a fraction and saw other human figures with what looked like long-lashed whips slung carelessly from their belts; one, two – and her mind and body froze as one of the figures resolved into the form of a man with black hair, a certain arrogance to his stance.

'Quinas!' She hissed the name aloud without realising it, and every muscle in Jasker's face locked rigid.

*'What?'*

On the verge of repeating what she had said, Indigo paused. She couldn't be certain; the phosphorescent nightglow shot through by torchlight was deceptive, and many men in this region had black hair.

'Indigo!' Jasker caught hold of her shoulder and shook her so violently that the spyglass fell from her hand and rolled noisily over the rocks. 'That name – *what was it?*'

Startled and disorientated, she blinked at him like a sleeper coming out of a trance. 'Wh – '

'Did you say, *Quinas?*'

The air was suddenly charged. 'An overseer at the mines,' Indigo said. 'I thought – ' A hot, indefinable emotion crackled between them. 'You know him?'

107

Jasker's face was haggard. 'He is the serpent who slaughtered my wife.'

Grimya sprang to her feet with a howl of distress as she and Indigo together felt the bolt of blind, crimson fury that erupted from Jasker's mind. For a shocking instant the sorcerer's outline was etched in fire – then he sank back on to the rocks, covering his face with both hands.

'I never thought to hear that name again!' His voice was distorted with pain. 'I thought him dead, I thought Ranaya had avenged that evil – '

'Jasker!' Gripping his shoulders Indigo jerked with all her strength, pulling him off balance. Eyes like white-hot embers met hers and she felt a renewed surge of insensate rage: then Jasker caught hold of himself, staring at her with a look of blank shock.

'Quinas . . .' His voice was a dead, dry whisper.

'He's alive. I met him in Vesinum; I – ' She stopped, not wanting to relate the circumstances of their encounter. 'He's a mine overseer, Jasker; that's what he told me. And just now, I believe I saw him. There are men mustering down there, and others with whips.'

'The shift's about to change. Before the miners are dismissed, their numbers are counted, to see if . . .' Jasker shook his head violently. '*Quinas . . .*'

'He's Aszareel's lieutenant, isn't he? *Isn't he?*' She shook him again, fiercely.

'Yes. One of the most favoured.'

'Then he'll know the secret of what lies in that valley. And he – ' she broke off, thinking quickly. 'Jasker, where is Aszareel now? Does he still preach?'

Another shake of the head; though now Jasker was beginning to come to his senses. 'No, I – don't think so. Shortly before they . . . shortly before I fled Vesinum, Aszareel disappeared. It was said that he'd gone into the Charchad valley to receive grace and to be transformed.' He grimaced. 'That, so his acolytes say, is the ultimate benediction to the faithful.'

'Then without Aszareel to lead them, Quinas is among the highest of the Charchad hierarchy?'

'Yes.'

A slow and unpleasant smile spread across Indigo's face. She, too, had a personal score to settle with Quinas, though of a far lesser order than Jasker's. And Quinas had been the architect of Chrysiva's misery . . .

She said, 'When the shift changes – do the overseers leave the mines with the men?'

'Half an hour or so behind them.'

'Then we may just be in time. Jasker, we must set a trap for Quinas as he leaves the mountains. I shall provide the bait, and your sorcery will be the trap's teeth.'

Jasker's eyes lit ferally. 'I would give a great deal to have my revenge on that festering, hell-bred . . .' He stared at his own clenched fist. 'What I would do to him, how I would make him suffer before he died . . .'

'No.' Indigo laid a restraining hand on his arm. 'I want him alive, Jasker.'

He looked at her, his eyes tormented. 'Alive?'

'Alive, and unharmed.' She felt black excitement stir in her, and her fingers tightened hard on his biceps. 'When I'm done with him, you may kill him as slowly and as agonisingly as your skills allow. But first, I want him to tell me how to find Aszareel – and how to reach the valley of Charchad!'

# Chapter VIII

*I don't care about the cause!* Grimya said with unhappy vehemence. *There must be another way. You can't do it, Indigo – you can't try to go into that valley!*

*Hush.* Indigo tried silently to soothe the she-wolf. *If we find Aszareel, there may be no need for such drastic measures. Don't see ghosts where there may be none.*

*But if we do not find him –*

*Then I will do whatever I must. You know that, Grimya. If the demon is to die, there's no other choice.*

'Indigo?' Jasker's soft voice broke in on their private exchange and Indigo turned her head, half rising from where she crouched in the lee of a rock fold. The sorcerer emerged from the darkness and she saw a faint, gold aura flickering like tiny phantom flames about him.

'I have summoned them. Are you ready?'

She nodded 'Tell me what to do.'

A sound, so faint that she might have imagined it, impinged on her ears; a soft whistling as though the air around her had been invisibly displaced. She felt a warm breath skim past her face, and she stood upright. Jasker smiled.

'Hold out your arms, as though you were a falconer calling your birds to you. Don't flinch: you will feel some heat, but nothing more.'

She did as she was bidden and Jasker closed his eyes, murmuring under his breath. Moments later there was a vivid shimmer in the air, and a brilliant green fireball materialised above her head, hovering briefly before it twisted in mid-air, divided, and coalesced into the flickering green and crimson forms of two salamanders which settled on her outstretched forearms. As Jasker had warned, she felt a surge of heat from their translucent bodies; but it was no more than the tingling warmth of sitting by a winter fire. Golden claws pricked her skin slightly, tiny, jewel-like eyes regarded her with an alien intelligence, and fiery scarlet tongues, fork-tipped, licked the air and made it sizzle.

Indigo saw Grimya back away from the shimmering elementals, but she herself felt no fear of them; rather a sense of awe that such creatures were willing to acknowledge her in such a way. She looked at Jasker, her eyes shining, and the sorcerer said:

'Go, then, Indigo. I'll be waiting.'

Grimya whined, disliking the sudden electrical charge in the atmosphere as the salamanders raised their heads and hissed. Indigo looked down at her and smiled reassuringly. *It's all right, love. They won't harm us. Go on, now – go ahead along the path.*

Grimya looked at her dubiously for a moment, but didn't reply. Instead she turned about and trotted away, and with a last nod to Jasker Indigo followed her.

They had taken the shortest route back down the flank of Old Maia, then had climbed through the gully by which Indigo had originally stumbled upon Jasker's stronghold, and hastened along the path that led back towards the river and the road. Other elementals summoned by Jasker – tiny, living flames that hovered and danced along the path – had lit their way, and they had arrived within sight of the gates just in time to glimpse the last miners climbing aboard the open wagon which would take them back to Vesinum. The overseers, Jasker had said, should emerge within the half hour, and Indigo and Grimya had settled down to wait whilst the sorcerer withdrew to make his preparations.

Indigo's heart was beating erratically as the mine entrance came into her field of vision. All the way

111

down the mountainside Grimya had argued against this plan, and even Jasker had at first counselled patience, saying that without more time for detail and precaution she would be running a great risk. But Indigo had overridden them both. They had been granted an unlooked-for opportunity to take Quinas by surprise, and she would not let it slip through her fingers. In the end Jasker had taken little persuading to see her point of view; his own hatred for the overseer was goad enough. Grimya, though, was still unhappy, fearing for her friend's safety, and only Indigo's promise that she would take every care she could had mollified the she-wolf enough to make her agree, finally and reluctantly, to take part.

Ahead of her, Grimya had stopped at a place from which she had a clear view of the mine track. The she-wolf looked back and Indigo heard her silent call. *I can see the place. There is no one about yet.*

*Very well. I'll move closer.* She advanced until she could just make out the guard-hut, an angular silhouette among the more natural shadows of the cliff wall; then Grimya cautioned: *No further. The little dragons shed much light, and you will be seen.*

Indigo nodded and dropped to one knee behind an outcrop. The plan she had outlined to Jasker was simple enough but should be effective; and, as she had said, she would make ideal bait for the trap. When they had clashed in Vesinum she was well aware that Quinas would have gladly killed her, had it not been for the fact that she was a foreigner, an unknown quantity who might have more influence than appearances suggested. In full view of half the town's population he would not have risked such an action; this time though, without witnesses and under the provocation she intended to give him, she counted on a very different reaction.

Torchlight flared suddenly by the hut, and long shadows sprang out across the uneven ground. Indigo pressed herself back against the rock wall, while

112

Grimya, belly low to the ground, streaked like a shadow across the mine track to disappear into the darkness on the far side. Voices and the muffled stamp of hooves cut the quiet; then came the metallic groan of the gates opening, and moments later three mounted men carrying flamboys emerged from the mines.

She recognised Quinas immediately. He was in the lead, his companions following with a deferential air, and in the torchlight his face was clearly visible. One of the salamanders shrilled on a high, excited note, and Indigo stepped out on to the path.

'Quinas!' Her voice sent echoes shouting among the rocks and the horsemen started, dragging their mounts to a halt. Quinas looked for the source of the call; and his face froze.

'You – '

Indigo smiled ferally. 'We have a score to settle, Overseer Quinas. And I mean to have satisfaction here and now!'

One of Quinas's companions hissed, 'What in the name of Charchad are those things?' but Quinas held up a hand, demanding silence. His horse stamped uneasily, fearing the salamanders; he jerked the reins viciously to quiet it and said:

'Well, *saia* Indigo. What manner of conjuring trick is this?'

'No trick, you scum. Simply servants of the Goddess Ranaya, whose name you and your kind have blasphemed!' She paced backwards, orchestrating her movements as she and Jasker had carefully prearranged. One step, two, three: she halted.

'What's the matter, Quinas? Are you afraid of my friends? Afraid they might burn your squirming black soul if you come too close?' The salamanders, on cue, rose on their hind legs, hissing, and Indigo held her arms high. 'That's no more than I would expect from a craven coward of the Charchad!'

Quinas's mutated eyes glittered redly. 'You heretical bitch's whelp!' He spurred his horse forward, forcing the animal when it proved reluctant. 'I should have dealt with you in Vesinum – '

'Risk your reptile's skin against a woman with a knife?' Indigo taunted. 'Not you! You prefer to show your manly strength with helpless children, don't you, Quinas? You prefer to kick and revile poor creatures like the miner's little wife – they make fitter odds for a crawling gutter-worm like you!'

One of the other men said explosively, 'Quinas, let me – ' but the overseer again gestured him to silence. 'Hold your peace, Reccho,' he said, and he was smiling coldly. 'This bitch seems determined to pick her quarrel with me alone, and it would be churlish not to oblige a lady.' He had the horse under control now, and began to walk it steadily, calmly, towards Indigo. 'If she's bent on suicide that's her privilege; when I've finished with her, you can have what's left if you're interested.'

*Grimya.* Indigo projected a silent thought. *Are you ready?*

*Ready!* came the swift reply. The girl took another two steps back, and said aloud: 'Fine words, Quinas. But you haven't the spine to put them into practice!'

The salamanders hissed again, threateningly, and their flaming tongues darted. Quinas sneered.

'Your little friends don't impress me, bitch. And they'll desert you soon enough, when you suffer the punishment of Charchad for your blasphemy!'

As he spoke, he drove his heels hard into his horse's flanks and the animal sprang forward, neighing a shocked protest. Indigo had been ready for his attempt at surprise, and she darted backwards, the salamanders rearing and shrilling, as Quinas spurred his horse after her.

'Jasker!' Her voice rang out harshly. *'Now!'*

A wave of tremendous heat buffeted her backwards as white fire struck like lightning out of nowhere, crackling across the track in Quinas's path. His horse shrieked, slewing, and realising the danger the overseer

114

wrenched its head around, yelling to his friends to get clear.

*Grimya!* Indigo flung all the power she could muster into the telepathic shout, and instantly there came an answering howl out of the darkness, the cry of a hunting wolf. Quinas's horse started to buck, trapped between terror of fire and terror of predators, and suddenly the overseer's two companions came blundering into the canyon, their mounts out of control as Grimya snapped and snarled at their heels. The horses collided, one man fell, and Indigo heard shouting from the mine gates as the sentries ran to investigate.

The salamanders were nearly hysterical now, shrilling and spitting fire, and she turned to yell back into the darkness, 'Jasker! Just Quinas – just Quinas!'

Fire erupted from the rock face, twin walls of roaring flame that trapped the three horsemen in a searing cage of heat. One of the sentries howled in pain as he ran up against the firewall and reeled back – and suddenly the salamanders launched themselves from Indigo's arms and speared into the air. For a moment they became streaking green fireballs, blindingly incandescent – then their bodies reformed, and with shrieks of triumph they dived down on the trapped men.

Unhuman screams ripped the air apart as the salamanders struck, the sounds of men and horses in agony. Indigo whirled round, and in the dark of the canyon behind her saw a human outline etched in sparks, arms raised, head flung back, fire crackling from his outstretched hands.

*'No, Jasker!'* she yelled, her lungs straining. *'I want him alive!'*

A wild surge of denial slammed into her mind, and she rushed forward, sprinting towards the shining form of the sorcerer. 'No, Jasker, *no!* Call them off! Grimya, help me!'

A dark, sleek shape appeared above her, scrabbling on the steep slope, and she heard Grimya's answering bark. They reached Jasker together and hurled themselves at him, careless of the sparks and the flames. He went down, roaring furiously, and Indigo screamed: 'Save Quinas! In the name of Ranaya, *save Quinas!*'

For a moment Jasker lay where they had pinned him, his expression registering stunned shock. Then, as though someone had struck him full in the face, intelligence returned to his eyes.

'*Ranaya* – ' He threw Indigo off, scrambling to his feet, and uttered a shrill whistle. Answering cries came from within the wall of flame, and the sorcerer ran, stumbling, towards the mayhem. Indigo saw him approach the firewall and plunge through it; moments later he reappeared unscathed, with a shapeless burden over his shoulders. His gaze met Indigo's and she saw hatred, venom – then he flung Quinas's scorched body down on to the rock and turned back to the fire again. He raised his arms, cried one word – and a river of lava came spilling over the cliff above the burning men, pouring down into the canyon with a titanic, rumbling roar. Chunks of flaming magma spun high into the air, the molten rock heaved like a great sea-wave – and suddenly the flames were gone, and the men and horses were gone, and all that remained was a twenty-foot high wall of solid pumice that glowed a dull, sullen crimson.

Indigo staggered back against the canyon wall, groping for some support that would stop her legs from giving way beneath her. Grimya ran to her side and she hugged the she-wolf's head against her thigh. Her heart was thundering under her ribs and she felt that there wasn't enough air left in the world to breathe. At last she managed to suck in a great, gulping breath – and saw Jasker walking slowly back towards her.

'Those men . . .' Her voice sawed in her throat; she coughed, trying to clear the constriction. 'They – '

'They're dead enough now.' Jasker's voice was devoid of emotion. 'And the mine guards won't get past that wall, even if they're not too frightened to try.'

Something flickered at the top of the rapidly solidifying barrier, and one of the salamanders appeared. It seemed to squeeze itself out of the rock, like a rabbit emerging from a hole, and for a moment it perched motionless, watching them. Then, fastidiously, it nibbled at something caught between two of its claws, raised its head, and its flickering tongue licked at its own muzzle. It cheeped once, a conciliatory sound, then winked out of existence.

Indigo felt sick. 'My quarrel was not with them . . .'

'They were Charchad. And the salamanders must have their reward.'

'But the horses – '

Jasker's eyes met hers, and her voice tailed off as she saw his look.

'You have your captive, Indigo,' he said quietly. 'Isn't that what you wanted?'

'I – ' But it was true; she had made her choice and the responsibility was hers. 'Yes,' she whispered.

Jasker prodded the prone form of Quinas with one foot. 'Best look at him, then,' he said distantly.

Now that it was over, Indigo could hardly bring herself to examine her prisoner. Swallowing nausea, she crouched down beside him and turned him over. His hands, face and clothing were scorched and the ends of his hair singed; otherwise he seemed unharmed.

'He's unconscious, but he'll live,' Jasker said.

'Yes.' She rose. 'We succeeded . . . somehow it seems hard to believe.'

Jasker stared down at the senseless captive, then shook his head. 'It was just the first step. We've a long way to go yet.' He glanced at the canyon winding into the dark ahead of them. 'There's no point in wasting more time. We'll get him back to the caves; then we'll see what he can tell us.' A grim smile made his face more haggard than ever in the gloom. 'That will be a *real* beginning.'

Near the entrance to Jasker's cave they were met by

117

three more elementals, tiny blue fireballs that danced agitatedly in the air above the sorcerer's head. Jasker paused, listening to something that only he could hear, then said to Indigo, 'The girl Chrysiva's condition has worsened. I set these creatures to watch her while we were away, and they tell me she is mortally sick.' He sighed. 'It's no more than I expected.'

Indigo looked venomously at Quinas, whom Jasker had carried unceremoniously up the mountain flank like a sack of flour. 'I'll go on ahead,' she said. 'I may be able to do something for her.'

'Very well.' Though the look in Jasker's eyes told her that he doubted it. 'At least give her some water. She'll have a feverish thirst on her by now.'

Indigo nodded, and began to run up the slope.

They had left Chrysiva asleep in the main cave. As Indigo entered, the girl stirred and tried to sit up; and Indigo blanched as she saw her face in the candlelight.

Chrysiva was close to death. The raddled flesh of her face seemed to have sunken and shrunk on to her skull, giving her a desiccated, corpselike look, and her eyes were wide and staring, pinpoint pupils entirely surrounded now by the bloodshot whites. Great patches of her skin had flaked, exposing raw redness beneath, and her hair was falling, giving a grotesquely piebald look to her scalp.

'Chrysiva . . . ?' Indigo struggled to keep the horror she felt from her voice, but knew the attempt was a failure.

'W . . . wa . . .' The girl coughed; pink-tinged spittle ran down her chin. 'May I – have some w-water . . .'

'Of course.' Indigo ran to where Jasker kept his water-skins and filled a cup. Grimya, who had followed her, stood a few paces away watching with worried eyes; as Chrysiva drank the she-wolf said:

*Her tongue has turned black. Is there nothing the man can do for her?*

Indigo started to reply, but stopped as a heavy tread in the passage beyond the cave announced Jasker's arrival. The sorcerer dumped his burden on the cave floor and said, 'He's stirring. I'd best make sure he's well secured before I look at the girl.'

Quinas was indeed beginning to regain consciousness. His limbs moved feebly, then he groaned and uttered a muffled curse. Seeing him for the first time, Chrysiva's watering eyes widened and she tried to sit up, feebly pushing the cup away.

'It's all right; be calm, now.' Gently Indigo held her back, and looked over her shoulder at Jasker. 'Truss him, quickly. The tighter the better!'

The overseer was still too weak and confused to protest as Jasker dragged his arms behind him and bound wrists and ankles with a rough cord. Then, hauling him up by his collar, the sorcerer dumped him hard against the wall.

'Nnn . . .' An ugly, gargling sound came from Chrysiva's throat and she clamped one hand over Indigo's forearm, nails digging painfully. 'Him . . . he is – he is – '

'Hush! Don't look at him, Chrysiva, don't let him upset you.' Indigo swung the girl round to face her and looked into her eyes, her own expression hard. 'He will die, Chrysiva. We will avenge your husband for you!'

A bark of cynical laughter cut across her words and she looked up to see that Quinas, fully conscious now, was staring coolly at her from the far side of the cave.

'Such sisterly concern,' the overseer said drily. 'Truly, I am touched.' He smiled. 'If you want to "avenge" the brat's husband, *saia*, you might as well say a prayer or two for her whilst you're about it. She looks as if she needs all the help she can get.'

Chrysiva burst into tears and Indigo whirled on Jasker. 'Get him out of the cave, Jasker!' she snapped. 'Get him out of my sight, before I cut his throat!'

Quinas said, 'Ah, *saia*, your compassion knows no – ' and the words cut off with an oath as Jasker's fist hit him full on the jaw.

119

'I have just the place for this refuse,' Jasker said.

'Then take him. Quickly, before I forget my own intentions.'

Chrysiva watched as Quinas – prudently silent now – was dragged away down the dark tunnel. Grimya, anxious to see that nothing went amiss, accompanied Jasker, and Indigo poured more water into the cup.

'Drink,' she said, holding it out. 'And then you must rest, Chrysiva.'

'No . . .' The girl blinked as though coming out of a trance, saw that the tunnel mouth was now empty, and turned to look at Indigo. 'No,' she repeated, and there was unexpected strength in her voice. 'I don't want to rest; at least, not in that way . . . *Saia* Indigo, you've been so good and so kind to me, I – I want to give you something in return. It's little enough repayment, but . . .' One hand fumbled at the folds of her robe but her movements were uncoordinated. 'I can't find it . . . please. Here. Pinned to my bodice . . .'

Indigo touched the garment – she could feel the irregular fluttering of Chrysiva's faltering heart beneath the fabric – and found something hard and metallic. A brooch. At the girl's urging she unpinned it and put it into the palm of Chrysiva's hand.

'Please, *saia*. I want you to have it. It was a gift to me, from . . .' tears blinded her eyes, 'from my husband. I know it's but a poor thing, yet it – it has meant very much to me. Please. I know you will keep it safe.'

Indigo's own vision blurred as she stared down at the brooch. It was, as Chrysiva said, a poor thing; a little bird crudely fashioned from pewter, the wings uneven and badly engraved, the pin askew. It must, she thought, have been made by some craftsman's unskilled apprentice, and was doubtless the only kind of adornment that an impoverished miner could afford for his wife. But to Chrysiva, it meant more than all the diamonds and emeralds in the depths of the Earth.

She said hoarsely, 'I can't take it, Chrysiva. It's

yours, and it must remain yours. And I want no
payment – '

'*Please.*' The girl thrust the brooch into Indigo's hand
and fiercely pressed her fingers into a fist around it. 'I
. . . will have no need of it soon, *saia*. And I want –
want to ask – '

'What? Only ask – I'll grant you anything, if I can.'

'I . . .' Chrysiva's lip trembled, her diseased face
took on a tight, private look. Then she shut her eyes
and whispered: 'Send me to Ranaya's breast, *saia*
Indigo. Let me join my husband on Her plains of fire.
I know I must go there soon, and I don't want to suffer
any more.' She drew breath and her eyes opened again,
hurt and desperate. '*Please*, Indigo – kill me, and let
me have peace!'

Appalled, Indigo drew back. She didn't know how
to reply, what to say – then she heard Jasker and
Grimya returning, and got hastily to her feet.

*Indigo?* Grimya sensed her distress immediately and
ran towards her. *What is the matter?*

'Chrysiva – she – ' Indigo's voice broke and she
shook her head, clutching the pewter brooch more
tightly in her hand. The sorcerer touched her shoulder
gently; she flinched, then looked at him in desperation.
'Jasker, can't something be done for her?'

The answer was in his eyes. And she thought of
what Chrysiva would suffer before she finally died, the
lingering, agonising horror of her final end . . .

'She has asked me to kill her,' she whispered.

'Ah, sweet Ranaya . . .' Jasker turned away, his face
haggard. 'Child – ' He moved to Chrysiva's side, crouched before her. 'Child, is this what you truly ask?'

Chrysiva nodded. 'You are a priest; you understand
such things. I beg you, grant me the wine and the fire,
as only a priest can do. Give me Ranaya's blessing and
let me go to Her.'

Jasker rose and paced slowly back to where Indigo
and Grimya stood. He looked old suddenly, worn and
tired.

121

'I can't do it.' He spoke so softly that she could barely hear him. 'It would be a mercy to her and Ranaya would give Her blessing gladly, but . . . Indigo, I can't *do* it. My own wife, when she . . .' He stopped, drew a deep breath. 'Those memories are too strong and too terrible. I would flinch, I would pull back at the last moment. The Mother help me, I would fail her!'

Indigo was staring at Chrysiva. In her hand the little pewter brooch was warm, and it seemed to symbolise something that her mind could not quite grasp and hold to. And she thought of Fenran.

Pain and misery and a long, tortured road into darkness . . . She could understand Jasker's emotion, for she shared it. To take the life of such a one as Chrysiva, in cold blood –

But it would not be in cold blood. It would be, as Jasker said, a mercy. Could she in all conscience place her own fine feelings above the desperate need of a woman in the deepest and most hopeless distress? She closed her eyes, and seemed to see Fenran's face before her closed lids; Fenran smiling and laughing and holding out his arms to her. *What would you do, my love?* she asked silently. *Would you have the courage to grant such a wish, or would you fail?* And she believed she knew the answer.

She turned away from Chrysiva and said very quietly, 'I have a crossbow . . .'

'Indigo.' Jasker laid a hand on her arm. 'My cowardice must not be allowed to compel you.'

'No.' Her fingers closed over his, trying to give reassurance. 'It isn't like that, Jasker. Truly, it isn't like that.' A little unsteadily she walked to where the girl lay, and knelt down.

'Chrysiva?'

Hope flickered in the bloodshot eyes. 'Yes, *saia*?'

'I will keep your brooch safe, I swear it. It will be as precious to me as . . . as it was to you.' Steeling

122

herself, she bent to kiss the girl's forehead gently. 'Speed you well, Chrysiva.'

The sharp, metallic sounds as she loaded a bolt into the crossbow seemed an obscenity against the quiet backdrop of Jasker's murmuring voice. Indigo was too far from the bed to hear the words of the blessing he gave, but she could discern an eagerness in Chrysiva's soft-voiced responses, a renewal of hope, and – though it only served to reinforce her sense of unreality – a joy. Grimya sat silently watching, and Indigo took a little comfort from the knowledge that the she-wolf did not condemn her; it was, Grimya had said sadly, better that they should all grieve a while than that Chrysiva should be in pain.

Jasker rose suddenly to his feet, making Indigo start nervously. She looked back; the sorcerer nodded, and Indigo's hands tightened on the bow.

Chrysiva's eyes were closed and she was smiling. Indigo stood over her and, feeling strangely detached as though a dream-self were watching her real self from a great distance, aimed the crossbow at the girl's heart.

Old days, other days, when her father had given her her first lessons in weaponry. She remembered those lessons now. The accurate eye, the steady aim, the quiet hand. And calm. Above all, calm.

She fired.

# Chapter IX

The last notes of the Island Pibroch shimmered in the cave and faded to a distant echo, and Indigo set the harp down.

'It was a poor elegy,' she said harshly. 'It's been so many years since I played it that I've all but forgotten . . .'

Jasker, who sat cross-legged before the shrine of Ranaya, spoke without looking up. 'It was beautiful.' His voice was filled with emotion. 'It brought me visions of things that I didn't know existed under the great sun. Vast stretches of water, places where the day never ends yet where the air is cold and clear . . . I saw endless green forests, and white mountains that shone like polished glass . . .'

'The southern glaciers.' A faint, wistful smile touched Indigo's lips; the image allayed a little of the seething dark rage tight within her, but only for a moment before her voice hardened again. 'But what use is an elegy to Chrysiva now?'

'It will speed her on her way to Ranaya.' Jasker made a last obeisance before the shrine, then moved back. 'Your music, and my prayers. We can do no more, Indigo.'

The harp uttered a discordant cadence as with a surge of frustration Indigo thrust it ferociously aside. She checked herself – the harp had done her no disservice, and to vent her anger on it was childish – and pushed her hands into the folds of her robe. She couldn't look towards the motionless shape, shrouded now in a piece of linen that Jasker had used as a

124
124

blanket, which lay by the tunnel entrance ready for its final journey. Jasker had told her a little of Ranaya's funeral rites, the committal of the body to earth and to fire, but she didn't want to think about that yet. Chrysiva was still too alive in her mind.

Unthinkingly her hands closed on the pewter brooch which had been the girl's gift to her, and she felt a mental knife-thrust of sick fury. When Jasker's formalities were done there would be another matter to attend to, and impatience was beginning to eat at her. She wanted Quinas's blood. She wanted his bones to gnaw on, his marrow to drain. She wanted his *soul*.

Jasker rose to his feet and the movement broke the vortex of her thoughts.

'I shall take her to the fumarole now,' he said quietly. 'Will you come with me?'

'No.' She shook her head. 'I think I'd prefer to be alone for a while.'

*I wish to go*, Grimya said. *To say farewell.*

*Go then, love. And say her a prayer for me.* Aloud Indigo added: 'When you return, Jasker, we shall have work to do.'

'Don't think I've forgotten it.' He paused by Chrysiva's shrouded form and looked back at Indigo with a pity in his eyes that she didn't want to acknowledge, let alone accept.

An aura flickered about Jasker's silhouette as he vanished into the dark of the tunnel with the dead girl in his arms, and when he was gone, with Grimya a silent shadow at his heels, Indigo gave way to a great shudder that seemed to twist her spine and vibrate to the roots of her being.

*Quinas.* Hatred blossomed like a poisoned flower within her as she thought of the overseer. Jasker had confined him in a narrow chimney deep in the volcanic tunnels, a cell of hot rock and sulphurous fumes where, as the sorcerer had put it, he would survive long enough to pray for death. He had already put the overseer to the test of the fire-cord, but the experiment had failed: unlike Indigo, who had been subconsciously willing to reveal the truth to him, Quinas had mentally fought the cord's influence with a strength that the sorcerer found surprising, and without at least a small measure of co-operation the cord was useless. Other methods would be required to persuade Quinas to speak.

Indigo didn't know what tortures Jasker might be capable of inflicting on their captive, but she admitted without a shred of conscience that no price would be too great for the information they wanted of him. If any living being could lead them to Aszareel and the true heart of Charchad, Quinas was the man. And he would do it. If she had to take him apart, limb by limb, sinew by sinew, with her own hands, he would tell her what she wanted to know. And when he was drained of all he could give, there would be the sweet, savage joy of retribution for Chrysiva, and for Chrysiva's husband, and for the countless others whose lives and hopes and dreams had been shattered by the evil that dwelt in that poisoned valley.

*'Ahh!'* It wasn't a word but a shapeless cry of protest, an attempt to articulate something that she couldn't even comprehend. Chained energy jack-knifed Indigo to her feet and she strode across the cave, only stopping when she all but collided with the far wall. She pressed her palms to the rock, feeling the subterranean warmth from the volcano's deep-buried heart pulsing through her fingers, and shut her eyes against the tidal wave of rage that threatened to unhinge her mind.

The power of fire. Jasker had told her a good deal about the nature of his sorcery, the energy that he drew from the heaving, molten seas far down in the Earth's core. Fire was his element: he was brother to salamanders, cousin to dragons, master of flame and smoke and molten magma. He had told her of his great ambition – to make contact with the titanic fire-spirits, first spawn of Ranaya Herself, who slept deep, deep beneath the volcanoes' dormant cones; to harness their

126

awesome power and to orchestrate their final
vengeance on the Charchad and all it stood for. But
though he had stretched his mind and his soul to the
limits of mortal endurance, Jasker had been unable to
wake those gargantuan powers. And –

*And it wasn't enough.* What burned in Indigo was
more than fire, more than the pent fury of Ranaya's
Daughters in their long sleep. Since her first encounter
with Jasker she hadn't consulted the lodestone, for she
had had no need to: she knew without a single spark
of doubt what it would tell her. North. To the valley
called Charchad. To the glowing, festering heart of the
corruption which it was her task, and hers alone, to
eradicate from the world.

A bitter sense of weary futility washed over Indigo
then, a feeling of hopelessness that no amount of
willing would drive away. She sat down, her back
slumped dejectedly against the wall, and drew out
Chrysiva's brooch to look at it. The dull pewter of
the little bird-shape glinted in the candlelight, and she
remembered an old Southern Isles belief that at the
moment of death the soul left the body in the form of
a white and ghostly seabird that flew away over the
sea, singing a final and beautiful song, to follow the
sun and at last become one with it. If she had been
able to glimpse Chrysiva's soul-bird, she thought, she
would have seen not a proud white gull but a poor,
crippled sparrow.

A tear fell suddenly on the pewter brooch and trembled there for a moment before trickling off on to
Indigo's hand. She had begun to weep without realising
it, and she brushed quickly at her eyes, squeezing the
lids tightly shut. Crying would achieve nothing. It was
the *anger* she needed to recapture now, the rage she
had held in check but which had been burning in her,
eating at her, since she had first set foot in Vesinum.
The brooch was a focus for her wrath, for the brooch
symbolised all the innocence, the hope, the *life*, that
the Charchad had corrupted in this land. And at the

root of that corruption, the soil from which it fed, was the demon which she, by her crime, had released into the world.

Her fist clenched on the brooch in a sudden, involuntary gesture as the fury burst on her mind with a hot desperation that made her feel queasy. Chrysiva's symbol; and her own, too, for wasn't it a bitterly poignant emblem of the curse she had brought upon herself? She had promised to keep the little pewter bird and treasure it. And she would keep that promise with a vengeance, for the brooch was now to her what it was once to Chrysiva: a token of something lost which she would strive to recover, no matter what the cost.

Footfalls in the tunnel: Indigo raised her head quickly and was in time to see Jasker enter the cave. The sorcerer's burden was gone, and his eyes were empty of all emotion. Behind him, Grimya walked with head low and tail dragging; her mind was closed and she seemed reluctant to meet Indigo's gaze but instead took herself off to the far side of the cave, where she flopped down and appeared to want nothing more than to sleep.

'It's done.' Jasker picked up a water-skin and filled a cup for himself. 'Her body and her soul are with Ranaya.'

Indigo rose to her feet. A sharp edge of the brooch had cut into her hand where she had been gripping it over-tightly, but she didn't notice. 'What's the hour?' she asked.

'Dawn, or thereabouts. Maybe a little later.' Jasker looked up, his face expressionless. 'Why?'

'Quinas.' She became aware of the pain in her hand now and it brought her thoughts into focus, sharp as glass in her mind. Jasker studied her face for a moment, then said:

'I doubt if he'll be ready to co-operate with us yet. Leave him a little longer; let his prison do some of our work for us.'

'No.' She shook her head. 'I've waited long enough, Jasker. For Chrysiva's sake I want what Quinas can give us – now!'

The sorcerer continued to watch her. 'For Chrysiva's sake?' he repeated quietly. 'Or for yours?'

'Hers, mine, ours – damn you, what *difference* does it make?' She turned away from him, hunching her shoulders with taut anger, then a moment later spun round again. 'You said you could break him, you *promised* it. If now you haven't the stomach for it, say so, and I'll do the task myself!'

'Indigo.' He came forward and laid both hands on her shoulders. Furious at his attempt to pacify her she tried to pull away, but he gripped her, forcing her to look at him.

'Very well,' he said at last. 'Since your patience is at an end, we shall go now and do what must be done. I would have preferred to wait, but no matter.'

She was trembling under his touch, every muscle alive with tension. 'Each minute we delay might see the death of another innocent like Chrysiva,' she said hotly. 'Is that what you want?'

'You know it isn't.'

'Then – '

'Then there's no more to be said.' There was expression in Jasker's eyes now, and what she saw there made Indigo feel shamed, though she fought furiously, silently against the sensation. At last Jasker released her and stepped back.

'If you're ready, come with me,' he said. 'Though I'd feel happier if you left me to do this alone.'

She gave him a searing look and he shrugged. 'Come, then.'

Grimya raised her head as they started towards the tunnel mouth, and Indigo paused, looking back at the she-wolf.

*Grimya? Will you come with us?* she asked silently.

*No.* The reply was vehement and unhappy. *I do not want to see.* A pause. *There is darkness here, Indigo;*

129

*a cruel darkness that I cannot understand and do not like. Please . . . are you sure this is right?*

*Of course I am.* She could sympathise with Grimya's simplicity that gave rise to such fears, but she couldn't share them. She forced a smile, but it wasn't convincing. *Sleep for a while. I'll be back soon.*

*I know. But when – '* The she-wolf hesitated.

*When what?* There was a faint tinge of impatience in Indigo's thought.

*No matter.* Grimya looked at her, sadly she thought. *I will try to sleep, as you suggest.*

She lay down again, head turned away, as Indigo followed Jasker out of the cave.

'He's stronger than I'd expected.' The sorcerer walked back to where Indigo stood at the top of the slope that led down into the shallow pit deep in the mountains. His bare torso was slickly filmed with sweat and his hands and arms smoke-blackened to the elbows. His eyes were like chips of ice-cold stone in their sockets, and when he smiled, the smile had not the smallest trace of humanity. 'But a few more minutes, I think, will see a change.'

Unwilling to meet his gaze, Indigo looked past him to where Quinas lay spreadeagled on the pit floor. The overseer was still conscious – Jasker had taken good care to see that he didn't lose his mental faculties – but his mouth hung slack, gasping slowly, silently like a stranded fish, and his eyes were blank with shock.

What she had witnessed in this hot, sulphurous and claustrophobic place had tested Indigo's faith in her own determination to have information at any price. She hadn't believed that any human being could be capable of inflicting such tortures as Jasker had worked upon Quinas, let alone with such steely and utterly detached dedication. The sorcerer had called upon the most subtle nuances of his art, and for upwards of three hours Quinas had writhed and shrieked and suffered under the touch of fire in every imaginable manifes-

130

tation. He had seared, he had bled, he had choked; he had been dangled over the chasm of complete insanity and been brought back with his mind intact but monstrously scarred. His body was now a battered hulk, hair burned away, skin blistering and peeling, fingers fused together where the flesh had melted and reformed. And throughout Jasker had been a man of stone, the skilled, precise and supremely indifferent orchestrator of his victim's torment. The worst of the Charchad murderers, no matter how mad or depraved they might be, were pale shadows by comparison.

Indigo knew that she should have been sickened by what she had seen. She didn't share Jasker's madness, nor his personal need for revenge. No loved one of hers had been Quinas's victim. She should have interceded, should have spoken up for mercy and justice, and begged the sorcerer to find another way. But even now, looking at the ruined shell of a man lying quivering on the burning rock floor, she could find no pity in her heart for him, only a diamond-hard core of hatred and disgust.

At last she met Jasker's gaze, and felt an answering flicker of satisfaction within herself. 'A few minutes?'

He shrugged carelessly. 'Perhaps I should have implemented it earlier; but there's one more little trick I have up my sleeve . . .'

'Use it, Jasker.' She felt a rivulet of sweat trickle down her spine and the sensation sent a hot surge through her. 'Break him.'

He smiled at her again. 'You'd best keep well away from the pit floor. And if you want to retire – ' Raised eyebrows asked a question, and Indigo shook her head.

'Very well. But have a care; the heat may be more than you'd bargained for.' He turned, strode back down the slope. Quinas turned his head to watch him, and Indigo saw the muscles of the overseer's face tense in trepidation, though he tried to keep the fear from his expression.

Jasker smiled again. He raised his arms as though

moving to embrace a lover: an instant later heat swelled in the cavern and burst like a storm-wave, a wall of blistering, suffocating redness that sent Indigo staggering back, gasping as the breath was snatched and burned from her lungs.

And in the shadows at the far side of the cavern foul black smoke belched out of nowhere, and something sprang to life within the smoke.

The creature was three times Indigo's own height, but as thin as a sapling tree. It was neither a dragon nor a giant salamander, though it had elements of both in its shimmering form. Eyes that were shockingly human looked out from a pointed, reptilian face; membranous wings were folded over a body that seemed to be molten, slowly pulsing; and a hand – a human hand, but covered with scales instead of skin – reached out in a gesture that imitated Jasker's own.

Fire spat between the elemental and the sorcerer, and Indigo saw Jasker flinch momentarily as the white-hot bolt crackled against his outstretched arm. Quinas's head was straining back, eyes starting almost out of their sockets as he sought to find the source of this new threat. And again, Jasker smiled.

'Sister of the magma, daughter of the molten earth; you are welcome here.'

The being hissed, the sound echoing in the cave's confined space. To Indigo's ears the hiss had the distorted but unmistakable form of a single word; *Feed*: and she felt her stomach turn within her.

The sorcerer took two measured paces backwards, and a cord of fire appeared in his hands. He stretched it taut, then with a nod of his head indicated the spreadeagled man on the floor and uttered five syllables in an alien tongue that seemed to be composed of inflections rather than words.

The elemental flowed forward, the smoke from which it had formed roiling with it. It hovered, swaying, above Quinas's head – then, so fast that Indigo's senses could barely register the movement, a tongue of white flame darted from the elemental's mouth and struck the overseer's right eye.

Quinas shrieked, his body flailing uncontrollably but uselessly against the bonds that held him. Indigo had a momentary glimpse of blackened skin and melted flesh where his eye had been, before the elemental curved in towards him again –

'No, sister!' Jasker held up the fire-cord, which blazed suddenly with blue light. 'Enough!'

The creature uttered a high-pitched whistle, protesting, but it was constrained to obey. It drew back and hovered, swaying like a snake trying to hypnotise its prey, and Jasker took one step forward.

'Quinas.' His voice was quiet, reasoned, chillingly indifferent. 'You have seen' – a soft laugh as he acknowledged his own inadvertent and unpleasant joke – 'the way in which my little sister of the magma likes to feed. A mortal man is a delicacy which she will take a long time in devouring; many days, perhaps. So I give you a choice. Tell me what I want to know – truthfully; and remember I have my own methods of testing for the truth – and I will dismiss her to sleep again in the molten rock from which she came. Refuse, and I will relax my hold on her and let her choose another morsel before I ask my questions again; and so the pattern will continue.' He smiled. 'I think you will tire of the game before she and I do.'

The elemental whistled again, as though in agreement, and Quinas stared back at the sorcerer. His remaining eye was completely red, whether with blood or with the effect of the bizarre crimson lens Indigo didn't know; and his twitching body now seemed beyond his control. When at last he tried to speak he could at first only gasp, his scorched mouth opening and closing spasmodically. Jasker waited, uninterested in his struggles, and at last a voice that sounded as though the larynx that formed it had been torn into shreds croaked:

'I . . . will . . . answer . . .'

Indigo felt her own lungs expel a hot breath, and Jasker nodded. 'Very good.' He tautened the fire-cord once more. 'Then, while my little sister waits to ensure your continuing co-operation, we shall begin.'

They needed no further torture. Quinas could barely speak and each word cost him fresh agonies, but slowly, falteringly, the information they wanted was revealed, until Jasker was satisfied that their prisoner could tell them no more.

'We have everything he can give us.' Jasker came slowly back to where Indigo crouched near the cave mouth. 'And it's enough.'

She nodded. 'We know that Aszareel is still alive, and dwelling in the Charchad vale,' she said softly.

'Yes. I'm not sure how to interpret that; no normal man could survive that place for more than a few days. But it was the truth, as far as Quinas knows it.'

'Aszareel isn't normal,' Indigo said with venom. 'He's – ' she broke off, shook her head.

Jasker sank down on to the rock beside her and pressed his fingertips to his eyes. He was close to exhaustion, and although the great elemental had departed, the cave was still suffocating and the heat and fumes were draining what strength he had left.

'We've no further use for that offal now,' he said tiredly, gesturing towards the pit. 'There's a fumarole nearby; I'll kill him and give the corpse to the salamanders that live there. They'll feed well for a while.'

Indigo's head came up sharply and she looked at the overseer who, mercifully for him, had lapsed into unconsciousness. Then she snapped viciously: 'No. We'll take him back with us. I want him to live for a while yet.'

'What's the point? He can tell us nothing more, and we have no further need of him.'

'I don't care. I want him to live. I want him to *suffer*.'

Jasker looked at her, disquieted. His own lust for personal revenge was more than satisfied: in fact he had found much of the torture distasteful, preferring cleaner methods when it came to retribution. A pragmatic execution and disposal now seemed only right. But Indigo felt differently. For her, Quinas's death wouldn't be enough.

A belated spark of humanity struggled through the numb weariness, and he tried again to reason with her. 'Let him die, Indigo. Let him go to the hell he deserves, and be done with him.'

Indigo didn't reply immediately, but sat staring at the man in the pit. But she didn't see Quinas's ruined body; instead, in her mind's eye, she saw the ravaged face of Chrysiva, and felt the little pewter brooch hot under the folds of her robe. Then Chrysiva's face changed and became that of Fenran, her own love, torn, bleeding, eyes blank with shock and pain, and finally his features crumbled away into the vicious, silver-eyed countenance of another being, one that had never been human yet which took its evil life from humanity; a being from which she could not be free until her quest was done. Her Nemesis.

'*No!*' she said vehemently.

Jasker sighed. He didn't have the energy to argue any further: let her have her way, if it eased some gnawing devil within her. 'Very well,' he said resignedly. 'We'll do as you wish.' He stood up. 'I doubt anyway that he'll come round for a few hours, and maybe by then – '

'By then you think I'll have changed my mind?' Fury flashed in Indigo's eyes. 'Don't presume to know me, Jasker!'

'*Saia*, I presume nothing.' Jasker turned back towards the pit, then paused. 'I am simply a little disconcerted to find that your capacity for retribution outmatches even mine.'

The brooch seemed to burn hotly anew against her skin, and Indigo said, 'I have my own reasons, Jasker.'

'Yes.' He acknowledged the point with a wry quirk of his lips. 'I'm sure of it.'

She turned away as he went to fetch their prisoner.

# Chapter X

Grimya sprang to her feet as they entered the main cave. For a moment Indigo felt the warm mental surge of her greeting: then the she-wolf saw what they carried, and the warmth shattered into a maelstrom of shock and confusion.

*Indigo!* Grimya's distress was like a psychic knife in the girl's mind. *What have you done?*

Indigo stared at her friend. For an instant she saw an echo of the image, both physical and mental, that she presented to Grimya, and cold fingers of conscience locked on her gut. Then she cast the feeling aside, as she might have cast away a worn and useless garment.

*We did what was necessary*, she responded curtly.

*But the man still lives . . .*

*Yes. And will continue to do so.*

*Indigo –*

'No!' She hadn't meant to voice the angry retort aloud, but it was out before she could prevent it. Jasker looked quickly at her, then at the wolf. 'No . . . ?' he queried, quite gently.

Indigo shook her head violently, refusing to elaborate, and the sorcerer watched as Grimya turned away. He hazarded that they had communicated briefly and not happily, resulting in Indigo's outburst, and experimentally he sent a soft mental probe in Grimya's direction. There was no response – she didn't even twitch – and Jasker sighed inwardly, realising that she either couldn't or wouldn't respond to him. Now the she-wolf moved towards the cave exit, her head hanging low. She looked back once, as if hoping that

137

Indigo would speak to her; but the girl ignored her, and slowly, dejectedly, Grimya padded out.

Jasker lowered Quinas's unconscious body to the floor at one side of the cave. Indigo sat down, back turned to him and shoulders hunched in a clear signal that she wished to be left alone. There was a peculiar blend of defensiveness and aggression about the posture, and Jasker suspected that the girl was balanced on a precarious mental knife-edge which could at any moment pitch her into utter exhaustion or the throes of uncontrollable wrath.

Pragmatically, he said in as casual a tone as he could muster, 'We should eat. It won't do to neglect necessities.'

'I'm not hungry.'

'Neither am I.' He glanced at their captive once more. 'To tell you the truth, I haven't the stomach for food at the moment; I'm too tired. But I'll make myself eat, because I must. And so should you.'

She turned her head, her face venomous. 'Damn you, Jasker, I said I'm *not hungry!* You sound like my old nurse – ' and she cut off in mid-sentence, jerking away from him again. Jasker thought he heard a faint whimper as though she were fighting back tears. He sighed and, too weary to pursue it, went to his small food store and began to prepare a makeshift meal for himself. His stocks – never bountiful at the best of times, as food was scarce and decayed swiftly – were badly depleted, but he scraped together a few wilting remnants of vegetables and some strips of dried meat which could be softened if need be with a little water. When he had finished, he turned back and saw that Indigo had risen and crossed the cave floor to stare down at Quinas. Her expression was cold and faraway, but in the unsteady light from the candles he thought he detected the unnatural shimmer of tears in her eyes.

'Indigo.' He set the food down and walked slowly towards her. She didn't flinch away when he put an arm about her shoulders and, encouraged, he went on,

138

'Indigo, you're grieving still for Chrysiva, and you must know that I understand only too well how you feel. But we've taken all we can from this creature in revenge.' He looked at the unconscious man before them, at the burned hair, the blistered skin, the ruined hands, the grisly black and crimson crater where his right eye had been. 'Wouldn't it be simpler now to let him die?'

Indigo shut her eyes and her teeth clamped hard on her lower lip. 'Yes.' Her voice was ugly. 'It would be simpler. But I want him to live.'

'Why?'

'Because . . .' She sucked in a deep, painful breath. 'Because every moment he stays alive, every moment he suffers, is a further retribution. Don't you understand?' She looked up at him, and Jasker was taken aback by the terrible expression in her eyes. She looked as though she had opened a door on to a world so blackly evil that it had drained the last vestiges of humanity from her soul, and had coldly and deliberately chosen to step through that door. Then swiftly she reached into her robe and held up something that glinted dully. 'She gave me this, Jasker. It was the most precious possession she had, and she gave it to me in gratitude before I killed her. Look at it. *Look* at it!'

He looked, but didn't attempt to touch the brooch. Harshly, Indigo continued: 'Each moment, Jasker, each *moment* that Quinas suffers, will be for Chrysiva!' Her fist clenched tightly round the little pewter bird. 'And he *will* suffer. He *will*.'

'For Chrysiva?' Jasker asked. 'Or for someone else?'

She froze, staring at him. 'What do you mean?'

'You know what I mean.' He gripped her shoulders, his thumbs unconsciously bruising, but neither of them was aware of the violence of the gesture. 'It isn't for Chrysiva, is it, Indigo? I know, because I've suffered that loss, too. It's for Fenran.'

Indigo's eyes widened. She hadn't realised that he knew Fenran's name, and to hear it spoken aloud was

139

a shock that brought all the memories, all the horrors, surging like a horde of howling devils into her mind. Breath caught in her throat and cracked into a sob.

'No,' she whispered. 'No, it – ' She started to shiver. 'You can't *understand*, you can't – ' Tears pricked her eyes, hot and stinging; and with the tears came a vast and violent upsurge of the feelings pent within her. She tried to fight the emotion, struggled to stop it from breaking through to the surface – and suddenly her self-control shattered into a storm of weeping.

'Indigo!' Jasker caught her as she sagged to her knees, and she reached out blindly towards him, the pewter brooch falling from her grasp as she clutched at him in a desperate and wordless plea for comfort. Not reasoning, not pausing to think, he held her tightly against him and his vision blurred as memories that were cruel kin to her own rose in his mind. Hair, long and thick and silky against his face, the smaller, softer contours of a woman's body, the smoothness of her skin . . . imagination and longing rioted together in the sorcerer and he kissed her face, her shoulders, the crown of her head; felt her respond and cling to him as though he were hers and she were his and under the benevolent smile of Ranaya it had never been any other way –

'Don't weep.' His voice was husky with emotion, the words muffled as he pressed his cheek close to hers. 'My dearest one, my sweet rose in a barren desert, don't weep.' And then he spoke a name that for two years had been only a stab of silent agony in his heart.

Something deep within him locked rigid, and the shock of what he had done cleared his head as abruptly as if someone had thrown a pitcher of ice-cold water in his face. Appalled, he looked down at Indigo. She was silent, motionless, and he knew that she had heard him and understood the significance of what he had said.

Very slowly then she raised her head. Her cheeks were wet with tears and her eyes red-rimmed. Her hands, which had been clasping his shoulders tightly, slowly unclenched and she wiped her knuckles across her flushed face.

'Jasker . . .' She paused, then drew away from him, letting herself sink down until she was sitting on the cave floor. 'I'm sorry. I was . . .'

He shook his head. 'No, *saia*. It's I who should apologise. I didn't think, didn't consider: for a moment I almost believed that you – '

'Yes. I felt the same.' Jasker thought she was going to cry again, but she pulled herself together. 'We were both very foolish, weren't we?' She blinked rapidly. 'You're a good man, Jasker, and our cause has given us a great deal in common. Friendship, sympathy, empathy even. But – '

He smiled sadly and finished the sentence for her. 'But I'm not Fenran.'

'No. And I am not your dead wife. It would be so easy to pretend, but pretence would be wrong.'

'More than wrong.' Jasker reached out and took hold of her hands. There was no tension in the gesture, only a kindness that was almost brotherly. 'It would be a travesty.'

Indigo nodded. There were no more tears left in her now, and as they dried she felt the storm of emotion shrivelling with them, leaving a dark, quiet void. In the depths of the void something simmered, but it was too remote to have meaning and she was too exhausted to pursue it.

Jasker released her hands and gazed down at the floor. His eyes were hooded and his thoughts private, and silence fell in the cave for a minute or two. Then at last the sorcerer rose to his feet.

'I shall leave you to rest,' he said. 'I think perhaps we both need the chance to be alone for a while.' He looked down at her, his face haggardly sad. 'And I'm sorry, Indigo. Truly, I'm so sorry.'

She didn't look up as he walked slowly out of the cavern. Although Indigo felt wearied to the bone, sleep

141

was beyond her. She sat cross-legged before the one candle that still burned in the cave, staring at the unsteady flame and breathing so slowly and shallowly that an observer might have wondered whether she were alive or dead. Behind her, Quinas lay unstirring, his ruined hands bound behind him and his body placed so that his face was turned towards the wall. She didn't once look at him; but she was coldly, cruelly aware of his presence.

Minutes or hours might have passed; Indigo neither knew nor cared. In his private sanctum deep in the volcano Jasker would be meditating or praying, trying to make amends for what he saw as his foolishness, and for breaking the taboo that forbade him from ever speaking his dead wife's name. Yet to Indigo, the spark that had sprung so briefly to life between them hadn't been folly, but rather the desperate need of two lonely and unhappy people to seek comfort in the midst of emptiness. She didn't love Jasker, any more than he loved her. But for one bittersweet moment they had superimposed the images of their lost lovers upon each other, and had been almost convinced by the illusion.

But almost was just that: *almost*. Illusions couldn't last, and Jasker neither could nor wished to take the place of Fenran. *His* hands were the only hands she wanted to feel on her skin, his lips the only ones she wanted to touch hers. Five years since she had lost him . . . how many more before she might hope to see him again?

On the floor before her, Chrysiva's pewter brooch lay shining with a bright patina in the candlelight. She had retrieved it from where it fell, and at last, slowly as though in a dream, she reached out and picked it up, weighing it absently in one hand. Chrysiva. Fenran. Jasker's wife. They all lived on in this small, crude symbol of a miner's love; this embodiment of what the power she hated with such a passion was doing to her world.

Hate. The quiet void that the emotional storm had

left behind filled suddenly with something black and burning and deadly. Though she gave no outward sign of it, Indigo felt that a furnace had opened deep inside her and that its white-hot flames were devouring her from within. But she knew the sensation, and welcomed it; for this was the rage that had sustained her since the night in Vesinum, the wrath that had driven her to the mountains and to Jasker, the loathing that had led her to watch unmoved as Quinas shrieked in the agonies of torture. Hate. It was strong, strong wine. And she was not done with drinking yet.

She stood up, and as she straightened it seemed for a moment that the cave filled with a red haze that all but blinded her. It cleared quickly – it was nothing more, she realised, than a brief miasma caused by tiredness and lack of food – but it seemed to crystallise the fury within her into a narrow, vicious and utterly clear beam that abruptly found its focus in one direction.

Indigo turned – and saw that Quinas had rolled over and was staring at her with his one remaining eye.

The hate surged. She smiled and raised her hands, clenching the fists as though tautening an invisible rope. 'Well, now.' Had she been capable of listening detachedly to her own voice, she wouldn't have recognised it. 'The sleeper returns to the world. What did you dream, Quinas? Of tormented women? Of disease? Of slavery?' Her lips curved in an ineffably cruel smile. 'Or of the kiss of fire?'

He didn't reply – she doubted if he was capable of speaking – but slowly, slowly the red lens came down over his eye, and a muscle in his ruined face twitched spasmodically.

Indigo's smile widened. 'Are you in pain? Yes; I believe you are. Well, it will be over soon, Quinas. Not soon enough for you, I'd warrant, but soon.' She dropped to a crouch and leaned over the captive. His appalling disfigurements didn't repel her; she was far beyond any such human reaction. 'The pain will end,

143

Quinas, when you have performed just one task for me. Perform it, and I will allow you to die. Fail, and I will spend many, many months enjoying the spectacle of your further suffering. You understand me, Quinas. Don't you?'

The crimson-lensed eye continued to regard her blankly, but this time the overseer's scorched mouth twitched. His throat worked convulsively and a toneless, desiccated whisper issued from him.

'M . . . m . . . ma – ad . . .'

Indigo laughed, the sound cracking the quiet. 'Mad? No, Quinas. I am not mad. I am *angry*. And my anger is not yet assuaged, nor will it be until the evil *thing* you serve lies flopping and gibbering and rotting to primeval slime at my feet!' In a sudden movement she stood up, and swung round to where her possessions had been neatly stacked by the wall a few feet away. She snatched up the crossbow, slammed a bolt home and then turned back to Quinas. Her hands caressed the weapon, moving slowly but with deadly purpose, and she said:

'You have told us of your master Aszareel, and you have told us where he is to be found. But it isn't enough, Quinas. I want more from you.' Suddenly she levelled the crossbow. 'Get up!'

Quinas hesitated, then made a barely discernible negative movement of his head. He tried to sneer, but it was a poor effort, and ghastly on his wreck of a face. 'And if . . . I will not,' he whispered, 'what shall you . . . do then, *saia*?'

Indigo laughed, quite gently. 'Look again, my friend. See where the bolt is aimed.'

His gaze travelled to the crossbow, took in the line between it and his own body. The bolt was pointed directly at his groin.

'No, it won't kill you,' Indigo confirmed softly. 'But it will cause you great pain. Yet more great pain, Quinas. Do I make my meaning clear?'

She couldn't guess what thoughts went through the

144

overseer's mind as he looked at the bow balanced steadily in her hands. But at last, though slowly and with a show of reluctance that was all the dignity he had left, Quinas started to struggle upright.

'In-di-go!'

Indigo spun round, bringing the crossbow up in a rapid reflex at the unexpected yet familiar voice from behind her. Quinas fell awkwardly back on the rock floor, and the girl stared over the bow's sights at Grimya who stood in the mouth of the exit tunnel.

The she-wolf's eyes gleamed in the dimness, their expression sad. *Will you kill me, too?* she asked silently.

'You startled me . . .' Defensive, Indigo turned the words into an accusation, and lowered the weapon. 'I thought – '

Grimya looked at Quinas. *You thought that I was another enemy?*

The overseer was staring at her, curiosity overcoming pain and confusion. Swiftly, Indigo switched to tele-pathic speech. *You should know better than to approach without warning!*

*I tried to speak to you, as we are speaking now. But your mind was closed to me.* Grimya padded further into the cave, then hesitated. *It is almost closed to me now. We exchange words, but I can't see your thoughts. Indigo, what are you doing? Where is Jasker? And why were you going to kill this man when you said you would not?*

*I wasn't going to kill him. Damn you, Grimya, you wouldn't understand!*

Grimya whined softly in the back of her throat, and lowered her head, dejected. *I might. But you will not let me try.*

Black anger surged in Indigo, and with a violent movement she flung the crossbow aside. It crashed against the wall, making Grimya flinch, and the girl strode across the floor before turning and facing the wolf again.

'Very well,' she said aloud. 'Very *well*, if you must know everything!' She no longer cared whether Quinas heard them; no longer cared for anything but her one intent, the one thing she meant to do and which Grimya had interrupted. 'Come here, Grimya. Come here and look.'

*Indigo, please . . . you are making me fear what is in your head . . .*

Indigo's face distorted into a vicious mask and she repeated savagely, 'I said, *come and look!*'

Slowly and unwillingly Grimya approached. As she drew near she saw that Indigo held something in her outstretched hand. The she-wolf had seen it before. An ornament, such as humans liked to wear, made of a silver-coloured metal. It had belonged to the poor, sick woman, and she had given it to Indigo as a gift, just before . . . but Grimya didn't want to remember that, for the woman's death had marked the beginning of the strangeness within her friend. And although she couldn't comprehend the reason, she felt that the little ornament had somehow been responsible.

'Well?' Indigo's voice was harshly interrogative. 'Do you know what this is?'

Grimya blinked miserably. *I know where it came from, but I do not know what it is called. Indigo–*

She was interrupted. 'It's a brooch. Chrysiva's brooch. Given to her in love, and taken from her, as her *life* was taken from her, in sickness and hatred and corruption! Are you capable of understanding what that means?'

*But it is only a piece of metal*, Grimya reasoned.

'No! It's far more than that; it's a *symbol*, a – ' words failed her and she shook her head violently. 'How can you possibly understand such things? How can you *possibly* understand what this brooch means? It was hers: it was Chrysiva's. And now Chrysiva is dead, murdered by the Charchad. And the Charchad is the demon, and the demon squats in that filthy, stinking valley, and spreads its ordure and its corruption across

146

the *world!*' She drew a great, gasping breath, and her body began to tremble with barely-controlled rage. 'I want that demon and all it stands for to die,' she hissed venomously. 'Whatever the cost, whatever the danger; I don't care.' Her eyes met Grimya's, and the she-wolf recoiled from the insane fire that burned as nacreous and as unnatural and as all-consuming as the light of the Charchad valley itself in her wild stare. 'Chrysiva will be *avenged!*'

Candlelight caught the little brooch as Indigo jerked her hand away, and for an instant the pewter winked as bright as . . .

As bright as silver.

In that moment, Grimya realised what had happened to her friend.

*Nemesis.* Images of the demoniac child with its unhumanly laughing eyes surged into the she-wolf's brain. Indigo's own *alter ego*, quintessence of the evil she had released from the Tower of Regrets. An influence which sought to destroy her, and from which she could not be free until the last of the seven demons was dead. And though Nemesis might take any form it chose, one constant would always betray it to vigilant eyes.

That constant was the colour silver.

Horrified, Grimya stared at Chrysiva's brooch. She should have known when Indigo began to focus her attention on the woman's dying gift that the influence working upon her friend was unnatural. But the fact that the metal was base and its sheen dull had misled her, and neither she nor Indigo had considered for one moment that other dangers than the Charchad might lie in wait for them. Now though, Grimya was certain of it. *Silver.* A momentary glimmer in the dim candle-light. Nemesis had returned to challenge them.

She raised her head to look into Indigo's eyes, and saw that it was too late for reason. Unknowing, Indigo was in Nemesis's grip. And the demon's hold on her was too strong for Grimya to break.

The she-wolf felt a quivering, spasmodic sensation

at the back of her throat; a reflex that made her want
to raise her muzzle and howl her distress to the sky.
She felt alone, bereft, lost – but a newer wisdom was
fighting through the animal instinct, telling her that
now, perhaps as never before, she must act of her own
volition. Indigo wouldn't hear her; her mind was locked
on another plane, shrouded in the black wrath that
drove her. But there was another. Grimya doubted
him, knowing he was mad and unwilling to offer him
her complete trust. Now, though, it seemed that he
was her only hope.

She whined softly, still hoping with a stubborn part
of her mind that Indigo would blink and look at her,
and that the insanity in her eyes would be gone. But
Indigo didn't hear her. Instead she crouched, the
brooch held tightly in her hand, and stared ahead as
though she saw into an alien and dreadful world, and
relished it.

She didn't even raise her head as Grimya ran from
the cave.

Sheer exhaustion had claimed Jasker, but his sleep was
punctuated by disjointed and unpleasant dreams. They
culminated in a nightmare during which, on another
level of consciousness, he thought he heard a voice
repeatedly calling his name, and when he woke with a
jolt from the dream he was momentarily disorientated
by the silence of his sanctum. He sat up, rubbing at
his prickling eyelids – then started afresh as he saw
Grimya at the cavern entrance.

The she-wolf's eyes were crimson with distress.
Panting, she looked at the sorcerer in mute appeal,
then to his astonishment she gasped, gutturally but
clearly,

'Please – hh-*elp* me!'

Jasker stared at her, wondering fleetingly if he might
still be dreaming. He'd guessed that the wolf was
capable of telepathic communication, but hadn't
bargained for this. At last he found his own voice,

though it was soft with incredulity. 'Grimya . . . you can *speak* . . .'

Grimya dipped her head in a manner that implied embarrassment, even shame. 'Yes. I . . . did not want you to kn-know. But now, I cannot . . . hh-ide it any longer. I need your h-help, Jasker!'

Amid the first shock of the revelation Jasker had paid little heed to what Grimya had actually said. But now, belatedly, it registered, and he felt a sharp stab of apprehension that erased the last traces of his weariness.

'What's wrong?' Muscles tensing, he started to get up. 'Has something happened?'

'Not y-yet. But I fear it will. It is In-digo. She – ' Grimya pawed the ground in frustration at her limited abilities. 'She is *sick*.'

Nauseous horror twisted Jasker's gut. 'Tongue of Ranaya, you don't mean the Charchad sickness?'

'No, not th . . . *at*. In her head. In her m-mind. It concerns the man, the hurt man. I tried to t-talk to her, but she . . . would not hear me. Please – I cannot explain it prr . . . operly. Come and see.'

He needed no urging. For Grimya to have broken the bonds of her secret – and he could well understand why she wished no one but Indigo to know of her peculiar talent – something must be very seriously wrong.

'Lead on,' he said. 'Ranaya alone knows if I can do anything where you've failed, but I'll try.'

They left the cave and Grimya hurried ahead along the maze of tunnels through which she had tracked the sorcerer. She found it hard to curb her impatience at his slower speed, and at last broke into a run as the main cavern mouth came in sight. Jasker saw her disappear through the entrance – then his heart nearly stopped as he heard a dismal howl echo back along the tunnel.

'Grimya!' He raced the last few paces, burst into the cave. Grimya stood splay-legged in the middle of the floor, ears flat to her head, and as he entered she turned to face him and whimpered one agonised word.

'*G . . . gone!*'

The cave was empty. Debris littered the floor, mostly Indigo's possessions, although a good few of Jasker's meagre belongings were mingled with them. It looked as though someone had searched the cave frenziedly before abandoning it to chaos. Grimya was right: Indigo had gone.

And so had Quinas.

# Chapter XI

Jasker swore softly, and sat down on the floor as his legs seemed unwilling to support him. Grimya ran to his side, tongue lolling. 'Wh-what are we to d . . . *do?*'

The idea that Quinas might have regained enough strength to overpower Indigo was ridiculous; he could only have left the cave as her prisoner and not she as his. But if the girl's state of mind was as Grimya implied, that thought was poor comfort.

'Grimya.' He turned to the she-wolf, made as if to take her hands then remembered that she wasn't human. 'Why would she have taken Quinas from the cave? Can you think of any reason?'

Grimya's head swung from side to side. 'Sh-she would not . . . *talk* to me. But she was . . . was . . .' She growled unhappily. 'I cannot explain. I don't know the proper w-w-word!'

'Angry?'

'Ye-*ess*. But more. As if she had . . . caught prey, but w-would not believe that she had k . . . killed it, and so tried to kill it again and again.'

Jasker understood the analogy. 'Obsessed,' he said. It was what he had feared.

'Ob . . . s . . . sessed.' Grimya repeated the word with difficulty.

'Yes. I've seen it in her, Grimya; and I understand it. You see, I too am obsessed with destroying the Charchad, and so I can sympathise with Indigo's feelings. But,' he laughed wryly, without humour, 'strange as it may seem, I don't think my obsession matches hers. Something drives her; something I can't even

151

begin to comprehend, and it makes my feelings shallow by comparison. When we took Quinas to the cave . . .' Abruptly he checked himself. 'No. You don't want to know about that; it isn't fair that I should burden you with it. Suffice it to say that I think we should find Indigo, and quickly.'

'I can trr-ack her,' Grimya said. 'As I trr-acked you. That will be easy. But – '

'But what?'

'There is s-something else, Jasker. S-*omething* I have not told you.'

Although the she-wolf's voice was capable of little inflection, her tone alerted the sorcerer. He frowned. 'What is it, Grimya? What haven't you told me?'

'I . . .' She licked her chops uneasily. 'I should not say. I have been told that I m . . . *must* not say. But if I do not w-warn you . . .'

She was very distressed, he realised, duty and instinct warring within her and causing her painful confusion. He reached out and stroked the top of her head, attempting both to soothe her and to convince her of his genuine concern.

'Grimya. If you have promised to keep a secret, then I understand and respect that; it's a very noble thing to do. But there are times when matters change in unforeseen ways, and if that happens, then to keep the secret will sometimes do more harm than good. Do you see what I mean?'

'I . . . th-*ink* so . . .'

'Don't you think that this may be one of those unforeseen times?'

'I . . .' Unsure of herself, the wolf turned away. She lowered her muzzle almost to the floor, considering, then at last looked up at him again. 'I do not know whether what you say is t-true. But I th-*ink* I must tell you. For Indigo's sake.' She paused. 'I m-must tell you about Ne-me-sis.'

A chilly shock went through Jasker. '*Nemesis?*' he said sharply.

Grimya blinked. 'You – *know* what it is?'

It was the word he had seen in Indigo's mind, the fragmented concept of a peculiarly personal evil which he hadn't fully comprehended. Jasker's pulse quickened.

'I have heard of it only once before,' he told the she-wolf, 'But it's important to Indigo in some way, isn't it?'

'Ye-ess,' Grimya admitted unhappily.

'And it has some connection with silver?'

Her eyes flared red and her lips drew back, exposing her fangs defensively. *'How do you kn-know that?'*

Anxious not to waste further time with detailed explanation, Jasker dissembled. 'It was something Indigo said to me. A hint, no more. Grimya, you *must* tell me about Nemesis, tell me everything you know.' He raised his head, glancing round the empty cavern as though some sound or shadow had alerted him, then shivered despite the heat. 'My instinct warns me that it's vitally important.'

'I under-stand instinct,' Grimya said. 'And mine speaks with the same voice. But . . . *ahh!* I w-wish I could sp . . . eak in your mind! But I have trr . . . ied, and you cannot h-hear me.'

So she *was* telepathic, as he had guessed. Silently Jasker cursed his own shortcomings, the peripheral skills that he had never developed. *If I had been a more diligent servant* . . . he thought; but it was too late for wishing.

He turned back to the she-wolf and said, 'I know it's hard for you, Grimya, but we must do the best we can. Please – tell me what you know.'

And so, haltingly but as quickly as she was able, Grimya told Jasker of the demoniac threat that dogged Indigo's every step, and of its manifestation through Chrysiva's brooch which had led to the savage and alien madness she had seen in her friend. Jasker listened, trying to help her when she couldn't find the words she wanted, and at last he had pieced together

153

enough of the story to make a clear – and unpleasant – picture.

He thought back to the images he had seen in Indigo's mind during the truth-ordeal. So much was explained now, from her almost unhuman single-mindedness to her vicious determination to prolong Quinas's ordeal, and he pitied her deeply. But mingled with the pity was a certain knowledge that to let sympathy cloud his judgement could be a very dangerous mistake. Indigo had lost control of her own motivations, and Jasker surmised that she was by now too strongly under the demon's influence to be capable of reason. The hold had to be broken – or, driven by the insane rage that Nemesis had so cunningly orchestrated, Indigo would hurl herself headlong and without rational thought at the enemy she sought to destroy, and that reckless obsession would be her undoing.

Which was precisely what Nemesis wanted.

Grimya had begun to pace back and forth across the cave. She was anxious to be acting rather than talking, and Jasker was well aware that time had been lost while she told her story. But to learn the truth had been vital; Nemesis wasn't a power to be reckoned with lightly, and without Grimya's forewarning he would have been unprepared to meet it.

The wolf said: 'I want to go after her. If I w-wait much longer, there will be no trr-ack to follow.'

'I'll come with you.'

'N-no. You will only . . . slow me.' She looked at him apologetically. 'A-lone, I can ff-*ind* her without being seen.'

She was right; he was no hunter, no tracker. But he had other skills . . .

'Very well,' he said. 'But take the greatest care. Ranaya knows I don't like having to say this, but if Indigo has, as you say, fallen prey to this demon, she may no longer look on you as a friend.'

Old memories stirred in the she-wolf's eyes, and she dipped her head. 'I . . . know that.'

'Then find her, and return to me here as swiftly as you can.'

'I w-will.' And without a further word Grimya ran from the cave. Jasker heard her claws scrabble on rock as she raced away down the tunnel, then he crossed quickly to the shrine of Ranaya. Sorcery couldn't help him now; he had never had a scrying talent, and Grimya's nose could find Indigo where his powers would only fail. Until the wolf returned with news of her whereabouts he could do little other than pray to his goddess.

Jasker knelt before the shrine and began to plead silently, fervently, for guidance.

To Grimya's dismay, Indigo's trail had been all but obliterated by the heat and by the pollution from the mines. She emerged from the tunnel network into the blistering sunlight of late afternoon, and was instantly assailed by the sulphurous stinks that blew into her face on a north-westerly wind and turned the air around her to a brassy haze. The rock was too barren to carry even a single footprint, and for several minutes Grimya sniffed at the ground, struggling to interpret and separate the smells of hot stone and old magma and the grimmer stench from the distant valley. At last, though, her nostrils encountered something she recognised. A hint, no more – but it led away along an old lava bed, up into the mountain slopes.

The heat made her gasp and the rock underfoot scorched her pads, but she ignored the discomfort and streaked along the gully, stopping every so often to check that the trail, still faint but just discernible, hadn't petered out. She tried to keep to shade where she could find it, but as she climbed higher into the peaks the patches of shadow became fewer, until she found herself on an exposed ridge that baked in the furious sunlight.

Grimya stopped to take her bearings. The wind was stronger here, ruffling her fur but bringing her little relief from the heat, and far below she could see the dense, phosphorescent smog that hung over the mines. Sullen fires glowed dimly through the smog where the smelting furnaces roared, and the air pulsed heavy and ominous with the stink and noise rising from the vale.

Grimya shuddered, not wanting to look at the scene. She turned her head to gaze along the ridge – and saw, some way ahead where the ridge dipped to form a narrow shoulder between twin volcanic cones, two slow-moving figures.

She only just prevented herself from howling her relief. One of the distant figures was unmistakably Indigo; though the haze impeded her eyesight the she-wolf recognised her friend's hair. And the other, shuffling, stumbling, moving as though every step cost him indescribable pain, was the evil man, the man they had hurt because he served the Charchad.

Grimya slithered down the side of the ridge to a level from which she would be invisible should either of the two people ahead of her turn and look back. Body flat to the ground, she slunk awkwardly along the steep slope, until she judged that her quarry would by now have reached the farther peak and be too concerned with climbing to pay any heed to what lay behind them. She wriggled back to the ridge's summit, and saw that she'd guessed rightly; they were some fifty paces ahead of her now, moving slowly into the red-brown folds of the peak's lower slopes.

Grimya hesitated. Jasker had told her to return as soon as she had news of Indigo's whereabouts; but loyalty and concern were tugging against the injunction. She knew Nemesis's intention as well as anyone, and she was desperately afraid for Indigo. She couldn't leave her to the demon's unchallenged influence – she had to try again to make her see reason. She *had* to.

She broke into a run, sprinting along the ridge, and as she ran she called Indigo's name.

The girl stopped and whirled round, bringing up the crossbow which she held in her hands. For a moment her eyes were blank, without a trace of recognition; then abruptly the she-wolf's presence registered in her mind and she snapped, 'You! What d'you think you're doing here?'

*Indigo, you must listen to me! There's danger, there is –* And Grimya's urgent mental message collapsed into confusion as she realised that Indigo's mind was utterly closed to her. She couldn't communicate, for her friend refused to hear.

Hastily switching to vocal speech, she gasped out, 'I – came to f-*ind* you. Indigo, there is dan-ger!'

Quinas had sunk down on to the bare rock, shuddering with giddy exhaustion, but Indigo didn't move. She stood staring down at the she-wolf, and Grimya was appalled by the cold contempt in her eyes, and by the aura of hatred that radiated almost tangibly from her. Suddenly, against the grim backdrop of the barren peaks and the sulphurous, pulsing sky, Indigo had become an alien creature. And the dully gleaming brooch, pinned like a proud badge of rank at her breast, was feeding the fires within her.

'Please,' Grimya panted, 'you m . . . ust hear me! The brr-ooch – it is Ne-me-sis, it is the demon! We did not understand at first, but n-now – '

She got no further, for Indigo's face twisted and she snarled, '*We?* So you've transferred your loyalty to Jasker now, have you? I should have expected nothing better of you!'

'*No*, Indigo!' Grimya cried desperately. 'L-listen to me! Open your eyes, *see* what the demon has done! You m . . . ust not go on, or you will be in grr-eat danger!'

'Damn your carping and your cowardice!' Indigo's eyes blazed, and suddenly she levelled the crossbow until the bolt was aimed directly at the she-wolf. '*You* listen to *me* – and carry this message back to your good friend Jasker. You and he may not have the courage to do what must be done, but I have! Tell him that I am going to the Charchad valley, with this piece of offal as my hostage, and that I mean to slay this demon where all his fine words and empty posturings have *failed!* Tell him that!'

Grimya swung her head from side to side in distress. 'Please, In-digo! I am not your enemy.'

'Enemy or friend, I neither know nor care. Go!'

'No! Come back with me, hear what Jasker has to s-s-say – '

'I said, *go!*' Indigo shouted, and her hands tightened on the bow. 'Or I'll kill you.'

Her finger was curling on the trigger, and as their gazes met, Grimya, to her horror, saw death in Indigo's eyes. She whimpered, backing away a pace, and Indigo sneered.

'I will count to three. And if you have not obeyed me by then, I will *kill* you. I *mean* it!'

Desolately, Grimya realised that this was no bluff. Her friend, her trusted friend, was insane, and if she didn't turn tail and run she would choke out her life on this sere slope with a crossbow bolt in her heart. Hardly able to believe the betrayal, she stared for one last instant at Indigo, her eyes silently pleading, but met only the white-hot wall of the girl's fury.

'One,' Indigo said.

Grimya whined.

'Two.' Her finger tightened on the trigger – and the she-wolf turned and fled. She slithered down the slope, almost losing her footing but not caring if she fell to the foot of the volcano and broke her neck. Grief swamped her; grief for her own failure, grief for Indigo and what she had become – but stronger even than the grief was a soul-tearing fear, as she raced with all the strength and speed she could muster back to the cave and to Jasker.

Indigo watched the she-wolf dwindle into the distance, and only when Grimya was out of sight did she at last lower the crossbow and, cold-eyed, turn away. Quinas lay where he had slumped; as she moved to stand over him he looked up at her and tried to summon a contemptuous smile.

'One word, and you'll finish the journey with a bolt through your leg.' Indigo spoke with remote indifference. 'Get up.' She waited while he clambered slowly and painfully to his feet, then prodded his spine with the bow. 'Move. We've a way to go yet.'

The overseer hesitated, and turned his ruined face to look at her. For a moment he seemed about to speak; then her expression made him think better of it and he clenched his teeth against the agony that tore at him with every step, to trudge laboriously on up the slope.

Indigo followed, watching his struggles unmoved and matching her pace to his. During the early part of the journey she had tried to make him go faster, threatening further torments if he disobeyed; but she had finally accepted that he was capable of no more than this snail's pace. Well enough; there was an hour or more of daylight left yet, and by the time the sun set they would be close enough to the Charchad valley for its own evil nacre to light their way.

She hadn't once paused to question the impulse that had made her drag Quinas from the cave and order him to lead her to the vale. All she knew – or cared about – was that she would no longer tolerate delay. When the overseer had finally broken under Jasker's skilled torture and told them the truth about his master and mentor Aszareel, she had felt the sensation then; the surge of hot, blinding desire to run from the torture-chamber, climb the slope of Old Maia and from there follow the route that, according to Quinas's gasping and agonised confession, would lead her around the mines and into the valley of Charchad. She had controlled the desire then, aware that to act without thought or preparation would be foolhardy; but later, when the combined goads of Jasker's dissembling and her own furious focus upon the pewter

159

brooch had begun to work on her, she was prepared to wait no longer.

Quinas had tried to protest, but she had her own methods of coercion, and her prisoner now bore several further scars – from a knife this time, rather than from Jasker's elemental fire – as witness to her powers of persuasion. The chances were that she wouldn't need him, but if luck went against her he could be valuable, and so she had considered the trouble of taking him with her worthwhile.

She didn't know what she would find when she reached her destination. Quinas had revealed all he knew, but she had been frustrated to discover that his knowledge was limited. He had never entered the Charchad valley, had never crossed the final, heavily-guarded ridge and looked down on the glowing pit from which his twisted religion had sprung. That privilege was reserved for those whom the Charchad deemed to be sinners in need of their deadly form of enlightenment. But as one of Aszareel's most influential acolytes Quinas knew the ways into the valley, and now the time had come for him to follow the example he had enforced so savagely upon others. As a guide, Quinas would lead Indigo into the heart of Charchad – and as a hostage, he would help her fulfil at last her seething desire to confront the avatar of the demon she meant to destroy.

Once or twice a small voice within her had struggled to be heard, saying: *and what then, Indigo? When you find Aszareel, how will you kill him and the demon he represents?* But she had ignored it, silencing it beneath an avalanche of angry contempt. To falter would be the act of a weakling; she would *not* be prey to the doubts that had caused Jasker to flinch from what must be done. The demon would die, she told herself – that was all that mattered. And in her wrath, in her lust for retribution, in her madness, she believed it.

At the sound of scrabbling paws Jasker sprang to his

feet, and turned in time to see Grimya race into the cave. The she-wolf slewed to a halt and collapsed, panting, her sides heaving convulsively as she tried to drag air into her lungs. Dismayed, he hastened to fetch her a dish of water and watched as, gasping her gratitude, she lapped and lapped until at last the worst of her thirst was slaked and she could speak coherently.

Jasker listened to her story with a sense of ominous despair that grew as the tale unfolded. When Grimya finished, he paced across the floor and stood looking down at the shrine.

By now the sun must be near setting, and from what Grimya had told him Jasker knew that he had no hope of overtaking Indigo before she reached the Charchad valley. Any attempt to follow her into that hell would be nothing short of suicidal, and though he had little enough regard for his own life, a doomed rescue bid would be a futile sacrifice. There had to be another way.

And then, as he stared at the little statue of Ranaya, an inner voice told him that there was.

It wasn't possible. He had tried, he had striven, he had forced himself almost over the brink of sanity and life itself to achieve it, and every time he had failed. Two years of struggling, and the door had remained barred to him. He *couldn't* try again. He didn't have the resources, the skill or the stamina.

*Then what,* asked the inner voice, *is the alternative?*

Jasker shuddered as his own mind answered the question with bleak certainty. For the first time he had a chance – perhaps the only chance he would ever have – to turn the tide that had overtaken his land and was slowly but surely murdering it. United, he and Indigo might have been able to raise enough power to smash the Charchad's stranglehold, until Nemesis's machinations had broken the link between them. But it was possible, just possible, that the link could be reforged – *if* he had the courage and the will to do it.

The remedy was in his own hands, and it was a

remedy that had so far failed. But this time, he had an unexpected and unlikely ally, who might unwittingly hold the key . . .

He turned and looked at Grimya. Her head came up and, seeing his speculative gaze on her, she scrambled to her feet and came towards him. Her tongue lolled and her eyes were glazed with weariness, but she was determined not to let exhaustion get the better of her.

'Jas-ker?' She looked up at him pleadingly. 'You have thh-*ought* of something?'

'I'm . . . not sure; not yet. I will need time – '

'But we hh-*ave* no time! Indigo is in dan-ger!'

'I know. But if we cannot physically bring her back, I must find another way.'

The wolf's ears flicked. 'You will use m . . . magic?' she asked dubiously.

*Please Ranaya that I have the capability*, Jasker thought, and aloud replied, 'Yes. It's the only means left to us, Grimya.'

'I . . . understand. But . . .' she looked towards the tunnel, her eyes uneasy. 'If I w-were to go after her again, perhaps – '

'No. You'd risk your own life for no good purpose.' He crouched down and gently touched the she-wolf's muzzle. 'Grimya, please trust me. I believe I know of a way to save Indigo, but if it's to stand a chance of succeeding, I will need your help, and you *must* do as I ask. Will you?'

She was uncertain, two instincts at war within her.

'*Please*, Grimya,' Jasker repeated. 'For Indigo's sake.' A shadow passed over his face, as though old memories had briefly but poignantly awoken. 'I don't want her to die any more than you do.'

Perhaps Grimya sensed something of his thoughts, or perhaps his words alone were enough to convince her; he didn't know. But at last she raised her head and said, though still with a trace of hesitation,

'Yess . . . I trr-*ust* you. And I will do whatever you want of me.'

He could have hugged her, but all he said was, 'Thank you.'

'Wh-at do you mean to . . . do?' she asked.

Jasker stood up. 'Before we can hope to rescue Indigo, we must break the hold Nemesis has over her,' he said. 'And that means using powers greater than those of the demon, to break through to her mind and make her realise the truth. That is where you must play a vital part.'

'But I c-cannot reach her,' Grimya reminded him.

'As she is now, no. But I believe that I can raise a power that will smash through the demon's defences – and I will channel that power to Indigo's mind through you.'

'A power . . . like the f-f-*ire*-dragons?'

'No.' Jasker's voice was sombre. 'Not like the fire-dragons, Grimya. Something far greater, far older.' He looked down at her with sympathy and respect. 'It will take courage, little wolf; all the courage that you and I can muster. But we can do it.'

'I am not af-raid. But what is this power, Jas-ker? What is it that you mean to do?'

The sorcerer's eyes took on a strange, distant expression, a look that Grimya had never seen in them before. Then, quietly, he said:

'I mean to summon Ranaya's Daughters from their long sleep.'

163

# Chapter XII

'It's no use.' Quinas's mouth stretched in a painful rictus that was his best attempt at an ironic smile. 'You may do what you will to me, *saia*, but you can't change the simple fact that I can go no further.'

Indigo stared down at him. In the gathering dark his face was a ghastly piebald of scar and shadow, and his one eye, catching the cold, greenish light that now filled the sky above the narrow gully, seemed to mock her. Anger seethed in her and she quelled an impulse to stretch out her foot and put him to the test by crushing his wrist under her heel. In truth, she believed him, for it was little short of a miracle that he'd been capable of stumbling on this far in his ravaged condition. For the last hundred yards or thereabouts he'd been reduced to crawling on elbows and knees – he had tried to use his fused and ruined hands, but the pain had proved too great – and had only covered the final ten paces when she gripped the end of the rope that bound his shoulders and dragged him bodily over the rough ground. But now she didn't doubt that he was finished.

She looked up and ahead to where the gully rose sharply to a ridge. The last ridge. That was what he had told her. The last ridge – and on the far side lay the vale of Charchad.

She turned back to her captive. His eye had closed and he was motionless; she prodded him with her toe.

'Wake up, you sewer-worm. I'm not done with you yet.'

The red lens flickered briefly. 'Water . . .' Quinas coughed on the word. 'If you have . . . a little water.'

Indigo would have spat in his face, but couldn't muster the saliva. She knew that she, too, was suffering from dehydration, but was reluctant to squander more of her small supply than was absolutely necessary. At least now, with the sun below the horizon, it was a degree or two cooler. All she needed was the energy to climb the next ridge; then she would rest.

'What now, *saia*?' Quinas's dust-dry voice broke into her thoughts. He had realised that she wasn't going to give him water, and the realisation made him less careful of his situation than he might otherwise have been. Again, he gave her the rictus smile. 'There are no vultures in these mountains to eat my body and give me the slow death you have ordained. So will you simply leave my flesh to melt from my bones in the sun?'

Loathing glittered in Indigo's eyes. 'I doubt that the sun would deign to touch your corrupted carcass,' she retorted. 'No, Quinas. I have a better end in mind for you.' Again she glanced at the ridge ahead. 'If you cannot walk, you will be carried. But, on your feet, on your knees or on my back, one way or another you will enter the Charchad valley.'

'No – ' The protest was out before he could stop it, and for the first time Indigo heard true fear in Quinas's voice.

'What's this? Is the noble follower of Charchad *afraid*?' She challenged him harshly, viciously, jerking on the rope so that he jolted with pain. Broken teeth clamped down on his lower lip and the overseer whispered: 'Yes . . .'

'Louder, Quinas. I can't hear you clearly enough!'

He drew a deep breath, then: 'I said, *yes!*' His eye fixed her, a dreadful, unblinking stare of naked horror. 'You cannot carry me. Not unless I co-operate – and that I will never do. You may hurt me, you may cut me or burn me or flay me; you may try to drag me bodily into that vale. But I'll fight you, *saia*. From somewhere I'll find the strength, and I'll fight you! And if I can no longer fight, then I will tear out the arteries in my own wrists with my *teeth* if I have to! But never, *never*, will I enter the Charchad valley, because I *fear* it!'

He slumped back, drained by the effort of his vehement speech, and Indigo gazed down at him. So Quinas was as terrified as his own pitiful victims of what lay in that vale. Quinas, acolyte of Charchad, loyal servant of Aszareel, could not face his master – and at the last he had been forced to admit it.

She began to laugh. The sound was ugly and unnatural, but it bubbled up into her throat and she saw no reason to stop it.

'Quinas,' she said. 'Quinas, the scourge of sinners, the lighter of funeral pyres, the tormenter of women.' She put the back of one hand to her mouth to suppress the gale of crazed mirth. Then the laughter died abruptly and her tone changed to one of scorching contempt. 'Quinas, the grovelling *coward!*'

'Yes,' the overseer said quietly. 'But honest enough to admit to it.'

Reflexively, Indigo fingered the brooch at her breast. This *amused* her. This admission, this last-moment confession from the self-professed man of strength and courage, was *funny*. Too afraid to confront that which he so zealously compelled others to worship . . . she snorted back a fresh burst of laughter and wiped her eyes, feeling unaccountably excited. The situation had a delicious irony: Quinas, the Charchad acolyte, would cower here among the rocks and shun his god, while she, alone and unafraid, climbed the final ridge to spit in that same god's face. Jasker would have enjoyed such a joke –

Indigo scowled, checking herself. She didn't want to think of Jasker, for he had proved himself no better than Quinas. Let him cower, too, safe in his caves. Let him mumble his prayers for the souls of Chrysiva and

166

all the others like her, for all the good they'd do. *Her*
time had come now. *Hers*, and no other's.

She stared up at the ridge, speculating, calculating.
According to Quinas this was one of the lesser paths
to the vale, and although every approach was guarded
constantly, there would be no more than two, perhaps
three sentries on duty. They would be looking inward,
alert for a sinner trying to flee, for no one entered
Charchad by their own choice.

Until now.

She slung the crossbow on to her back, settled it,
then turned back to Quinas for the last time. Another
cruel jerk on the rope; another wince of agony. Indigo
smiled.

'Well, my cowardly friend, I have decided to grant
you a little of the mercy which you deny to others. I
have no more need of you – so you shall lie here and
see the beginnings of my triumph.' She bent down,
putting her face close to his. 'The end of Charchad,
Quinas. Think on that, while you wait for the sun to
rise and drain the last of the life from your wretched
body. The *end*!'

'*Saia*–' He made as though to reach towards her but
fell back, too weak. His breath was short, and speaking
was difficult. 'I beg you . . . don't do this!'

'I am deaf to your pleas, Quinas. Entreat the moon,
entreat the mountains – entreat the sun when it rises.
They might hear you: I will not!'

'Indigo.' He used her name for the first time since
his capture. 'Please – you are throwing away your life!'

Her answering smile was a cool and supercilious
sneer. 'Look to your own life, Quinas, whilst you still
possess it. Make the most of the little you have left!'

She wanted to make some final gesture of contempt
towards him, but could think of nothing appropriate.
Let her actions be enough in themselves. Long before
she returned, Quinas would be dead meat. She hefted
the bow on her shoulder, drew her knife from its

167

sheath, and walked away up the gully towards the ridge and the deadly glow beyond.

Quinas didn't move until the last faint sounds of Indigo's progress had faded into the ever-present background of throbbing, subterranean vibrations from the mines. Even then, when he had shifted his position to one more tolerable, he forced himself to count the passage of another minute before he risked sitting up.

His head swam from the effects of food and water deprivation and for a moment he thought he might lose consciousness; but he fought the spasm, dragging it under control at last. His breath rasped in the hot night air and pain was a constant fire throughout his body. But his will was unscathed. And his strength was by no means as depleted as he had led Indigo to think.

He knew now that she was utterly insane. The sorcerer who had put him to the torture was a feeble ghost by comparison; Indigo's madness was of an order that transcended anything remotely human. And it was that madness which had enabled Quinas to use his strongest weapon, and use it well. For in the throes of what she saw as her triumph, clouded by her obsession with revenge, Indigo had been only too ready to believe his little charade.

He guessed that she would by now be nearing the end of the gully. If he had judged correctly that gave him just the time he needed, and he twisted his body about, struggling firstly to his knees and then, awkwardly, to his feet. Several times during the journey from the caves he had tried surreptitiously to loosen the ropes binding his upper arms to his sides, but had failed. No matter; the bonds would hamper him, but he'd cope.

Pausing to catch his breath he glanced along the canyon again and smiled faintly. He had always been a good orator, a good actor; but this time he'd excelled even his own expectations. Indigo had been easy prey for his pretence of exhaustion and terror, and his final

168

plea to her not to go into the valley – a refining touch which had occurred to him on the spur of the moment – had sealed it perfectly. Satisfied that she had bested and shamed a craven coward, she had strutted away from him, leaving him, she thought, to die.

Quinas chuckled softly. He had no intention of dying yet. And Indigo, together with her unsuspecting companions – though their punishment would be meted out later – had a lesson in store. A lesson that he would take great pleasure in administering.

Loose shale slithered under his feet as he turned about, supporting himself against the rock wall. Some ten paces back along the gully was a narrow side-runnel, cut by lava in the days when these old volcanoes were active, that turned steeply downhill. Indigo hadn't noticed it, but Quinas had, and knew where it led. It was just wide enough to traverse, and, determinedly ignoring the pain that shot through him, the overseer slid his battered body through the gap and merged with the darkness.

Indigo slithered to a halt as the path she had been following ended abruptly at the solid wall of the ridge. To her right the gully's side had been shattered by a rock fall at some unguessable time in the past, and the last few feet of the path sheared away in a treacherous slide with few footholds. She caught her breath – getting air into her lungs was becoming more and more of an effort – and paused to take her bearings.

From where she stood to the top of the ridge was a climb of no more than fifty feet, and though the slope was acute she didn't foresee any problems. She smiled ferally, then took a few disciplined sips from her water-skin, enough to wet her throat but little more, before gripping the rock face to her left and swinging herself across the final, broken section of the path. For a moment she stood with her face pressed to the ridge, still smiling, savouring the excitement, the increasing, adrenalin-fired sense of triumph. So close now. Just minutes more, and the final goal would be in sight.

Indigo thought of Quinas, and laughed with soft, crazed pleasure. Perhaps she should have killed him – but it had seemed so much more fitting that he should be left for the elements to finish in their own good time; and to meditate meanwhile on his failure and on the imminent ruin of his depraved cult. The chuckle faded and she wiped her mouth, licking a few drops of water that transferred themselves from her lips to her hand. Then she looked up at the crest of the ridge: and drew in a stunned breath.

The crest was a silhouette that stood out stark and ragged against a backdrop of shimmering, phosphorescent light. A line of furious brilliance edged the rock like a ghastly halo, and through the cliff face Indigo felt a peculiar, rhythmic vibration that seemed to penetrate skin, flesh and bone. It fuelled her sense of anticipation and, heart quickening, she set her foot on the slope and began to scale the ridge.

The vibration and the light increased as she climbed, and by the time she was half way up the slope Indigo was bathed in reflections from the eerie radiance. As she neared the crest she went more carefully, keeping her body pressed flat to the rock where she could. She didn't know how close to the ridge the sentries might be stationed, and was anxious not to risk betraying her presence by an incautious sound or movement. The sharply-etched silhouette of her goal came nearer, nearer . . . then her groping hands reached the crest, and slowly, breathlessly, Indigo raised her head above the edge of the ridge.

Searing green light erupted in her face and she jerked back with an involuntary gasp, turning her head away as the brilliance swamped her vision. She covered her eyes with one hand to protect them, and through the latticework of her fingers saw her hand, the arm beyond it, the rock before her, shining with cold, green fire that sparkled with motes like silvery dust. Her skin

tingled; she risked allowing her hand to slide slowly
down her face, letting her vision accustom gradually to
the incredible radiance . . . and at last she was able to
look, for the first time, into the Charchad vale.

She couldn't move, couldn't utter a sound as her
senses strove to assimilate what her eyes took in. The
valley was like a gigantic fumarole, a vast well that
plunged giddyingly down into the bowels of the Earth
– and from the well's depths a titanic, monstrous incan-
descence blasted into the sky, bleaching the valley walls
to green-white skeletons, hurling its terrible radiance
up and out into the night. Grisly shadows shifted on
the far cliffs, beams of nacreous colour that mocked
the mine searchlights played at random through the
huge, shimmering spaces. And far down, where the
incredible light collapsed into a roaring, strobic
inferno, she thought she glimpsed nightmarish shapes
moving through the maelstrom with an ominous and
implacable purpose.

Indigo clutched at the uneven rock. *As if the sun
itself had fallen to Earth.* Jasker's words came unbidden
to her mind and she felt her teeth start to chatter
uncontrollably. She couldn't tear her gaze away from
the vale; her skin tingled with heat and cold together
and all she could do was stare and stare at the appalling
scene laid out before her.

It was an abomination. An aborted nightmare, a
cancer on the face of the world and on the body of the
Earth Mother. And Quinas and his ilk *worshipped* this
monstrosity, revelled in its power, adored it . . .

Heat flared in her head, the white heat of renewed
rage as the feelings which had eaten at her soul since
Chrysiva's death flooded back in double measure. She
didn't fear what lay in the Charchad vale. Aszareel,
the demon, whatever the name or nature of the misbe-
gotten power that had conjured this horror to life,
she was its equal and more. Indigo clenched her jaw,
bringing the chattering under iron control. She felt
bloodlust, a wild and eager awakening of a killer

171

instinct that drove deep into her gut. A thousand curses on the cowards and the whimperers whose resolve had failed them. *She* would not fail. She would face the demon of Charchad, and the demon would die. For Chrysiva and all the others, it would *die*.

Movement on the periphery of vision alerted her. She jerked back, pressing her body hard to the rock and unconsciously showing her teeth in a vulpine snarl. The ghastly light played over her hands, etching the bones so that for a moment she looked to her own eyes like a living skeleton; she ignored the phenomenon and cautiously turned her head a little to the left.

Two figures moved along a narrow ledge a short way below her vantage point. They were dim and shapeless in the glare, and until they drew closer – which, at their leisurely pace, would take some minutes – it would be impossible to make them out in clear detail. But it seemed a logical assumption that these were the sentries of which Quinas had spoken.

A broad, savage grin spread across her face. She drew back, moving as quickly and lithely as a snake until her head was below the summit of the ridge, then twisted about and unslung her crossbow, setting a bolt into place and drawing back the string. She could shoot, reload and shoot again in seconds, and Charchad acolytes died as surely as any other mortal creatures. Only two guards: they would be easy pickings. And when they were gone, nothing would impede her.

She writhed forward once more and peered over the crest. The two guards were closer now, so close that she could discern their true shapes. And her heart almost stopped beating, for whatever else they might have been, they weren't human.

Once, perhaps when they were dragged squalling from their mother's wombs, they had had the potential to grow into men; but the Charchad had warped that potential into something so far beyond humanity that Indigo's stomach turned over with shocked revulsion. They still clung to the basic human structure of two

172

legs, two arms, one head; but the grip was precarious, for they bore a closer resemblance to the walking foetuses of some gruesome troll than to anything remotely mortal. Dead, parchment-thin skin was stretched taut over their naked and outsized skulls; slack mouths filled with brown fangs drooled over jowls that swung bloatedly above torsos as fleshless and flaccid as the corpses of rotting fish. And from their stunted arms and legs grew six-fingered appendages tipped with broken, blackened claws that scraped and scrabbled on the rock as they heaved their misshapen bodies along the ledge.

Despite her dehydration, bile clogged Indigo's throat and seared her tongue with a taste of rusting metal. She couldn't continue to look at the grotesque sentries: not caring about range or timing, she shut one eye and sighted along the crossbow, aiming quickly, oblivious to which of the two shambling figures was the better target, and fired.

Recoil hammered against her arm. The string sang a murderous note, and the steel bolt slammed into the face of the nearer of the guards. He – it – screamed, the sound horribly reminiscent of a slaughtered pig, and, even as his companion shuffled about in confused chagrin, pitched from the ledge and plunged into the coruscating light and into oblivion.

Feverishly, Indigo fumbled for a second bolt. Her hands felt like bears' paws, clumsy and uncoordinated, but at last she got the bolt home and swung the bow round to aim at the remaining sentry, who was still turning and turning in bewilderment on the ledge. She heard her own breath rasping in her ears; dragged back the string –

And something struck her a giddying blow on the back of her skull.

She opened her mouth to cry out in pain and protest, but no sound came. Instead there was a huge vortex of nausea that rushed at her from nowhere, making the surrounding scene start to spin like a mad carousel.

The crossbow clattered on the rocks and Indigo rolled over, limbs losing co-ordination and flailing like a young child unexpectedly pitched off balance. She saw faces above her, swimming and indistinct like dream images, and felt an irrational storm of indignation. Then something that felt like fire and ice together cracked out of the darkness and tore into her face like the sting of a monstrous bee, and she passed out.

'Wake her.'

Brackish water splashed against Indigo's face. She tried to protest but her vocal cords wouldn't obey her; all she could do was turn her head in an effort to evade the assault, but it did little good. There was an insistent, muted thundering in her ears and the ground under her seemed to be shaking. And she could smell something dense, heavy, metallic, clogging her nostrils.

'More.'

She knew the voice but couldn't give it a name. Someone she had –

Another shock of water hit her, and nausea erupted from somewhere deep down. Instinctively she rolled, just managing to turn her head aside before a foul mixture of bile and sputum poured from her throat. Retching, she dragged herself backwards on her elbows, still disorientated and reluctant to open her eyes.

'All right: that's enough. She's conscious now. Turn her over.'

Hands pawed at Indigo's body but she didn't have the co-ordination to fight them off. Then a shadow fell across her and her cheek was slapped, lightly but with purpose.

'*Saia* Indigo. I would suggest that you look at me. There seems little point in prolonging this farce unnecessarily.'

Her eyelids fluttered, opened. For a moment her eyes refused to focus; then abruptly the scene about her resolved.

She was in some kind of building, a rough, window-less hut made from sheets of carelessly cut and rusting iron. The air stank, and by the greasy light of the lamp hanging from a ceiling hook she could make out the crude table and two chairs, the board on the wall with its chalked lists of figures, the piles of slates and notched lead tally-sticks in one corner. The office of a mine overseer, crowded now with some half-dozen men. They must have brought her down into the valley while she was unconscious, and now the noise, the stink, the polluted dust clogging the air told her she was in the heart of the mining region, completely cut off from any hope of rescue. And in the midst of her captors, his mutilated smile ghastly in the murky lamplight, was Quinas.

A vicious oath whistled between Indigo's lips. Quinas was dead meat; she had left him in the gully, unable to move, waiting only for the sun to rise and blister the last of his life away. He *couldn't* have turned the tables on her.

But the impossible had happened, and now Quinas presided over the group of men from some kind of makeshift litter. A bandage hid his bald scalp and ruined eye, and salve had been smeared on the lesser burns, giving his face a slick, oily sheen. A smile of unadulterated triumph cracked his scorched mouth.

'Well, *saia*.' He spoke gently, an obscene parody of affection colouring his tone. 'We have, it seems, apprehended a sinner in the act of sinning, so to speak.'

His companions grinned unpleasantly. To judge from their clothing and demeanour Indigo surmised that they too were mine officers; overseers like Quinas perhaps, or foremen, or gangers. Each wore the glowing badge of a Charchad acolyte, and each suffered in some small way from the Charchad sickness; flaking skin, falling hair, webbed fingers, a nose that was beginning to crumble . . . One carried a whip with a plaited thong; it was this, she realised, that had cut her face, leaving her cheek sore and bleeding, and Indigo didn't doubt

175

that at the smallest provocation the whip's wielder would take pleasure in using it again.

*Fool!* a voice in her brain railed. *You should have killed him! You should have plunged your knife into his corrupted heart and watched him vomit out his life at your feet! You should –*

Someone caught her by the hair and dragged her into a sitting position so suddenly and violently that her head swam again and the self-recrimination collapsed under a fresh wall of sickness. This time she held the spasm back, refusing to lose the last pathetic shards of her dignity, and her teeth clenched hard.

'I should have slaughtered you . . .'

'Indeed you should.' Quinas inclined his head. 'That was your weakness, dear Indigo. But wishing isn't the same as doing, is it?'

Her head was clearing now, and in the wake of physical recovery came something else that she couldn't yet quite grasp. *Charchad.* She had come to . . . but no; that wasn't it. Something else. Something Grimya had said. She had seen Grimya, on a ridge near the peak of Old Maia. Or had she dreamed that part of it?

'You have offended us, Indigo.' Quinas's soft, cajoling voice intruded on her efforts to remember. 'And though we of Charchad are merciful, those who persistently offend must be punished. You understand. Don't you?'

His words were meaningless. There was something else, something far more important . . .

Nemesis.

'She doesn't hear you, Quinas,' someone said laconically.

'Oh, but she does. Don't you, Indigo?'

The brooch. Grimya had said something about the brooch.

*'Don't you?'* Fingers took her jaw in a pincer hold, and in the same moment she remembered. The brooch. *Nemesis.*

176

'No-o!' It was a cry of pain and anguish and bitter regret as the last bonds of Indigo's thrall shattered and she realised what she had done. *Grimya!* her mind shrieked silently. *Grimya – Jasker – I betrayed you, I failed–*

The scream dropped away into cold silence. With a great effort Indigo forced herself to look at Quinas's face again, and what she saw made her quail as she realised that his desire for revenge drove just as deep as her own. She, more than anyone, was responsible for the ruin that had been worked on him and which meant that he must face the rest of his life as a mutilated hulk. Now, through her crazed stupidity, he had turned the tables on her. He, and her Nemesis. And now that she was his victim, he would see to it that her suffering more than matched his own.

And all for a worthless piece of base metal . . .

One of the overseer's mutilated hands reached out to touch her cheek as lightly as a falling leaf. She saw the fused stumps of his fingers, and her gut recoiled at the caress. Quinas smiled.

'You are a sinner, Indigo. It grieves us to witness such sins as you have committed against Charchad; but we know our duty.' Other voices murmured assent. 'Sin, Indigo. Sin. And what is the punishment for sin?'

Silence. They waited for her to answer, but she couldn't, dared not –

'The vale. The road to the ultimate enlightenment.' The stunted fingers stroked her face again and she shut her eyes tightly. But she couldn't shut out the voice, the gentle, mocking, persuasive voice.

'You sought our master Aszareel, Indigo. You sought him, when only the chosen of Charchad are privy to such an honour.' A terrible quiet hung in the air momentarily, then Quinas's soothing voice continued.

'But we have decided to be merciful.' Something brushed her eyelids and it was all she could do not to scream. 'We have decided to grant you the enlighten-

177

ment you crave. It is a privilege given to few, but we believe that you have earned it. Are you not grateful?'

Someone sniggered, quelled it. Indigo opened her eyes again and saw that the overseer was leaning over her. His face bore an obscenely sepulchral smile.

'You are to make a journey, my dear. A journey from which there will be no return.'

Another breath of laughter, like poison in her ears. Quinas's hideous smile widened. 'To the deepest reaches of the pit of Charchad, Indigo. To look, in the moment before you die, upon the face of our lord Aszareel!'

# Chapter XIII

They forced her to drink from a battered tin cup, clamping her jaws open and pouring the bitter liquid into her mouth when she tried to fight them. It took three of the Charchad acolytes to hold her down and she still managed to spit most of the draught back in their faces; but none the less enough went down her throat for the drug it contained to take effect.

The numbness came first. She felt it beginning in her hands and feet, creeping slowly along her limbs towards her torso, and though she exerted all her willpower she could do nothing to stem it. Ten minutes after swallowing the draught she was pulled to her feet, and when she tried to struggle, her muscles simply refused to respond. She could still stand unaided, but beyond that she had no more physical self-control than a doll; and as her captors dragged her to the hut door in a grotesque, loose-legged parody of walking she felt her mental faculties also starting to lose their grip as the drug's potency worked in her veins. Sick, soul-numbing terror was lodged like a parasite in her gut, but she couldn't respond to it; she felt remote, as though she were watching herself from a distance that increased with every moment. Yet on another level her senses were still painfully her own, and working at fever pitch. And overriding all else in her mind was a sense of utter desolation and remorse.

She had failed. Driven by emotions that she hadn't had the wit to examine or control, she had opened herself to the ultimate folly of recklessness; and Nemesis had been waiting to exploit that folly. She should have seen the danger inherent in Chrysiva's brooch, the correlation between its dull silvery sheen and the ever-present threat of her demon. And when Grimya proved wiser than she was, she should have listened.

But *should* and *if* were of no use to her now. She had scorned her only friends for the sake of blind, vain fury, and that vanity had led her to the mad belief that she could face and conquer the evil of the Charchad vale without them. Now all she could hope for was a relatively swift death, and she had no one but herself to blame.

In its dark, astral realm of poison thorns and black stars, Indigo thought, Nemesis must be laughing.

The door swung open, banging against the iron wall and making the whole hut shake. Oily smog swirled into Indigo's face; her eyes began to water and she tasted sulphur and burnt dust at the back of her throat as she was hustled out into the eerily glowing nightscape of the mines.

She was met by a battering chaos of noise. The filthy air pounded with the near-subliminal thunder of machines, from the great cranes on their towering booms to the gape-mouthed diggers and vast hammers worked by teams of sweating men as they attacked the rock faces. More straining slave gangs hauled lines of ore-trucks along a rattling, rumbling network of rails; these men chanted as they toiled to keep their steps in rhythm, a doleful, groaning dirge like some hell-inspired shanty. Steam hissed and roared, disembodied voices shouted orders; somewhere, someone screamed in pain or fear or both. Through the grim miasma the beacon torches flickered on their high poles, their light diffused by the smog into shapeless and ghostly smears in the churning night.

Indigo was dragged over the rough ground. Her eyes were streaming by now and she could see no more than a few paces ahead. They passed under the tall gantry of one of the torches, and in the sudden flaring brilliance she made out the blurred shapes of other figures who seemed to be waiting for them.

Someone who carried a whip and whose accoutrements glinted metallically strode out of the glare to meet Indigo's captors. Words were exchanged, but the background din buried them; the only recognisable sound was a bark of laughter. Then hands shoved her roughly forward; unable to control her muscles, she fell sprawling among booted feet and was instantly hauled up again. Metal clanked; she felt something clamp about her ankles, and realised with dull shock that she was being shackled to one end of a crocodile of ragged men. She tried to protest, but her frozen throat could only utter a peculiar mewling sound which drew no more than a brief, apathetic glance from the captive next in line.

More clanking, and a second set of shackles locked on her wrists. Her arms were released; she stood upright but only just, blinking confusedly at her tormentors. There was a movement among the group of overseers, then Quinas appeared, supported by two of his cohorts who had carried his litter from the hut.

'Well, *saia* Indigo.' The familiar, hated voice slid like a cold knife into the tangles of her thoughts. She didn't have the wherewithal to turn her head, and someone had to take hold of her chin and wrench her around until her eyes focused vaguely on Quinas's face.

'It is customary at these moments to offer the Charchad's blessing to those who are about to receive enlightenment.' In the hot glare of the torch overhead Quinas's disfigurements made him ghoulish. 'Your companions have already partaken of that sacrament; but it seems, sadly, that you are not in a fit condition to share their boon.'

She continued to stare at him, but even if she had been capable of speaking she couldn't have thought of anything to say.

Quinas smiled. 'It seems something of an anticlimax that our final parting should be shorn of the proper

181

ceremony: but I've learned to view such small disappointments philosophically. So it only remains, Indigo, for me to bid you farewell. For the last time.' And he nodded to the waiting jailers. 'Take them on to the vale.'

An overseer at the head of the line of prisoners jerked hard on the chain he held, and the men shambled forward. Indigo was pulled along with them, her head wobbling on her shoulders. For a moment the hellish scene tilted as she almost lost her balance, then as she managed to right herself she caught one last glimpse of Quinas before he turned away. His face was in shadow, out of range of the torchlight, and she couldn't see his expression. Only his remaining eye caught a stray reflection, and it glowed like the eye of a reincarnated demon.

Indigo's teeth chattered; a convulsive, involuntary reflex. She couldn't speak, but as the line of captives shuffled into the darkness her lips moved slackly to form a single, silent word that sounded as a confused and desperate plea in her ravaged mind.

'Gr . . . Grimya . . . ?'

Before they set out, Jasker gave Grimya the last of his food. The she-wolf protested that she was too worried to be hungry, but he insisted. The supplies, he said, would be rancid long before they could hope to return, and they needed to sustain themselves for the work ahead. He had already eaten enough for his needs; now Grimya must take what was left.

At last, though reluctantly, she gave way. While she ate, Jasker sat poring by the light of a candle over a small map, the result of six months' exploration of the tunnels, shafts and galleries that riddled the volcanoes. It was a crude effort, drawn with a paste of soot and oily wax on to a smoke-dried animal skin, and by no means complete: in his underground wanderings Jasker was well aware that he had explored no more than a minute fraction of the vast network. But the map would be sufficient to guide them to their destination. What might happen beyond that point was a subject he preferred not to dwell on, aware that matters would by then be in greater hands. But – and he glanced obliquely at Grimya, who in spite of her protestations was now licking the platter clean – if luck went against them and this proved to be a one-way journey, at least they'd be spared the ignominy of dying hungry.

With a sigh, Jasker folded the map and tucked it into a small hide sack which he settled over his shoulder. He didn't want to burden himself unnecessarily, but to go into the volcano network empty-handed would be suicidal, and he had packed a few basic essentials such as rope, candles, knife, together with a full water-skin. He'd committed the first part of their route to memory; there was no further need for delay.

Grimya was eager to set out, but was surprised when instead of setting off through the cave's interior tunnel Jasker led her out into the hot night and away up a steep and difficult path which she hadn't seen before. The path was formed from a vein of obsidian, fused to glasslike smoothness and perilously slippery; Grimya struggled gamely to maintain a foothold and keep up, but when finally they reached the top she was panting heavily.

Jasker pointed to a low, dark crack in the mountain wall ahead. 'There's a cave on the other side of that gap, which leads to a passage. That's where our way lies.'

Grimya didn't like caves. Her natural element was the cool openness of forest and plain; confinement distressed her, and although she had adjusted as best she could to the claustrophobia of Jasker's hideaway, she found its atmosphere oppressive. The thought of wriggling through that narrow gap into stifling, sulphurous darkness made her heart quicken unpleasantly, and despite her determination to be courageous, she had to admit that she was afraid of what lay ahead. She would have given a great deal not to have to continue this journey, but forced the thought from her mind even as it took form. For Indigo's sake, she must go on.

Jasker had already dropped to a crouch and was squeezing through the rock slit. Grimya looked up at the titanic cone of Old Maia towering into the evilly glowing sky, and her hackles rose involuntarily. The greatest and oldest of Ranaya's Daughters, a sleeping but lethal giantess. And they were searching for her heart.

A soft call, echoing from the crack, told her that Jasker was safely through. Grimya shook herself from head to tail, attempting to slough off more than the prickling heat of the night; then she flattened her body to the ground and squirmed through the gap in Jasker's wake.

They walked for an incalculable time in almost perpetual darkness. Early on, Jasker took a candle from his sack and attempted to ignite it; but the tunnel soughed and echoed with strange, hot draughts, and the guttering flame refused to stay alight for more than a few moments at a time. At last the sorcerer abandoned his attempts to keep the candle burning. For a moment he considered calling a salamander, one of his little brothers of fire; but to summon and contain the elemental would take power, and he dared not risk depleting his resources in however small a way. For the time being at least, they must do without light.

It was an eerie journey. The air smelled of sulphur and tasted like iron; its oppressiveness grew as the tunnel wound and twisted ever downwards. At times the passage roof rose so high that their footfalls created unnerving echoes; at others the walls closed in so that they were forced to squeeze sidelong through a barely negotiable gap. Now and then a dim and distant flicker of orange-red light would erupt from some adit in the tunnel wall and hurl their shadows briefly on to the rock before dying away, and from somewhere far

184

below came a constant, rumbling vibration that even Grimya's sensitive ears couldn't quite hear, but which they both felt in the core of their bones.

The she-wolf couldn't disguise her fear. The smallest untoward sound, the slightest movement of air, was enough to make her jink and cower, and the deeper they penetrated into the mountain, the worse her feelings grew. They traversed a natural gallery, moving cautiously along a narrow ledge that overhung a huge, dark drop; then through another tunnel whose bizarre acoustics made their footfalls sound like the tramping of an army, and on over a spine of basalt spanning a vast fumarole that blew hot, sulphurous winds into their faces and glowed with a molten life of its own. Several times Jasker paused to consult his map, but it was merely a precaution; memory and instinct were proving sure guides, and he knew that they were drawing closer to their ultimate goal.

The sorcerer was well aware of Grimya's terrors, and in truth he shared them; these subterranean tunnels were no place for any living creature, animal or human. He only hoped that it would be possible to reach their eventual destination. He had seen the place once, during his original exploration, but since that first unplanned visit he hadn't had a reason – no, he corrected himself sternly; he hadn't had the *courage* – to return. There was no merit in deluding himself about that, and every justification for the dread he felt. But now that he must face it again, he prayed silently that in the intervening time some natural event hadn't rendered the place inaccessible, for if it had, his plan would have no more relevance than a handful of volcanic dust.

He wondered how near Indigo was now to the deadly vale. Much, he knew, would depend on whether she still had Quinas with her. If the overseer lived, his presence would slow her progress and that improved Jasker's chances of reaching his destination before she reached hers. But if Quinas had succumbed to exhaustion, or if Indigo had simply lost patience and killed him, it might already be too late.

Unconsciously, he quickened his pace, forcing Grimya into a rapid trot to keep up. To the best of his knowledge – and Jasker was prepared to admit that his knowledge, and the map, might be flawed – they were now very close to their goal. The air in the passage through which they hurried was foul with the reeks of dust and hot rock and semi-molten metal: beneath their feet, and not too far beneath, the natural laws of geology were being twisted out of kilter by the colossal heat of the volcano's boiling core. He was trying to calculate how much further they must have to go when abruptly Grimya's ears pricked forward.

'Light!' she said hoarsely. 'I s-see light!'

In the tunnel's darkness Jasker had been concentrating on keeping his footing on the uneven floor, and the she-wolf had glimpsed the first tell-tale glow before it registered on his mind. Now, though, his eyes caught a faint, flickering reflection on the wall ahead.

They had arrived. Old memories lurched to life in Jasker's mind, and he felt a thick, clagging sensation at the back of his throat that wasn't caused by the stinking air. He wanted to swallow but couldn't induce saliva, and he halted, staring at the angry glow and touching one hand to the rock beside him.

The wall's surface was hot, and he could feel a slow, insistent pulse vibrating through it. The light ahead of them illuminated an acute curve in the tunnel, and just beyond the turn, he remembered, the roof had caved in to create a sloping wall of rubble whose only egress was a narrow gap at the top. Beyond that barrier was the tunnel's end, and their destination.

The sorcerer took four slow, steady breaths, trying to calm his uneven heartbeat. Then, with a brief glance to ensure that Grimya was following, he walked on to the curve in the tunnel.

Nothing had disturbed the fallen rocks. The hot light shone lividly through the gap at the top, throwing the

186

slope into deep shadow and making it hard to judge distances and angles for an ascent. Grimya eyed the rubble uncertainly.

'Can you climb it?' Jasker asked her.

She dipped her head. 'Y-*ess*. But . . . what is that light? And the noises? They are . . . not reassuring.'

Jasker had been trying to ignore the disturbing sounds that were impinging on him from beyond the barrier, but Grimya's question forced his awareness to focus. If he closed his eyes and allowed his imagination free rein – something which he wasn't overly anxious to do – he might easily have believed that the discordant stirrings were a kind of unearthly music, the sound of alien souls singing in a scale and a tongue which no human mind could hope to interpret. Strange harmonies that defied comprehension, impossible whisperings, shivering cadences without pitch or rhythm yet containing their own eldritch integrity. Logically, Jasker knew that the sounds were nothing more than the shifting of random air currents through huge honeycombs of rock; but logic couldn't combat the effect of those chilling echoes, nor could it banish the conviction which had gripped him on his first encounter with this awesome place: that what he was hearing was the vast, unhuman voice of Old Maia herself. Grimya, unhampered by the flaws of the human ear, must be hearing that voice in her marrow . . .

He spoke softly. 'It's nothing more than movement of air, Grimya. There's no need to be afraid.'

He wished he could have trusted his own reassurances as he began to climb the rubble slope. The fallen rock was hotter than the tunnel wall, so much so that he couldn't maintain each handhold for more than a few seconds. And the climb was trickier than he remembered; loose debris made the going treacherous, and progress was frustratingly slow. But he was almost half way to the top when, sensing something amiss, he looked back over his shoulder and saw that Grimya hadn't followed him. Instead, she had turned and was

187

facing back the way they had come. Her ears were pricked alertly forward, and her posture was tense.

'Grimya?' Nervous impatience gave Jasker's voice an edge; if the climb and what lay beyond it must be faced, he didn't want to prolong the ordeal any longer than necessary.

Grimya growled, an uneasy rumble in her throat, but she didn't look at him.

'Grimya! What is it?'

At last the she-wolf turned her head. Her eyes, lambent with reflected light, looked feral and suddenly alien, and she drew back her lips in a snarl.

'Something is wrr-*ong*!'

Cold, phantom teeth bit into Jasker's stomach. 'Wrong?'

'In my mind. A . . . disturbance. I . . . *hheard* it! But now it has gone.'

His first irrational fear that someone or something had been shadowing them through the maze of tunnels died, but was instantly replaced by another foreboding. *In my mind*, Grimya had said. Was it possible that the wolf had picked up some psychic scent of danger?'

Clinging to his precarious hold, and ignoring the fact that his palms were scorching, Jasker said urgently, 'Try to hear it again, Grimya. *Try!*'

'I . . . cannot . . .' She shook her head violently as though trying to free herself from some invisible assailant, and backed a pace, her body quivering. 'It will not c-*come* . . . no. Wait. It . . .' And suddenly she raised her gaze to him again and this time her eyes were filled with fear. 'It is Indigo! Jas-ker, it is her voice! She is trr-rying to call to me!'

Jasker felt as though the blood in his veins had been driven out by a flood of icy water. It wan't possible: not unless –

'Listen again!' His voice cracked on the last syllable, and it took a great effort to drag himself back into any semblance of cohesion. 'What is she saying? *What?*'

'I don't know! I c-c-cannot hear her clearly; it is as

if . . .' Words failed Grimya; she yipped in distress, then resorted desperately to her first warning. 'Something is *wrrrong*!'

The spell that had shackled Indigo to obsession and mania must have broken, shattering the barriers she had created between herself and Grimya and allowing their telepathic link to be re-established. But the link was flawed, and Grimya had been unable to interpret it with any coherence.

Revelation came as sharply as a knife in the gut. Only one thing could have released Indigo from Nemesis's thrall; and the stink of the air, the shifting light, the distant whisperings of Old Maia, were suddenly no more than a remote backdrop to the sick fear that clogged Jasker's mind.

'Grimya, listen to me.' He tried to keep his voice calm, aware of how easily the she-wolf's distress – and his own – could erupt into panic. 'We have very little time left. We *must* go on, and quickly. Follow me – and if you love Indigo, don't be afraid of what you're about to see!'

She gave him an agonised look that negated any further need for words; then her claws scrabbled on the rock as she bounded towards the slope.

They completed the climb in breathless, scrambling chaos. Jasker forced himself not to think beyond the next precarious handhold, but, like a black litany, he constantly and silently cursed his own complacency. He had known that time was running against them, yet he had paid no more than lip-service to the urgency of their cause. Now, awareness of every minute wasted, every second squandered, drove him like a predator on the heels of its victim, until, with a gasp that almost emptied his lungs, he dragged his body the last few feet to the top of the slope.

As his head came level with the opening, light flared into his face and a stench of hot sulphur blasted through the gap. Jasker didn't pause, but thrust his

189

body into the narrow egress, and forced himself through.

His senses were suddenly and violently assailed from all directions as the sounds, the heat, the smells, the taste of ancient, molten minerals on his tongue, combined in a single assault. Unconsciously, Jasker had shut his eyes tightly as he writhed into the opening; he didn't want to look, needed to preserve his last defence. But then he felt Grimya's lithe form beside him as she, too, wriggled through the gap: and he heard her shocked whimper as, unprepared, she saw what he had not yet dared to face.

To falter now would be the act of a coward. And with an abrupt surge of bitterness, Jasker knew that cowardice had stood for too long between himself and his duty.

*Ranaya, Mother of Magma, Lady of Flame, forgive my weakness and grant me Your blessing!* He uttered the litany with silent desperation, as a condemned man might shout wordlessly to the heavens when all earthly hope was gone.

He opened his eyes.

# Chapter XIV

On his map he had dubbed it simply 'the heart', for it defied all rational attempts at greater definition. When Ranaya had given birth to the eldest of her three daughters, in a titanic blast of fire and smoke and magma that shook the surrounding land to its roots, the power of that first eruption had ripped like a giant fist through millions of tons of rock as the forces pent under the Earth's crust sought an outlet. The mountain's core had melted in the onslaught, and as the shattering bolt of energy punched upwards to spectacular freedom it tore a huge, vertical shaft through the mountain, an aorta from the molten heart of Old Maia.

No artist in his worst nightmares could have imagined the vista that greeted Jasker and Grimya as they emerged from the tunnel and on to the network of twisted ledges that formed the walls of the vast fumarole. Above them those walls soared dizzyingly upwards, pitted with vaulted arches that had formed from the solidifying rock as the volcano settled back into quiescence. Mineral veins, fused by unimaginable heat and pressure, formed shimmering bridges between the vaults; pyroxenite and magnetite and hornblende in a vast spiderweb of sullenly shimmering colours that vibrated with the eldritch echoes, far louder here with no rubble to muffle them, of the random, burning air currents that hooted and soughed among their tracery.

Jasker's fingers were buried in Grimya's fur, clenching as he strove to drag himself back from the terror into which his flailing senses threatened to plunge him.

He could feel the vast, hot draughts that sighed up from unimaginable depths like the exhalations of a sleeping titan, and he fought back an insane, vertiginous impulse to launch himself out from the ledge and into those enormous winds, to be carried on their tide and soar among the glittering webs overhead. He sank to his knees, the prayers that he had silently rehearsed for this moment forgotten, and his free hand clutched at the hot rock wall as he battled, or so it seemed, with every muscle in his body to force himself to look down.

A huge, dim spectrum of light opened before him as his gaze turned at last into the depths of the shaft. Quiet, orange fire shot through with tongues of white heat and the grimmer, deeper reds of smouldering magma, rising from a place where solidity had no meaning, where heat and flame and the slow shift of molten elements were the only laws that governed. He was looking into the deepest core of Old Maia, through her bones and her sinew to her eternally beating heart. And in his own bones, as he gazed down into that unhuman place, Jasker heard the muted, thundering, roaring undertone that was the raw voice of his goddess.

The rock wall had burned his palm. He realised it when physical sensation sliced through the trance into which he had fallen, and he withdrew his hand and stared at it, for a moment not comprehending the significance of the reddened skin and the swelling blisters at the base of each finger. As comprehension returned he thought instantly of Grimya, and turned to see her beside him, trembling with pain, her paws braced and her jaws gaping wide as she panted desperately.

'Jas-ker . . .' Her voice cracked as she struggled to speak to him. 'I – c-cannot breathe. I am . . . afraid. And I . . . h . . . *hurt!*'

'Great Mother . . .' He whispered the words so that the echoes wouldn't come shouting discordantly back, and reached into his sack to pull out a hide cloak which he'd packed among his supplies. Folded beneath her, it would offer the she-wolf at least some measure of protection from the heat. And water . . . they must both drink, before the supply he carried evaporated away, and hastily he unslung the skin. He'd brought no dish, but was able to pour enough into Grimya's mouth to slake the worst of her thirst. When she was done, he held the skin to his own lips – then paused as with abrupt, intense clarity he realised that he had been about to commit a sacrilege.

He had reached a turning point. This was the moment for which he had been preparing for so long, when the diverse threads of his entire life intertwined at last into one single strand. His early years in Vesinum; his growth to manhood and the discovery that he had been called to a vocation; his marriage and the brief, sweet joy it had granted him; the grisly death of his wife; the inexorable rise of Charchad – all those disparate events had been leading him to this one place and this one chance.

He thought of Indigo, shackled to a yoke that he, in the unceasing torment of his latter years, understood all too well, and ready to pay any price to free herself from that torture. Could he do less than she had done? Jasker didn't need to answer his own question, for in this instant of revelation he believed he saw the purpose for which the supernal hand of Ranaya had drawn together the tangled skeins of their linked destinies.

Lady of Flame, Mother of Magma, Sister of the Burning Sun. To drink now would be to fail Her, for it would spurn the element to which his existence was dedicated. He must trust to Her power and Her strength, for if hope still existed, She would take it and shape it and give it life.

Grimya's eyes flashed gold with shock as Jasker threw his head back and laughed, a wild, joyous peal that the hot winds snatched and flung up into the shaft of the great fumarole to ring through the vaulted network. The sorcerer's hand clamped on the water-skin and he hurled it out over the depths, watching it turn and spin, a speck on the shuddering air, spiralling into a slow fall, sizzling as it dropped and water flashed into steam, into atoms, into nothing, as the goddess of the volcanoes took her sacrifice and transformed it into fire.

Jasker laughed again, and Grimya saw a shivering bolt of brilliance sear from him to hang above the giant shaft. Light exploded into the form of a glittering salamander that spat scarlet fire and shrilled a super-natural challenge to the singing, echoing vault. A second elemental sprang into being at its side, and a third; shimmering in the pulsing light from the fuma-role. A blue-white fire cord had appeared in the sorcerer's hands; he held it taut, his hands smouldering, then turned to the terrified she-wolf at his side.

'Grimya.' Jasker's voice was unnaturally calm, but she heard the undercurrent of pure madness cracking through the façade. His eyes seemed to stare through her, into another world. 'You must find Indigo again, and link your mind with hers. You must become the medium through which I channel my power, and between us we must give that power to her. Do you understand?'

A long, convulsive shudder racked Grimya's body. 'I . . . under-stand,' she whispered hoarsely.

'Help me, Grimya. When the power begins to rise, I may not be able to control it. Don't fail me, little wolf – find Indigo quickly, and pray that she can hear you!'

The cord in his hands flared lividly as he turned back to face the fumarole, and the salamanders dancing in the air above them gave voice to a wild cry. Ears flat to her head, sides heaving as she panted with a mixture of pain and fear, Grimya shut her eyes and struggled to direct her mind towards Indigo. Her consciousness fled the shaft, fled through the tunnels and over the rocks and slopes of Old Maia, searching, seeking; and suddenly she felt the quivering surge of another, distant consciousness flicker briefly across her path. She tensed, concentrating harder, and the sensation came again; stronger this time but distorted, as though it had lost the ability to focus.

*Indigo!* Her silent mental projection blended in her head with the deep humming emanating now from Jasker's throat as the sorcerer began his conjuration. Hot light flared against Grimya's eyelids and slowly the humming began to change to vibrating, long-drawn words.

*Indigo!* Grimya cried again. *Hear me! Hear me!*

Far below them, a deep and distant rumbling answered Jasker's insistently chanting voice. The salamanders started to sing a counterpoint, in an octave so high that even Grimya could barely hear it, and frantically the she-wolf strove to capture and hold the elusive thread of Indigo's awareness that trembled just beyond her reach.

*Indigo!* She flung every last fraction of energy her mind could muster into the call, her body writhing with the strain of effort. And suddenly a wall seemed to collapse before her, and a great surge of fear and rage and desperation smashed into her consciousness from outside, hurling her thoughts into chaos.

In the heart of Old Maia, thunder shouted with a huge, grim voice. Jasker stood with arms upraised, his body wreathed by blue-white brilliance as the fire cord blazed in his hands. Below him, the orange light was beginning to change to deep, furious crimson. The temperature was rising, wind blasting through the shaft and roaring among the shining network of ore-veins, drowning the sorcerer's litany as Ranaya's ancient energies started to surge within him.

And Grimya, unaware, her mind locked with and lost in the mind of Indigo, howled across the distance that separated them as in that moment she saw what her friend had come to and what she faced.

*We are too late!*

When they reached the end of the pass, Indigo could only stare in dull stupefaction at the great gates that barred any further progress. The line of captives shuffled to a halt but she instinctively tried to stumble on, her reflexes numbed to unquestioning acceptance of the seemingly endless walk; as the chains at her ankles tautened an overseer saw her, shouted an angry order to stop, and the thong of a whip cracked across her unprotected breast. She didn't feel the pain, only blinked like an animal waking slowly from hibernation and fell back into line.

How long had it taken them to shamble to this final rendezvous? Her sense of time was in ruins; it might have been minutes or hours since that last glimpse of Quinas's triumphant face in the torchlight, and recollections of all she had seen and heard since then were no more than a jumble of random images in her head. She remembered a wide road whose surface seemed to be covered with ashes which the prisoners' feet kicked up into filthy clouds at every step, and she had seen a sliding, oily turbulence which she knew must be the river as it ran alongside the track. Then there had been a terrible, thundering sound, growing louder and confusing her until it resolved into the roaring of the great smelting furnaces past which the road was taking them. She had felt the heat of their massive fires, and had seen the clouds of steam roiling from the cooling-pits to thicken and saturate the darkness. There had been men moving in the hot, smog-filled turmoil, ant-figures dwarfed by their surroundings; those who saw the condemned creatures passing by had quickly averted their gazes.

Then as the furnaces fell behind, the valley had begun to narrow until there were no more buildings, no more machines, no more men. The ash road petered out and they trudged instead through a steep pass that climbed into the surrounding mountains between two high peaks. Now, the only light was the cold green radiance that filled the sky overhead, creating shifting, unnatural shadows on the rocks. An overseer's yelled imprecation to hasten the prisoners on echoed bizarrely, making Indigo think for a moment that other voices were shouting down at them from the high cliffs. Then something huge and dark and angular loomed out of the night ahead, and they were at the end of their road.

The gates, thirty feet tall or more, were slung across the pass on massive hinges hammered into the rock. They had been in place no more than four years, but already their iron surfaces were blackened and corroded, the metal eaten by the polluted air. The bar that held them shut would have withstood almost any onslaught from the far side, and as the overseers strode forward to wrestle the bar from its supports Indigo's damaged mind realised for the first time what must lie beyond.

Very slowly she turned her head – she was just capable of exerting a little control over her muscles – and looked at the prisoner beside her. He was staring at the gates with what appeared to be a mixture of awe and resignation; his mouth gaped slackly and a slow drool of spittle ran unheeded down his chin. Beyond him one other man also gazed at the gates; the rest concentrated their attention fixedly on the ground beneath their feet. No one moved, no one uttered the smallest sound of fear or protest.

A metallic crash that rang deafeningly between the cliff walls heralded the sound of the bar falling. As the noise faded back towards silence the gates creaked ominously, and Indigo felt a responsive shiver strike at the base of her spine. She wasn't frightened – the drug had rendered her incapable of any such depth of feeling – but for a moment only, unease had moved like a worm within her.

A heavy clank, the echoes more subdued this time but still enough to startle her, and the gates began to swing back. A thin, vertical line of furious green brilliance appeared, widening rapidly until she was forced to look away; then she felt a tug on the shackles, and heard the slither of loose stone under the pressure of feet as the captives began to move towards the entrance and the grim valley beyond.

'Not you!'

A hand clamped on her upper arm, hauling her back as, too numb to reason or argue, Indigo would have shuffled in the wake of her fellow prisoners. She looked uncomprehendingly into the face of one of the guards, who had interposed himself between her and the men. He was smiling. She didn't understand.

'Eager, isn't she?' Another of the guards came towards her, unclipping a heavy pair of cutters which hung from the belt at his waist.

'She'll have her turn. But not with this miserable crew of gutworms.' The first overseer fingered his Charchad amulet, then gestured impatiently. 'Hurry up with those; I don't want to leave the gate open any longer than I have to.'

His companion crouched down, and metal snapped as he cut the chains that bound her to the other captives. She was pushed roughly out of the way, lost her balance and fell, grazing her elbow as she hit the ground. As she struggled dizzily to sit up, she saw the overseers herding the line of men towards the shimmering space between the gates. Cold radiance flooded over them, haloing them in bitter green light; one – the man to whom she had been next in line – hesitated for a moment, looking back, and she couldn't judge whether his expression was one of pity or pleading. Then the pass rang to the slamming of the gates behind the last man, and they were gone.

Echoes faded, and suddenly the night seemed unnervingly quiet. The mountains had muffled the racket of the mines to nothing more than a faint, dreamlike murmur in the far distance, and the pass was still. Indigo hadn't attempted to climb to her feet, but simply sat where she had fallen, staring at the overseers as they turned back from the gate.

There were only three of them. She hadn't registered that fact before, but now, as the information filtered through to her mind, she wondered why the prisoners had accepted their fate so stoically. Had they chosen to fight, their guards would have been hopelessly outnumbered; yet they had made not the smallest protest, but had walked into the Charchad vale like uncomprehending sheep to the slaughterer's blade. What would become of them now? she wondered. Would they die, swiftly, brutally, before the valley's sickness could worm its way into their bodies? Or would they wander in that green, nightmare world until the flesh rotted on their bones and they became what Chrysiva had been turning into before a crossbow bolt ended her suffering?

At the thought of Chrysiva, Indigo's mouth twitched. She couldn't help the reflex, nor the peculiar sensation that followed on its heels and made her want to speak. But the words she sought eluded her. Earlier, before the Charchad acolytes had forced her to drink their filthy concoction, she knew that she had had a dreadful revelation about the events that had led her to her present predicament, but now she couldn't rally her powers of reasoning sufficiently to call it back. She felt dread, yes; but it was meaningless, as though it belonged to someone else and she was experiencing it vicariously. Was it a dread of dying? She thought so, but couldn't remember why death should matter so much.

Boots scraped on rock, and the small sound made Indigo realise that she had almost fallen into a stupefied trance. Now her eyes refocused, and she saw one of the overseers standing over her. His companions lolled against the cliff wall, watching with jaded interest.

'Well, now.' A metal-tipped toe prodded her knee; she flinched, but the reflex was slow, 'Still in the land of limbo, eh?' He reached into his shirt and his hand closed round something in an inner pocket. Indigo couldn't see what it was.

'Any last requests before you leave us?'

One of the other men uttered a snort of laughter. 'She's young enough and handsome enough,' he called out. 'I'll give you a wager I know what she'd like before she goes!'

For a moment, speculation flickered in the overseer's eyes. He looked Indigo up and down, his gaze dwelling for some while on her breasts and groin. Then he shook his head.

'It isn't worth it. We've all got wives at home who know how to please us and how to be grateful. This one wouldn't be grateful, and where's the pleasure in that? Besides, she's a foreigner. Never know what you'll catch from foreigners. No: we'll follow Quinas's orders and leave it at that.' He weighed in a clenched fist the small object he'd taken from his pocket, then added: 'You know, I almost feel sorry for her.'

'Sorry?' Lazily, one of the other men pushed himself away from the cliff and sauntered towards them. 'Why, for the blessing of Charchad?'

'Like I said, she's a foreigner. Try to show a foreigner the Light and they won't see it; we know that.' He shrugged. 'Seems a waste, that's all.'

His companion was now standing at his side, and leaned to spit inches from Indigo. 'You're getting old and soft, Piaro. Heresy has to be punished, remember? That's what Charchad tells us.' He laid a hand on Piaro's arm, a comradely gesture, but it carried an uneasy hint. 'For your own sake and your family's, don't ever forget it.'

'I'm not about to.' Then Piaro shook off some private thought. 'The others will have been taken down by now. Let's get this over with, and we can all go back to Vesinum on the morning wagon and get some sleep.' He dropped to a crouch, and for the first time as his hand unclenched Indigo saw that he held a small metal phial. The stopper came out with a faint, unpleasant sound and Piaro nodded to his companion.

'You might have to hold her chin while she swallows it. Don't let it spill; it's the only one we've got.'

They expected her to try to fight, but she didn't, for she felt desperately thirsty and saw no reason not to take a drink if it was offered to her. She felt disappointed when, instead of water, she tasted acute sweetness that cloyed on her tongue; but it was better than nothing and she swallowed convulsively.

'What will that do?' Piaro's companion asked.

'It's an antidote to the first drug she was given, that's all I was told.' Piaro straightened and put the empty phial away. 'Quinas wants her to have all her wits about her when she goes through.'

'Why?'

'How should I know? Maybe it's a last lesson for her.' His hands were sweaty; he wiped them on his thighs then reached down again to take hold of one of Indigo's arms. 'Come on. No sense in hanging around needlessly, and the other side'll be waiting.'

The world lurched as Indigo was pulled to her feet, and she thought confusedly: *an antidote?* She was being hurried along between the two men, so fast that her feet could barely scrape the ground in any semblance of rhythm. The gates loomed before her, and the third man was moving to haul on the great handle. *Light.* Green and hideous and so brilliantly livid that she gasped and tried to shake her head in protest – she was being propelled towards it, and her body was beginning to tingle with the cramps of returning sensation.

A voice impinged on her mind: Piaro's. 'Wonder what happened to the dog?'

'What – dog?' His companion was panting with effort; paralysed by the cramps, Indigo had suddenly become a dead weight.

'I heard she had a dog with her. Before, in Vesinum.'

201

*Dog?* Indigo thought. And something climbed out of her confused memory to grasp hold of her . . .

A grunt. 'It won't last long around here. Fresh meat that'll be, for some lucky bastard.'

*Grimya* . . .

The second overseer uttered an imprecation as Indigo's paralysis abruptly released her and she started to writhe in her captors' grip. 'By the Light, the bitch is coming out of it already! Shift her, Piaro; she's trying to get away – ' and he swore again as Indigo screwed her head round and tried to bite him. It was a feeble effort and her teeth snapped on air; a second later a hand struck her face and she subsided.

'Leave it.' Piaro spoke sharply as the other man made to hit her again. 'Just get her through, and get those damned gates shut!'

She made one last effort to fight them as the fast-acting antidote surged through her, but it was too late and too ill co-ordinated. A wall of blistering radiance struck her full on as the gates reared high overhead – then she was hurled forward and felt herself falling and rolling down a steep slope, her breath snatched from her lungs in an inarticulate cry of protest as the gates of the Charchad vale slammed with a shuddering crash at her back.

For a while – she couldn't tell how long, and when she tried to count the passing seconds her judgement collapsed into confusion – Indigo lay utterly still. Her limbs were tingling in the wake of the cramp; instinct told her that control was returning swiftly to her body but she didn't dare test it. And as the effects of the drug were purged from muscles and sinews, so her mind, too, was clearing, and with it her memory.

For one moment she was consumed by a red-hot surge of fury at herself for the blind stupidity that had led her to this. But the feeling subsided as she realised that recrimination would achieve nothing, and in the wake of the anger came an extraordinary sense of calm. What was done was done: the slamming of the giant gates behind her had been final confirmation of the futility of regret, and she had a simple choice. She could abandon the last of her hopes, or she could face what lay before her and, while she still had life and strength, fight it with all the power she possessed.

Indigo didn't know whether she had the courage to practise the brave words she was preaching; but she tried to comfort herself with the thought that if her resolve failed – as she feared it would – it would make not one whit of difference to her fate. She had nothing to lose now. Quinas had dealt his last card.

If only she could have made contact with Grimya –

No. She mustn't consider that thought. In the Charchad vale she was beyond the reach of Grimya or Jasker; even had they been able to come to her they could do nothing to help her, and she would not be the instrument of their deaths as well as her own. She was alone now. And there was only one direction in which she could go.

Indigo raised her head from the uneven ground, and opened her eyes to stare into the valley of Charchad.

She was better prepared than she had been the first time, but still nothing could soften the surge of shock and sick horror as the huge, incandescent vista opened before her. From the ridge, her first vantage point, the vale had appalled her; but this . . . she felt as though her ribcage was tightening within her flesh, threatening to crush her heart as she stared down and down into the vast pit of light. Monstrous waves of radiance pulsed up from the depths to sear the valley sides and drench her in green fire. Her skin ached, as though she were bathing in a solution of some strange, thin acid; her eyes were streaming, and as she stared helplessly at the far wall of the cliff where shadows stalked and shifted and made grisly patterns, she realised how helplessly insignificant she was in this place, a tiny, lost speck against the titanic backdrop.

Abruptly the world seemed to lose all reality, and dizzy nausea gripped her. The scale was too vast, the power too great – she couldn't stand against this, *couldn't* –

A stray sound, closer to, impinged on the distant, chaotic roaring of Charchad, and stabbed through the thrall of panic that threatened to smash her resolve beyond repair. Indigo's body jerked spastically and she scrabbled to her hands and knees, crouching like a nervous animal as her watering eyes tried to refocus.

Dim, light-blasted shapes were moving on the slope below her. For a moment she thought they must be the men who had been forced through the Charchad gate, wandering aimlessly in the deadly radiance – but as she blinked water from her eyes and her vision momentarily cleared a little, she realised that she was wrong. There were only two figures, and there was nothing aimless in their movements as they climbed the slope towards her. Reason tried to deny it, but instinct told Indigo that she was their objective.

*The other side will be waiting.* Her stomach clenched and contracted fearfully. There could be no doubt now: these beings, whatever they were, were coming for *her*. She started to shiver, and an urge to scramble to her feet and run flashed through her mind – then died. Run? Where? Back to the iron gates, to hammer on them with her fists and demand that they be opened? No. She must face and meet what was stalking out of hell to claim her. There was nowhere else to turn.

A new surge of light heaved up from the maelstrom below, and a massive, distorted beam played across the valley slopes, haloing the approaching forms in a filthy rainbow of colour, so that for the first time Indigo could see them clearly.

The sentries on the ridge might once have been human: these walking nightmares had not. Though their semblances were a parody of the human form, the planes and angles of their bodies were hideously out of kilter, as though they owed their existence to some obscene otherworld from which they had manifested warped and incomplete. These were no earthly

204

servants of Charchad. These were the demoniac shades behind the mortal evil, first get of the monster she had been pledged to destroy – the true children of Aszareel.

Five more steps, six, seven . . . Indigo counted them like a child silently repeating a lesson, until, only a single pace from her, the beings halted. White, lidless eyes stared into her own, and when they reached out to take the chain that dangled from her shackled wrists, she didn't protest, but rose slowly to her feet, shifting her gaze from their distorted faces to look calmly at the insane landscape beyond. She had accepted the inevitable, and acceptance had its own narcotic power.

The demons didn't speak. Perhaps, Indigo thought with a distant fragment of her mind, they were voiceless. Metal jingled; she felt a slight tug on the chain, and with the dreamlike serenity of a sleepwalker she stepped between her captors and on to the long, steep path down into Charchad.

# Chapter XV

'Grimya! Grimya, open your eyes!' Jasker's voice rose above the growing thunder from the fumarole, and he shook the she-wolf's huddled, immobile form. 'Come back!'

Grimya whined like a frightened cub but made no other response. Jasker doubted if she could even hear him, for her mind was lost in the consuming horror of what she was witnessing in Indigo's mind. He had to break her trance – she was the link, the *only* link.

'Grimya!' Goaded by an upsurge of frustration and fear, the sorcerer's voice rose to a bellow that echoed raucously through the shaft. *'In Ranaya's name I command you, look at me!!'*

A great convulsion shuddered through Grimya, and her golden eyes snapped open. For an instant her stare locked with Jasker's, and a mad, distorted picture tumbled through his brain. Blinding green radiance, terrible shapes that had no place on the Earth, a treacherous slope that pitched down into hell – for a split second before the image vanished Jasker knew that he was seeing the valley of Charchad through Indigo's eyes.

The frustration redoubled, making him want to scream. Grimya's despair had intensified her telepathic power to such a pitch that for one moment she had broken through the blocks in his own mind, allowing his vision to merge with hers. But it had been fleeting, incomplete. He *had* to recapture it.

Wildly, Jasker looked over his shoulder at the fumarole and saw that the light had deepened to blood-crimson, pulsing now with the rhythm of a massive, slow heartbeat. Old Maia was alive: she was awakening from sleep, slowly, steadily, relentlessly; and she was waiting. But her patience was running out.

He clutched at the she-wolf's fur, his sweat-soaked face distorted with frantic energy. 'Grimya, listen to me! You *must* hold open the gateway in your mind! Link me with Indigo – let me through to her again!'

An awful cry came from the she-wolf's throat; neither a howl nor a whimper but with ugly echoes of both. '*I – c . . . c . . . an't!*'

'You must! *Try!*' He hugged her, but in her confusion and distress she struggled to pull away from him, and he was thrown back. It was no use: he couldn't reason with her – but neither could he stem the power now; the evocation had been performed and nothing could revoke it. With or without Grimya, he *must* re-forge the link!

Jasker turned, scrambling back over the ledge to crouch at the brink of the shaft, and burning air sawed in his lungs as frenziedly he shouted to the giddying vault.

*'Mother of Fire, aid me and lend me Your strength!'* Desperation made his voice crack; echoes shrieked back at him and the salamanders screamed.

And far down in the Earth, Old Maia exhaled a titanic breath.

A shattering concussion hit them like a wall as a blast of wind roared out of the fumarole. Jasker was snatched off his feet like a dry leaf, felt himself pitching backwards, saw Grimya flung, yelping, against the rubble at the tunnel entrance. Then tne blast was gone, leaving him sprawled face down on the ledge with his lungs emptied and the concussion's aftermath thundering in his ears.

Ranaya had heard him, and She had answered! Scorched skin puckered and cracked as Jasker dragged himself to his knees, but the pain meant nothing. *The Goddess had spoken.* Slowly he raised his head, then realised that the spectrum through which he viewed the world had shifted from its natural place. Red – orange – yellow – Grimya, only now staggering to her feet and shaking her head in confusion, was a crimson shadow with eyes like coals; the ledge had taken on the sullen, fiery hues of molten lava. And he . . . he turned his hands palms upward, shaking, staring at their darkly glowing outlines, through them to the golden veins that moved and pulsed within the flesh, pumping fire through the network of his body –

The power was inside him. He could feel it burgeoning, invading his being, and he wanted to scream and laugh and weep with the glorious terror of it. *This* was what he had desired yet feared to grasp, and it was fear which had led him to fail so many times in the past. But now the concept of failure was beyond him. The power was his and he knew how he must use it.

He rose, and his eyes were hot and proud and vengeful as he turned to focus on the crouching she-wolf.

'Grimya.' Jasker's voice shook as his body struggled to contain the forces unleashed within it. 'Will you help me in what I must do?'

Grimya gazed back at him. Her heart was pounding still from the shock of Old Maia's huge and emphatic utterance, but the thrall that had frozen her mind was broken.

*The man was a man no longer.* Jasker's form was etched by a glittering gold corona, and though within its frame his body and his face were unchanged, the she-wolf sensed the chaotic movements of something vast and beyond mortality, an energy that blazed and sang through the sorcerer's very essence. *Demon!* her mind shrieked. But Grimya knew the ways of demons, and she cast the warning aside even as it sprang into her brain. Not a demon. Not kin to Nemesis, not a thing of evil. She could give it no name, and her simple instinct wasn't enough to enable her to understand, but she knew what Jasker had become. And, knowing, she felt reverence and pity well within her like the surge of a calming tide.

'Jas-ker . . .' She spoke his name huskily, though she couldn't help but wonder if it meant anything to him now. Ignoring the rock's burning heat that singed the soft fur of her underbelly, she crawled towards him. Her ears were back, showing her uncertainty, but her tail twitched with a convulsive and involuntary expression of hope. 'S . . . *save* her. Save Indigo. I can . . . hhh-*elp* you. I can. I will!'

'Little sister.' He smiled down at her, and Grimya's body began to quiver uncontrollably. 'Ranaya will bless you for what you do tonight.' And, bending, he touched one hand to the top of the wolf's head.

Old Maia, first of Ranaya's daughters, sighed. And as the great, gentle breath set the vaulted skeins of ore humming and singing like an eldritch choir, Jasker turned towards the fumarole, his arms upraised and shining in their halo of unearthly brilliance. Though Grimya couldn't see his face, his expression was rapt, triumphant, the harsh lines of bitterness and hatred and deprivation falling away as, through eyes that were suddenly blurred with tears, he gazed up into the shaft towards the invisible night sky.

Ranaya, Mother of Fire, moved within the marrow of Jasker's bones as he began to speak.

The peripheral torches were being extinguished. Dawn was less than two hours away, and as the huge sirens boomed across the night to herald the end of the shift, the outermost beacons were hauled down from their gantries to gutter into darkness. In the mineshafts, men set down their tools and turned their faces from the mineral veins in silent thanksgiving; those who were tardy, or who had to tramp through the deeper galleries and tunnels to reach the outside world, would have to negotiate the uneven slopes to the ash roads and the gathering-point in darkness, and chance that a turned

209

ankle wouldn't lay them up and reduce their earnings to nothing for the next few days.

Quinas was to return to Vesinum on the morning wagon. Not a dignified means of travel for an overseer of his standing, but to summon a private carrier would take time, and his colleagues were anxious that he should be put into the care of a skilled physician as quickly as possible. They had urged him to try to sleep, but he had refused to heed them, savagely insisting that he intended to await Piaro's report. Piaro had finally returned, and had confirmed that all had gone according to plan. Now, Quinas was as comfortable as they had been able to make him in the tallyman's hut, and need not be woken until the wagon was at the mine gates.

Simein, who was a staunch devotee of Charchad and one of Quinas's most trusted coterie, had taken it upon himself to see that nothing should disturb his friend and mentor during the few hours before the wagon's departure. He stood a few paces from the hut door, watching the extinguishing of the first torches and fingering the haft of the whip that hung coiled at his belt. At his breast his Charchad amulet on its slim chain shone like a small, disembodied eye, brighter now that the lights of the mines were diminishing; the unnatural glow from the sacred stone cast odd, angular shadows across the planes of Simein's face, emphasising the pocked and flaking skin that was the first outward stigma of his enlightenment.

The mines were abnormally quiet. In the distance the smelting furnaces roared, but the more immediate racket of the diggers and hammers and trundling ore-carts seemed muted, as though the night had wrapped them in a vast, muffling shawl. The moon had set; the only shadows were those cast by the remaining torches on their towering poles. And, although he couldn't put a finger on the cause, Simein felt ill at ease.

He looked up, past the cluster of rough buildings, over the heaps of waste dug from the mountains and left to rot in the blistering sun, to where the highest of the mountains brooded in silent silhouette over the scene. Just for a moment he thought that he'd glimpsed a peculiar, sourceless shimmer above that menacing peak, but after a few seconds of watching, his eyes registered nothing and he turned away again. An after-image from the torches; no more. He had better things to do than indulge in idle fancy.

In the mountains, where men had burrowed through endless tons of rock to hew out a high-ceilinged gallery, something spoke with an unhuman voice that set the tunnels echoing. The last group of miners who had answered the siren and were heading for the open night and a day or two of freedom paused in their tracks, feeling the tremor that shook the old passages. Glances were exchanged, but no one spoke. Such shiftings in the deep rock were a natural hazard. There was nothing untoward in this new manifestation; it was simply the familiar shuddering of a sleeping giant, and the miners set the incident aside to concentrate on thoughts of home as they continued on their way.

Outside, there were sparks on the foul air in the pre-dawn gloom. No one heeded them; and no one paid any attention to the new rumbling that added an arhythmic undertone to the thundering pulse of the mines as the next shift trudged silently, dourly, to their labours.

Again and again she had tried to claw back some sense of reality, but in the howling maelstrom of the Charchad vale, reality had no meaning. Dragged by her demoniac captors, blinded by the vast radiation, buffeted by yelling, unnatural winds, Indigo fought to hold on to her sanity as the nightmare descent went on and on. Reason had collapsed under the onslaught of the twisted forces that battered the valley; form and perspective were warped beyond recognition, so that one moment she seemed to be forging through a

211

heaving sea of liquid glass, the next drifting helplessly above a void so vast that her struggling senses couldn't assimilate its dimensions. Terrible shapes moved all about her: winged things that flickered in the searing beams of light; bloated, misshapen horrors lurching like wraiths through the pulsating brilliance; something enormous and translucent, undulating . . . The crackling din from the depths of the vale beat constantly against her skull, and blending with it were human screams of torment, and other voices, not human, shrieking in fury or delight or sheer, unfettered madness.

Indigo knew that her senses couldn't withstand the bombardment for much longer before she, too, became as mad as the denizens of the monstrous vale. She battled to keep a hold on her mind, but the hold was slipping, threatening to spin out of control and pitch her into a state of gibbering insanity from which there would be no return. Her body had become a blazing star of pain, as if the nacreous radiation were eating into her flesh and slowly consuming her; ice and fire burned together in her veins and every breath she took was rasping, choking agony. The courage that she had sworn to cling to was in tatters now: hope was failing, resolve was failing –

The chain attached to her shackled wrists jerked suddenly taut. Indigo lurched off balance and fell to her knees as, like houndmasters dragging a cur to heel, her demon guards hauled her to a stop.

Glaring, livid light, more brilliant and more deadly even than the pulsing beams filling the valley, blasted her eyes, and she cried out in shock and terror as she realised that she was sprawling on the brink of a pit whose vertical walls plunged down into invisible, coruscating depths. Vertigo hit her in a violent wave; she felt unhuman hands grip her arms, thrusting her forward; felt the ground beneath her giving way to nothingness –

*As though the sun had fallen to earth – the heart of*

212

*Charchad, the final fortress, the domain of Aszareel –* Indigo screamed an inchoate protest as the world tilted wildly and her flailing body pitched into the pit.

She hit solid ground with an impact that cut off the scream and drove the air from her lungs in a rattling gasp. A lost, random shard of logic startled her into the realisation that she had fallen only a short distance; not enough to break a bone or even to stun her. And yet –

The rock on which she sprawled – if it was still rock, and had not been warped into something unimaginable – was breathing, moving under her, alive and hideously alien. And beneath the heaving stone surface, something yammered a dreadful parody of laughter.

The rock split. Through the blasting glare she saw the pit floor crack across inches from where she lay, and flung herself back as belching, roiling darkness erupted from the chasm and coalesced into a dense column that towered above her. Black radiance poured from the column, staining her skin, and Indigo stared up at it, appalled by the realisation that this was no simple manifestation but something sentient and aware.

Suddenly the column shivered, and a rent appeared in its pulsating heart. Indigo felt a violent tug on her consciousness, as though whatever monstrous intelligence lurked within the column was reaching out to her, taking hold of her mind and crushing her willpower to shards. Her gaze was compelled towards the widening rent; she tried to fight the compulsion and jerk her head aside, but it was too strong –

An eye, lidless, white-irised and shot with veins the colour of rotting meat, opened in the split and stared back at her. And a voice that had no tone and no timbre, but none the less was redolent with the corruption of pure evil, spoke emphatically in her head.

INDIGO.

Her stomach recoiled and contracted; she clapped a

hand to her mouth as a vomiting spasm threatened to overcome her.

I HAVE BEEN WAITING FOR YOU.

As the voice spoke she felt as though worms were writhing in her head; images of filth and decay clamoured within her, and fear surged in their wake. This was the ultimate monstrosity of Charchad, into whose hands Nemesis and her own blindness had led her. And this horror contained the corrupted, mutated soul of what had once been a human being.

Her mind was starting to give way. She could feel it, as she felt the slithering of the worms conjured by the voice: not a violent cracking and splitting and plunge into madness, but a slow ebbing of her sense of reality. Weaponless, defenceless, she stood alone before a living devourer. No power in the world could help her now; she was condemned. And in the face of that knowledge, her terror suddenly had no meaning.

Slowly, aware of the floor shifting, breathing under her feet, Indigo rose. Her hands clenched, as though unconsciously she grasped and tightened an invisible cord between them, and she met the stare of the pulsing, diseased eye before her.

'Aszareel.' Loathing, contempt, accusation: they were like a new drug in her veins, pushing her closer towards the brink of insanity. She welcomed the sensation, for it gave her delusions of strength.

The obscene voice rustled in her mind. YES. I AM ASZAREEL, AND YET MORE THAN ASZAREEL. YOU SOUGHT ME, AND YOU HAVE FOUND ME. WHAT WILL YOU DO NOW INDIGO?

She smiled, her eyes glassy and wild. 'I came to kill you.'

SO YOU DID. A sound like laughter rumbled somewhere beneath her. THEN KILL ME, IF YOU CAN. YOUR EFFORTS WILL BE INTERESTING TO OBSERVE, AND WHEN THEY ARE EXHAUSTED, I SHALL TAKE MY TURN.

*You cannot die*, the Earth Mother's emissary had told her. But a demon could inflict far worse than death . . . Indigo looked down at her hands In the black glow they seemed like the hands of a corpse, shadows without substance.

*Shadows without substance.* She looked up again.

'No. I came to destroy Aszareel, not a false shade.' Recklessly, goaded by the crazed fatalism that was rapidly replacing all semblance of reason, she took a step towards the black column. 'Save your disguises for your grovelling minions, demon, and show me your *true* form!'

It was madness, a challenge that she couldn't hope to follow through to its inevitable conclusion, but Indigo was beyond caring. If she was to die with her task uncompleted, she would at least die facing the demon in its entirety.

The eye flashed with colours that she couldn't identify, and Aszareel laughed again. Beneath Indigo, the ground moved with a convulsion that almost threw her off balance.

AH: SO YOU WOULD SEE ME AS I AM? NONE HAS HAD THAT PRIVILEGE FOR A LONG TIME. BUT FOR YOU, INDIGO, I WILL MAKE AN EXCEPTION. The black column pulsed, as though some enormous force were trying to burst from within it, and its fabric seemed to bulge outwards. The eye distorted, swelling until it was twice the size of Indigo's head, and a foul stench filled her nostrils.

SEE ME. The air began to thicken. SEE WHAT YOU IN YOUR ARROGANCE HAVE SET YOUR-SELF AGAINST. The dark radiance was intensifying, deepening; and the ghastly voice was no longer solely in her head but reverberating all around her, echoing between the pit's sheer walls.

The column began to disintegrate. It was like watching the melting of some foul tar under blistering heat: the towering pillar lost its shape, shuddering, then slowly collapsed in on itself, boiling, bubbling,

215

falling back from the disembodied eye which continued to glare through the miasma. But now Indigo could see that there was something else beyond the eye; a shape materialising in the murky darkness, generating a sickly light of its own. The outline was recognisably human: yet something about its dimensions was hideously wrong . . .

The form solidified and took on perspective. A small, wizened man sat cross-legged in a pool of black scum. He was hairless, and where his spare flesh should have been clothed in skin, white scales with the phosphorescent aura of a putrid fish shimmered and shifted over his body. His stomach was obscenely bloated, black veins crawling over its surface and throbbing, engorged with something that wasn't blood. One eye, set above a ragged cavity where his nose had rotted away, stared at Indigo, and in its gelatinous depths moved awesome, alien intelligence.

And Indigo could see beyond the decaying, mutated remains of what had once been a human being, into a dimension where huge, perverted tides shifted in gangrenous seas, where disease and necrosis and putrefaction crawled from primeval depths to twist and devour anything that had life. She felt the decayed, distorted fingers of unfettered evil touch her mind, felt her muscles and tendons locking into freezing paralysis –

Aszareel smiled. Red-flecked saliva dribbled from the corners of his mouth, and a toad's tongue, black, corrupt, unfurled between the yellowed stumps that were exposed as his lips drew back. The smile widened, further, further, gaping impossibly; the warped head began to split in half, and with a hiss of foul gases released from a long-dead corpse, the hinges of the demon's jaw cracked, and blinding green nacre poured from its throat.

INDIGO. Earthly dimensions couldn't contain the voice; it dinned in her ears, shattering her hold on the desperate defiance that had sustained her and beating

216

against her mind and body like a massive wave. SEE THE FACE OF CHARCHAD, INDIGO WHO WOULD SLAY DEMONS! LOOK ON THAT WHICH ASZAREEL HAS BECOME, AND KNOW THAT YOU WILL SHARE HIS FATE!

The wizened figure raised one hand. And its arm grew, stretching to an impossible length, defying nature and reason to reach out through the churning murk towards Indigo. She tried to throw herself back, but couldn't move: her feet wouldn't obey her, her body was held fast – the demon was reaching for her; its hand had swelled to nightmare proportions and she saw the fingers spreading, clawing, curling inward to grasp and enfold her. And its form was changing. The warped semblance of humanity was breaking down, and through the shell of what had been Aszareel erupted a vastness and a darkness that breached dimensions to burst into the world and surge towards her. She had no voice; she was strangling, her mind screaming but unable to break the paralysis as finally, irrevocably, her sanity began to shatter and the last barriers were smashed down –

In the heart of Old Maia, Grimya's self-control was suddenly drowned by a wave of terror. As Indigo's defences collapsed, the link between them had been violently re-established, and the she-wolf felt the flood of Aszareel's triumph, of her friend's horror and despair. She flung her head back, howling above the fury of the ancient volcano, and her howl metamorphosed into a frantic cry.

'Jas-ker! Jas-ker!'

The psychic shock-wave of her fear struck Jasker like a physical blow, and triggered a surge of energy that fountained from the depths of his being as the last psychic dam within him gave way. For one ecstatic moment he became omniscient – he was Grimya, he was Indigo, he was the boiling, raging heart of Old Maia – and he shrieked with the glorious madness of attainment as he felt the power rising, racing, blasting

217

through his veins as the first titanic upsurge came roaring out of the fumarole in a crescendo of light and noise.

'*Now!*' His crazed voice dinned in the she-wolf's ears. '*The power, Grimya! NOW!*'

A wall of energy smashed against Grimya's mind like the onslaught of a gigantic cataract. She howled again, every hair on her body standing erect, and felt the power enter her, fill her, blast through her as she became a living channel for the white-hot fury of the volcano. Her cry and Jasker's scream rose on the back of Old Maia's thundering voice –

And a new voice joined with theirs, shrieking through their linked minds as, in the pit that was the heart of the Charchad vale, Indigo caught fire.

# Chapter XVI

*INDIGO!!*

The voices of Jasker and Grimya, and the roar of
the volcano, exploded into her mind out of nowhere,
and she yelled as the first stunning wave of power hit
her. Brilliant red light erupted about her, tongues of
astral flame leaping in a blinding corona about her
frame, and through their savage flare she saw the
monstrous hand of Aszareel flinch back and heard the
demon's shocked cry.

*Power!* Raw, untameable, it surged through her
brain in a single, glorious instant of revelation. She
tried to scream Jasker's name, a paean of hope, of
vindication, of furious joy, but the primeval energy was
beyond control, and the cry ripped from her throat in
a wordless banshee-shriek that wrenched all the hatred
and rage and burgeoning madness from her mind in
one instant of pure ecstasy.

Aszareel howled. He flung his arms skyward, clawing
at the air as though he would pull the churning green
maelstrom of the vale down upon them, and Indigo
saw tongues of fire catch among the fingers that had
reached out to crush her. The demon's head jerked
backwards; a black, foetid gale stormed from his mouth
towards her and she laughed wildly as the torrent of
filth met the flames that blazed around her and flashed
into nothing. The power was increasing, burning
through the pit's miasma; she drew a great breath,
calling the enormous energies into her blood and her
bones, revelling in them –

*INDIGO!* The voice was both Jasker's and Grimya's,

borne on the inferno that filled Indigo's mind and her body. Through eyes that streamed with heat and pain and joy she saw the thing that was Aszareel coiling changing; saw it grow to five times her own height, rearing above her while the sick orb of the demon's eye turned first to yellow and then to green as deadly radiance began to emanate from it in massive, pulsating waves.

*Take the power, Indigo!* This time it was Grimya alone who howled in her mind, and her cry was all but eclipsed by a sound that broke through from the astral dimensions and into the physical world, a deafening bellow that shook the valley walls. *Take it, NOW!*

The fire that wreathed Indigo flared from crimson into blinding white. She felt the bolt coming, felt it erupting from the molten heart of Old Maia, the hammerblow as it smashed through Jasker, through Grimya, into her own body. She couldn't contain it: the energies were too great to withstand and she knew she was about to be torn apart –

*DON'T TRY TO HOLD IT, INDIGO! USE IT – USE IT!*

Lightning tore through the Charchad vale, splitting the foul radiance with a titanic crack. It struck the eye of Aszareel, and the demon screeched as its body burst into flames. It writhed, the putrescent skin blackening, crackling as physical fire leapt from its face to its arms to its obscene torso; and its screeching rose to an ear-splitting shriek as astral flames took hold of the cancer beyond its earthly form. Other screams melded with the demon's death-cries; unhuman voices howling in fear and protest and disbelief as, linked inextricably with their master, Aszareel's hellborn minions caught the backwash of fire and burned in their tracks, flapping things and crawling horrors and mockeries of men shrivelling in the onslaught of the flames that spanned dimensions to devour them. Indigo heard their grisly chorus, and fell to her knees, convulsions racking her as the echoes of the power flooded the Charchad vale.

She flung her head back, hurling the energies from her in a final spasm, and heard Aszareel screaming, felt him shrivelling, melting, dying, as his perverted soul collapsed into the last throes of disintegration –

Then a new voice boomed out of the night.

In the mines, where men sweated in the claustrophobic warren of shafts and tunnels, the ancient rocks shook and rumbled with echoes that had not been heard in the region for millennia. Thirty miners had but a few seconds' warning before the roof of the gallery where they toiled caved in to bury them under ten thousand tons of stone. By the tally-hut, where Quinas still slept away the time before the arrival of the morning wagon, the ground shuddered to a gigantic subterranean vibration that toppled one of the torch gantries, bringing its blazing beacon crashing down in an explosion of sparks. In the distance a scream cut through the pulsing air – then the southern sky lit up with orange fire, and seconds later the first roar of the awakening volcano drowned the racket of the mines with its primordial thunder.

Old Maia heaved, a giantess rousing after centuries of sleep. In her cone, magma rose in a blazing turmoil of unleashed energies as the eruption blasted a thousand-foot column of fire and ash and molten rock into the sky. And on the far side of the valley, the forges and lakes and slag-heaps of the smelting furnaces were lit by an answering explosion of fire, and a third, as the huge peaks that formed the triumvirate of Ranaya's Daughters answered their sister in awesome harmony.

In the Charchad vale, the deadly radiance that had been the demon's greatest weapon exploded in an instant of howling, blinding mayhem, and the sky turned black as the last shreds of Aszareel's burning essence were consumed. Indigo felt the power leaving her in an agonising jolt, and as the white corona flashed out of existence she sprawled on the floor of the pit, limbs flailing, body thrashing, lungs heaving as she fought to breathe, to live, to stop herself from following

221

Aszareel and his hell-horde into the mad vortex of destruction that had sucked them from the world like leaves in a gale. She felt the ground hump beneath her, heard the thunder of Old Maia and her sisters as fire ripped through the darkness. And in her battered, tormented mind, she heard the last word that Jasker, her friend, her saviour, servant of Ranaya, was ever to utter in the mortal world.

*RUN!!!*

Grimya sensed it coming, but her only physical fore-warnings were the sudden explosion of crimson light in the fumarole, and a sound that was, to her horrified mind, like the herald of the end of the world. The ledge on which they stood shook under the onslaught of the rising tide, and a hurricane wind howled through the shaft, hurling her off her feet. Struggling to regain her balance, the she-wolf felt a wave of heat hit her full on, and as her fur singed and her eyes streamed she saw Jasker, wreathed in fire, standing on the brink of the shaft. His arms were outspread as though he welcomed a long-lost lover; his hair was smouldering, his hands catching light as the fire-cord he held blazed into new brilliance, and beyond his mad, sparking silhouette the salamanders sang an eldritch song above the voice of Old Maia.

'RUN!!' The sorcerer's voice beat against Grimya's ears as the volcano thundered its final warning. 'RUN!!!'

His eyes were burning in their sockets as he stared down into the fumarole, beyond the Earth's crust, into Her molten heart. And as the wall of magma rose towards him, he saw a vision of the multitude of under-ground veins, the chasms and the tunnels that linked Old Maia to her sisters. And he heard the vast voice of Ranaya, Mother of these three avengers, nurturer and slayer and inspirer, roaring out of the Earth's core to speak his name and call him home.

Grimya, her instincts goaded into life by the

222

sorcerer's last wild cry, leaped for the tunnel mouth, scrabbling up the rubble slope to the narrow gap. At the top she paused – and as she looked back, the first blinding coruscation hurled Jasker's form into silhouette, and a pillar of solid fire blasted up through the fumarole. In the fire's heart was a gigantic face, harsh-planed and angular yet with a terrible, serene beauty. Burning hair streamed about it like flares from the sun, and the eyes were twin infernos. The blazing lips moved, and a voice seemed to reverberate through the ancient mountain, ringing in Grimya's mind with a power that made her whimper in terror and awe.

*YOU ARE THE DEAREST OF MY SONS.*

Jasker fell to his knees, arms outflung. His hair caught fire, blazing in a wild halo that almost rivalled the brilliance of the goddess. And for one stunning instant Grimya saw his form change into that of a golden dragon, body shimmering, great wings clashing like living flames, before a column of white-hot fire flashed from nowhere in the place where he stood, and he was engulfed.

Thunder bawled in the shaft, and the rubble under the she-wolf's paws shifted violently. From somewhere in the tunnel network came an answering rumble. Panic surged through Grimya; she couldn't assimilate what she had seen, nor drag her senses into any form of coherence. Instinct and instinct alone awoke muscle and sinew and nerve, and she twisted about as the debris beneath her shook again, flinging herself towards the gap. As she reached it, the fumarole seemed to swell and contract like a vast throat expelling breath – and in the wake of the towering fires, lava exploded out of Old Maia's heart.

With a strength she didn't know she possessed Grimya's hind legs powered her through the gap, and she leaped for the tunnel floor beyond. The ground beneath her heaved as she landed; she rolled, sprang up, and, ears flat to her head, tail flying behind her, streaked away as the first wave of boiling, churning magma began to sear its way through the rubble wall. She had no idea of her direction, no conscious memory of the route by which they had reached the fumarole, but intuition drove her onwards, upwards, the rising heat a deadly goad at her back as she sought a way – *any* way – to the outside world. A cataclysm of noise dinned in her ears, echoing through the tunnels and galleries; she glimpsed towering flames, rock collapsing into magma; she raced through blinding, choking smoke in which sparks danced like maddened fireflies, leaped hissing streams of molten metal, fled frantically through crevices bare seconds before their walls smashed together to cut her off. And at last there came a lessening of the heat, the taste of new air – fouled, but new air none the less; and though her lungs and throat were too seared for sound, she wanted to yelp and howl with relief as she realised that she had reached the first cave with its low slit of an exit.

She flung herself flat, writhing through the narrow gap – and emerged into mayhem.

High above her, the sky had turned to an insane sea of black and scarlet as fire belched from the cone of Old Maia. Rivers of lava were already beginning to pour down the volcano's upper slopes, spreading among the peaks like a network of blazing arteries. Colossal explosions ripped through the night, shock-waves shaking the mountains and churning the air into buffeting chaos as in the distance Old Maia's sisters gave an answer to her challenge.

Grimya sprawled on the slope, her sides heaving as she struggled to breathe. Her body was all but para-lysed with pain and exhaustion, and in her mind images clashed and whirled in an uncontrollable furore. *The fumarole, the heat, the incredible power; Jasker screaming in triumph as his body burned, the awesome face of Ranaya – and Indigo, plunging towards final madness as the demon of Charchad rose to slaughter her –*

Reason came back with stunning force, and Grimya

sprang to her feet. For a moment she stood rigid, head raised, striving to project her consciousness beyond the night's insanity.

*Indigo!* Her whole body quivered with the effort of the mental cry. *Indigo! Hear me! If you live, hear me!*

In her mind she saw only fire, and frantically she tried again.

A glimmering on the edge of the chaos in her head – a spark of life, human, moving, faintly aware of her but unable to reach out and help her forge the link –

'Indigo!' This time Grimya yelped aloud, though the sound was lost in the thunder of Ranaya's Daughters. Indigo was alive! Hope burst into the she-wolf's mind, eclipsing her exhaustion and terror – then there came a crack and rumble, and ten feet away the slope split, shattering the obsidian path. Glaring light erupted from the crack, and flames sprang into the night as lava forced its way from the crevasse. Grimya's eyes flared as she realised the extent of the danger that both she and Indigo were in. If they were to stand any chance of escaping from the inferno, she had to find her friend before time ran out and the valleys were engulfed.

She spun round, her claws scrabbling for purchase on the treacherous surface. The air was thickening by the moment, clouds of ash whirling into her face on the hot wind and the burning nightscape alien and perilous before her. Fear clutched at the she-wolf's heart, but she drove it back, knowing that she dared not waste another moment. Like a fleet shadow she sprang forward, and raced away into the churning darkness.

Indigo didn't want to get up. The foul dust of the pit floor was clogging her mouth and nostrils, and broken shards of rock stabbed painfully against her stomach and legs; the booming thunder was growing louder, and she could smell fire. But although she knew she should raise her head, every part of her battered mind and body protested the idea. She didn't want to open

225

her eyes and look; she wanted only to lie where she was, her face pressed to the ground, until the world went away or unconsciousness claimed her. And she didn't want to heed the tiny, faraway voice in her head that called her name with increasing urgency, pleading with her to *listen*, to *hear*.

Grimya's desperate attempts to make contact might have come too late if the valley floor hadn't heaved suddenly and violently under Indigo, flinging her sideways and shocking her out of her semi-conscious daze. Her hands flailed; instinctively she thrust outward to save herself – and came fully to her senses to find herself crouching in the pit, staring through billowing smoke and the tangles of her own hair at a circle of blackened ashes.

*Aszareel.* As the last traces of stupor vanished, Indigo remembered. The demon was dead. Jasker had succeeded: he had raised the ancient, dormant power of the Fire-Goddess, and channelled that power through her mind just as the last shards of her sanity were breaking down. With Aszareel had gone all the demons of the Charchad vale: and something else, something she couldn't yet recall –

A titanic rumble cut across the chaos of her thoughts, echoing deafeningly through the valley. Wildly, Indigo looked up, and the revelation hit her like a hammer-blow. Smoke, blotting out the sky – churning clouds of ashes and sparks raining down on the valley – the green radiance of Charchad had been destroyed, and in its place the night was lit by three vast columns of fire. The roar of a new explosion rocked her backwards, and for an instant she was bathed in crimson brilliance that lit up the entire scene – then the first wave of lava poured over the rim of the vale and came tumbling like an avalanche towards her.

Indigo leaped to her feet and ran. The pit wall loomed from the murk and she clawed her way up, ripping her clothes, gashing her leg, falling at last over the edge and scrambling upright again. Fireballs of

226

blazing magma were plummeting from the sky now; she saw one searing down at her, setting the filthy smoke alight, and hurled herself out of its path as it crashed to earth. Flaming shards hurtled in all directions and she screamed as one struck her arm; her sleeve caught fire and she beat the flames out as she ran, burning her hand and forearm. More fireballs glittered overhead, sparks leaped dazzlingly in the air, singeing her hair; to her left the river of lava was widening, increasing speed and veering in its course, and she swerved aside, taking a steeper route but one that would carry her away from the deadly flow. Hot ashes, almost ankle-deep in places, scorched her feet, and she could barely breathe; each time she inhaled, her throat and lungs filled with smoke. She pulled up the hem of her skirt to cover her mouth and nose, but it made little difference; choking, blinded, she neither knew nor cared where she was heading, too desperate to get clear of the smoke and ash to think beyond the next staggering step. Once, not far off, she thought she heard voices crying out, and she slithered to a halt on the steep incline, peering wildly about. But the smog was too dense for her to see anything; the booming echoes of the eruption drowned any further cries and she hadn't the breath to shout back into the murk. If there were any other living souls in the Charchad vale, she couldn't hope to search for them and survive, and she turned back to the slope, groping her way on and up.

Then suddenly there was a break in the rock above her. Not the path from which she had first looked down into the Charchad vale, not the place where the great iron gates barred any hope of exit, but a jagged gap between two of the lower mountain peaks, its edges thrown into harsh relief by the flaming sky. Gasping, Indigo flung herself towards it, and sprawled full-length on to the backbone of a sharp, narrow ridge. The impact knocked the last of the stinking air from her lungs and she retched, giddy with sickness. Dragging

227

herself to her knees, it was almost all she could do to raise her head and look down on the far side, to the smelting furnaces and the mines beyond.

The valleys were in chaos. Men were running from the furnaces and the cooling lakes, racing along the ash road in a desperate bid to reach the mine gates before they were overwhelmed. Some might reach safety, but most had no chance, for nine massive torrents of lava were converging on them from all sides, plunging out of the peaks and splitting into fifty tributaries that seared towards the valley floor to cut off all but a few escape routes. She saw a hurtling fireball smash down in the midst of a group of fleeing men; antlike figures spun away from the devastation, twisting and writhing as they burned; some flung themselves into the river, but the river, too, was burning as its polluted surface caught fire. Huts, machines and gantries were ablaze, colossal tongues of blue flame belched from adits as gases trapped in the rocks exploded. And, vast and grim against the sky, avatars of destruction, the three gigantic peaks of Ranaya's Daughters vomited fire and lava and thundered their fury into the night.

Her eyes streaming, Indigo dragged her gaze away from the horrors below her. Nothing could save the doomed men, and to follow them into the valley would be suicidal. There *had* to be another way out –

And suddenly, through the mayhem of confusion, a familiar voice broke into her mind.

*Indigo!*

Indigo shrieked, 'Grimya!', then choked as shock made her swallow a mouthful of the roiling smoke. For almost a minute she was doubled over; then as the worst of the spasm receded she looked wildly around, her heart pounding with renewed hope. Grimya was alive, and trying to find her –

*Grimya!* She concentrated furiously, pushing the mental call out with all the strength she could muster. *Grimya, I am here! I heed you!*

A deafening bawl from Old Maia shook the crags, and through it she heard the she-wolf's answering cry.

*East, Indigo! Go to the east! I will find you!*

Indigo needed no further urging. She climbed to her feet and turned, stumbling along the ridge to where a harsh but scaleable slope of scree and boulders led on to the neighbouring peak. Her legs ached savagely, her scorched hands and feet and face felt white-hot with pain and it seemed that all the air in the world had burned to ashes: but she scrambled and slithered over the scree to sounder rock beyond, and began to cross the mountain shoulder.

She was half way to the next ridge when a flare of light above made her look up. What she saw almost stopped her heart.

The second of Ranaya's daughters was, from here, a towering but distant menace beyond a chain of crags. Indigo had thought herself safe enough – but the forces unleashed by the eruption had shattered the volcano's southern face, and a cataract of molten magma had burst from its prison to flow down the mountainside, into the surrounding peaks, through gullies and chasms and over rocks, burning its way towards the valley floor. Three separate lava rivers were now blazing down the slopes where Indigo clung – and she was directly in their path.

She couldn't move. Terror rooted her feet and hands, and her mind was paralysed; she could only stare in dawning horror at the danger. She might outrun the first of the murderous streams, but would be trapped between it and the second. And if they converged, or if yet another tributary came cascading over the crags high above, then she would be overrun, to die shrieking in flames –

The rock beneath her shook to an enormous, rumbling vibration. Not thinking, not pausing to reason, Indigo started to run, zig-zagging, leaping from foothold to foothold in a desperate and futile bid to outrun the oncoming lava. She knew she couldn't do it; the slope was too steep, she was certain at any moment to miss her footing and pitch down the side of the mountain –

*Indigo! Wolf!*

Grimya was crying out in her mind, her voice wild and frantic. But Grimya couldn't help her; the lava was coming; she could feel its raging heat, feel the shuddering slope about to give way beneath her –

*Wolf, Indigo! WOLF!*

With a shock that almost hurled her off balance Indigo remembered, and realised what Grimya was trying to communicate. *Wolf.* The power, the shapeshifting power that she had learned so cruelly and so unexpectedly in the astral world of demons – but she couldn't do it, not here, not now; it was *impossible!* She hadn't the strength, her mind was in chaos; she had only seconds before death struck her down, and, terrified beyond all hope of control, she opened her mouth and screamed.

The scream metamorphosed into an ululating howl, and she felt the change as a massive jolt of energy that slammed from her subconscious and into her body. Her balance went; she reeled, stumbled, fell forward –

And was running, on four legs that jackknifed her over the rock, brindled head down, scarlet jaws gaping, hearing Grimya, her sister, her blood-kin, urging her on as she streaked, far faster than any human could have run, towards sanctuary.

# Chapter XVII

There was smoke and there was heat, and there was roaring fire that tore the darkness apart. She could barely breathe and her body was in agony, but still she ran, for she was no longer Indigo but *wolf*, animal, goaded by instincts that owed nothing to logic or thought, but which drove her on to the one goal of survival. Hideous stenches assailed her, vile tastes scorched her mouth, but still she raced on, until the world was a crimson whirlpool, battering her senses, endless, meaningless, insane.

Grimya found her less than a minute after she collapsed on the shoulder of a ridge that led up into the easternmost peaks. Though the rock was hot, and shook sometimes to the distant quaking of the volcanoes, the lava flows had not reached these slopes; here, they were safe enough.

Indigo sprawled on the ground, legs splayed out, head twisted to one side. Her eyes were glazed with exhaustion and her tongue lolled as she struggled to breathe; her singed fur was matted with a thick coating of ash, and when Grimya tried to rouse her she could barely lift her muzzle a few inches.

They couldn't stay on the ridge. Dawn was close; the sun wouldn't be able to break through the dense canopy of ash and smoke that now hung over the entire valley, but once it rose, the heat – near intolerable now – would kill any living thing that had not found shelter. Grimya had seen a cave a short way off; it was small but would serve them, and she forced Indigo to rise, nipping at her shoulders and the nape of her neck until she staggered to her feet. Her thoughts were incoherent; though close to exhaustion herself, Grimya knew that alone her friend would not have survived for much longer, and silently thanked the Earth Mother that she had been able to find her in time.

The sky was shot with rivers of blood-red fire as the two wolves limped slowly and painfully along the ridge and on to a path, inches deep in ash, that wound along the mountain face. The cave was little more than a slit in the rock above the track, but the ash had not penetrated inside it, and it was relatively clear of smoke. Grimya coaxed Indigo through and watched anxiously as she slumped down on the floor.

'We c-can rest s . . . *safely*.' She spoke aloud, not certain that her friend would hear her telepathic voice. 'Until we are . . . recovered.'

Indigo shuddered. For a moment her form seemed to hover bizarrely between the animal and the human – then she sighed, and Grimya found herself gazing down at the huddled body of a girl who, scorched, singed, tattered and exhausted beyond recall, had already fallen into a coma-like sleep.

The she-wolf looked back at the cave entrance. Sparks still danced in the air outside, and she padded to the opening, staring out into the insane night. The thunder, she thought, seemed less now, and the fury of the eruptions was ebbing, as if Ranaya's Daughters were almost done with their wrath. She shuddered, trying not to remember the things she had seen tonight, the fear and the horror and the pain. She, too, should sleep; but before she rested she wanted to look for one last time at the deadly vale in which Indigo had so nearly perished, and at the ruins of the evil power which Jasker had given his life to destroy.

She felt a howl rising in her, making her flanks and her shoulders quiver. And though her lungs barely had the strength left to draw breath, she raised her muzzle to the sky and sang her night-cry to the invisible stars.

It was her own requiem for Jasker, and though she knew it was inadequate, it gave her a little comfort.

The howl died to a faint whine, and Grimya licked her muzzle. A stray eddy of smoke assailed her eyes; she blinked it away, then turned her head to gaze across the sea of peaks to the last high ridge that marked the boundaries of the Charchad vale.

There was no vale. Instead, there was a jagged gap where one huge crag had split apart. And beyond the crag's shattered remains, glowing now not with the green nacre of radiation but with the deeper, hotter reds and golds of fire, the valley of Charchad and all the horrors it contained lay buried beneath incalculable tons of stone and slowly cooling magma.

Jasker was walking towards her. His figure was wreathed in warm, dim light like the glow of a hearth fire, and he seemed to tread not on solid ground but on a haze of smoke that eddied about his feet.

Indigo sat up. Her body felt light and a little unreal; she was aware of an aching thirst, but beyond that her only sensation was one of extraordinary peace. It was still dark – the only light came from Jasker's aura – and she held out a hand towards the sorcerer.

'Jasker? I thought . . .' But she couldn't finish, for she didn't know what it was she needed to say to him.

He smiled, then his lips moved as though he were replying to her, but she heard no sound. And his eyes, she realised, weren't the eyes of a mortal man, but quiet, unfocused pools of orange-gold.

She knew then what Jasker's fate had been, but she didn't want to acknowledge it and couldn't bring herself to ask the question that would confirm it beyond all doubt. Jasker smiled again – and his countenance began to alter. The grey-white hair darkened to black, the gaunt face softened, becoming younger and suddenly heart-rendingly familiar, until Fenran, her own love, looked back at her from the halo of light.

233

Only the blank, golden eyes remained unchanged: and then Jasker's voice spoke quietly, warmly in her mind.

*'I am with my Lady now.'*

The halo began to fade. It died away, like embers slowly cooling, until the face that was both Jasker and Fenran merged with soft shadows and was gone.

'Fenran . . . ?' Indigo whispered. 'Jasker . . . ?'

Only echoes answered her. The darkness was complete and she felt bereft. Then a voice at her back spoke her name, and, heart quickening with irrational hope, she turned.

A tall, graceful figure stood behind her, clearly visible even in the velvet blackness. Indigo looked at the stern and beautiful face, at the flowing hair the colour of warm earth, into the milky eyes that gazed unblinkingly back with an unhuman blend of detachment and compassion, and remembered Carn Caille and the bright being who had come to her in the aftermath of battle; and a forest glade where snow fell with silent intensity and her true quest had begun.

She said, and the words were both a challenge and a plea: 'The demon is dead.'

The Earth Mother's emissary, her mentor, her judge, did not reply, and fear clutched at Indigo's heart.

'We slew it.' Her voice rose sharply, shrilly. 'We destroyed it. It is *dead!*' The fear threatened to swell into panic. 'Isn't it . . . ?'

A sad smile touched the entity's lips. 'Yes, Indigo: it is dead. This dream is over now, and it is time for a new dream to begin.'

Indigo bowed her head as a confusion of emotions welled within her. Relief, sorrow, bitterness – and, presiding over them all, a weariness that made her soul ache. The emissary looked down at the tangled crown of her hair, and said: 'You have learned a great deal, child, and you are stronger now. Try to take comfort from that, for it will lighten your burden in the times to come.'

Indigo felt tears start to trickle down her cheeks, and

wiped them away. She would *not* weep – but she had to loose the tight, hard knot of pain inside her, had to give her emotions some expression. She looked up and said miserably, 'I thought . . . I saw Fenran. I hoped . . .' But the words wouldn't come, for she knew the hope was unfounded.

The bright being's voice was gentle. 'With each victory you gain, Fenran's torment is a little lessened, for the forces that bind him are weakened. Keep hold of that, Indigo, and have faith.'

Indigo lowered her gaze again. She knew she should take comfort from the emissary's words, but it was hard; so hard.

The being said: 'Wake now, child. It is time to move on.'

'I – ' Then she stilled her tongue as she realised that there was only darkness where the bright entity had stood. The darkness shivered, shimmered – and she opened her eyes to find herself confronted by dim, sulphurous daylight filtering in through the entrance to the cave.

*Indigo!* Something warm and mammalian moved quickly beside her, and Indigo looked up into Grimya's amber-gold eyes. Tears started again and she flung her arms around the she-wolf's neck, hugging her, unable to speak for some minutes until at last the suffocating intensity of her emotions eased a little, and she sat back.

Grimya nuzzled her face. *You have slept for a very long time*, she said concernedly. *I think that we both slept, for I remember many strange things happening, but I believe they must have been dreams.*

'How – ' Indigo's throat was swollen and arid, and her voice caught on the word: she tried again. 'How long has it been?'

*I do not know. The thunder stopped a long time ago – many days, I think – and the fire-rocks and the ashes are no longer falling. But the sun has not yet driven away the clouds.*

235

Indigo could remember little of those last, mad hours. The memory would come, she knew, but not yet; and she was glad of that small respite.

'Aszareel – ' she said. 'He is dead, Grimya.'

*I know.* The she-wolf licked her own muzzle, as she so often did when she was disturbed or confused. *The . . . bright one told me so.*

'Bright one?'

*The one who came to us in the forest of my homeland, and who granted me my boon. I saw that one again, in my dream.*

So the emissary had not forgotten Grimya . . . and suddenly Indigo felt the resurgence of an old bitterness as she recalled that long-ago meeting. A boon, Grimya said. What manner of boon could it be to face an endless future under the shadow of her quest, unageing, unchanging, destined to wander the world until the seven evils she had released were finally expunged? The she-wolf had no crime to expiate, and no lost love to strive to regain. Yet she had left her home and everything she knew to share Indigo's burden: and it had brought her to this . . .

Grimya's quiet mental voice intruded on her unhappy thoughts, and she realised that the she-wolf had read what was in her mind.

*Do you think my answer would be different now, if I were offered my boon again? It would not. I am your friend, Indigo, and where you go, I shall go too.*

'You shame me, Grimya. Your faith is greater than mine.'

*It is not. Simpler, perhaps, for the ways of humans often seem to me like a tree with tangled branches. But not greater. You know that. In your heart, you know it.*

Did she? Indigo wondered. She thought of Fenran – *with each victory you gain, his torment is a little lessened*, the emissary had said – and realised that Grimya was right. She *did* have faith. And perhaps, as the she-wolf believed, faith was enough . . .

Slowly, Indigo rose to her feet, and walked unsteadily towards the cave entrance and the smog-filled day beyond. Her body had been battered to the limits of endurance, yet all she felt was a dull aching. She thirsted, but the thirst was bearable, though by now both she and Grimya should be dead for want of water. Immortality, it seemed, had its ironic compensations . . .

She reached the entrance, and stepped out on to the mountain slope. They were near the summit of a high peak, and through the sulphurous clouds she could see the range stretching away on all sides. Blackened with ash, empty, silent, the crags loomed through the eerie light like visions from a nightmare. There was no sound from the mines, and no green glow to stain the sky with its cancerous radiance. Only a faint glimmering in the distance, a flicker of orange-red fires as veined rivers of still molten magma moved slowly across the devastated valleys.

How many had died in that inferno? The fire-goddess's vengeance had made no distinction between the guilty and the innocent; though a great evil had been banished from the world, the cost of the victory was savage. And Indigo knew that the shades of those victims would walk in her dreams for a long time to come.

She heard the soft sound of Grimya's paws on the rock, and looked down to see the she-wolf standing beside her.

*It had to be*, Grimya said, and her eyes were filled with sorrow. *Without it, the demon's sway could not have been broken, and the sickness and the suffering would have gone on and on.*

'I know.' Indigo remembered Chrysiva, and the torments that that innocent girl had undergone while waiting for death to claim her. But in her present mood, it was hard to take comfort from the thought that there would be no more victims like her.

*I think that Jasker understood*, said Grimya. *He knew*

*what the goddess's vengeance would mean. But he knew, too, that there was no other way to save his land and his people.* She blinked. *I think he must have loved them very much.*

Tears started into Indigo's eyes, blurring the dismal vista before her. Yes; Jasker *had* understood: he had known what the sacrifice must be, and for the sake of his goddess, and for those whose lives were being torn apart by the horror that dwelt in the Charchad vale, he had been ready to become a part of that sacrifice.

She said softly: 'Will you tell me of Jasker, Grimya? Will you tell me how he died?'

*I will tell you. But – not yet. I do not think I could find the words yet.*

'No. Not yet.' Indigo wiped her eyes, and for a few moments gazed at the churning sky. High above, a dim smear of paler colour showed among the ash-clouds, and she realised that it was the sun, still lost behind the dense canopy but slowly, surely, dispelling the murk and the darkness to bring light back to the land. And again she heard the words that the sorcerer, who had proved such a true and steadfast friend, had spoken in her mind, in her dream.

*I am with my Lady now . . .*

She wished she could have mourned him in the proper way, with music and a lament to speed his soul on its last journey. But her harp, together with all her worldly possessions – save the crossbow and knife, which Quinas's henchmen had taken from her – lay buried beneath a hell of rubble and lava in the ruins of Jasker's cave. The thought made her want to cry again. To grieve for the harp was shameful when there were so many greater losses to be borne; but it had been very precious to her, for it was the gift of Cushmagar, the blind bard who was both her tutor and mentor, and the only link she had left with the home she had lost.

Indigo sighed, and dropped her gaze from the faraway smear of the sun to look down the slope to

238

where faint shadows were beginning to touch the rocks. And what she saw there made her heart contract and miss a painful beat.

*Her harp.* It stood unmarred, unblemished, on the ash-choked path, and the strings shimmered with the faintest of vibrations, as though she had but moments ago set it down. Indigo stared at it, certain that it must be a mirage, a wishful delusion conjured from her tired mind. But the harp's image didn't fade or waver – and suddenly she was scrambling down the slope, and, reaching the path, fell to her knees beside the harp, heedless of the ash which rose in sluggish clouds around her. For a terrible moment she dared not reach out to touch the precious instrument, desperately afraid that she would find only empty air and the echoes of an illusion: but then her hand moved convulsively, almost against her will, and she felt the smoothness of polished wood beneath her fingers.

The harp was real. The strings gave off a sweet, melancholy sound when she touched them, and as the echoes of the chord rang softly among the mountains she knew that this small miracle was a sign and a tribute from the Earth Mother's emissary, a symbol of hope in a place that had known only desolation.

As the harp's last notes died away, Grimya's anxious face appeared above her, peering into the gloom.

'In-digo?' the she-wolf called aloud.

Indigo couldn't answer her. She was hunched over, the harp cradled in her arms and her tears falling on the polished wood and the shining strings as she wept, for Jasker, for Chrysiva, for so many others whose names and faces she had never known. Grimya watched her with anguished pity, but quieted the instinct to run to her and try to bring her comfort. For a little while, she knew, Indigo needed to assuage her grief alone. The she-wolf whined softly, then withdrew into the cave and lay down with her muzzle on her front paws, gazing out with unfocused eyes and trying not to think on all that was past and gone.

At last, Indigo raised her head and knew that the storm within her was over. Her tears were drying, and though her throat and lungs were stifled and her heart felt drained, she was strangely tranquil. As she rose to her feet, gathering the harp carefully in her arms, she thought that perhaps, like the ravaged land around her, she too had been cleansed; and that in the wake of pain there might be peace, of a kind.

She looked up to the cave, and at her soft mental call Grimya appeared and ran down the slope to her. The she-wolf pressed her head against Indigo's thigh, not speaking, conveying with her touch a feeling she could not express in words.

The dim shadows were growing longer; behind the canopy of cloud the sun was beginning to slip towards the western horizon. Indigo put a hand to her breast, feeling the familiar shape of the lodestone in its pouch, and recalled the words of the Earth Mother's emissary. *This dream is over now, and it is time for a new dream to begin* . . .

She drew out the pouch, and laid the little pebble on her upturned palm. Tiny, vividly luminescent in the gloomy daylight, the fleck of gold shimmered at the stone's heart and pointed eastward. Along the track and over the final ridge; away from the mountains and the devastation and the unmarked graves of so many souls, towards the distant sea and another quest.

How long would it be this time? she asked herself. How many more years of wandering and searching, before a new evil cast its shadow on another land and she must again face the consequence of her own foolish, reckless deed?

Even the Earth Mother, in Her wisdom, didn't know the answer to such a question. Indigo sighed, and shivered as though casting off a shadow of her own. Then she looked down at Grimya. The she-wolf's golden eyes met hers, and Grimya said softly, in her mind, *There is no reason to linger. Better that we should go on our way, and leave this place to its healing.*

*Yes.* Indigo, too, communicated in silence, not wanting to sully the quiet that had descended, and turned to look down for the last time on the ravaged landscape below. Ash clouds still drifted across the wasted vista, and the glowing veins of lava, arteries carrying the life-blood from the now quiescent hearts of Old Maia and her sisters, moved slowly and seemingly without purpose through the valleys that had once shuddered to the racket of human toil.

A victory? Perhaps. But the victor's crown was a bitter one, and there would be no glory in her dreams.

Indigo whispered, so softly that not even Grimya heard her, 'Farewell, Jasker. May you find the peace that was denied to you while you lived.' Then she shouldered her harp and, with the wolf pacing beside her, turned away from the desolated land and began to walk slowly, wearily, along the gently rising track towards the first, distant glimmer of the eastern stars.

The ash that still fell steadily, silently from the sky filled their footprints like sand trickling implacably into an hourglass. Within minutes there was no trace of any living soul having passed that way, save for one last sign that all but the most vigilant observer might easily have missed. And gradually the soft, dark, implacable rain was burying even this tiny artefact, as though granting it, finally, its own eternal and lonely grave.

A crudely fashioned pewter brooch . . .

**THE INITIATE**
*Book 1 of the Time Master Trilogy*
Louise Cooper

The Seven Gods of Order had ruled unchallenged for an aeon, served by the Adepts of the Circle in their bleak Northern stronghold. But for Tarod – the most enigmatic and formidable sorcerer in the Circle's ranks – a darker affinity had begun to call. Threatening his beliefs, even his sanity, it rose unbidden from beyond Time; an ancient and deadly adversary that could plunge the world into madness and chaos – and whose power rivalled that even of the Gods themselves. But though Tarod's mind and heart were pledged to Order, his soul was another matter . . .

**THE OUTCAST**
*Book 2 of the Time Master Trilogy*
Louise Cooper

Denounced by his fellow Adepts as a demon, betrayed even by those he loved, Tarod had unleashed a power that twisted the fabric of time. It seemed that nothing could break through the barrier he had created until Cyllan and Drachea – victims of the Warp – stumbled unwittingly into his castle. The terrible choice Tarod has to make as a result has far-reaching consequences . . .

**THE MASTER**
*Book 3 of the Time Master Trilogy*
Louise Cooper

Tarod had won his freedom – and lost the soul stone, key to his sorcerous power. Cyllan, the woman he loved, had been taken from him in a supernatural storm. With a price on both their heads, Tarod had to find her before the Circle did. Only then could he hope to fulfil his self-imposed pledge to confront the gods themselves – for they alone could destroy the stone and the evil that dwelt in it. If touched by the evil in the stone, Tarod would be forced to face the truth of his own heritage, triggering a titanic conflict of occult forces, and setting him on the ultimate quest for vengeance . . .

# THE DARWATH TRILOGY
Barbara Hambly

Book 1

## The Time of the Dark

For several nights Gil had found herself dreaming of an impossible city where alien horrors swarmed from underground lairs of darkness. She had dreamed also of the wizard Ingold Inglorion. Then the same wizard crossed the Void to seek sanctuary for the last Prince of Dar and revealed himself to a young drifter, Rudy. But one of the monstrous, evil Dark followed in his wake and in attempting to help Ingold, Gil and Rudy were drawn back into the nightmare world of the Dark. There they had to remain – unless they could solve the mystery of the Dark. Then, before they could realise their fate, the Dark struck!

Book 2

## The Walls of Air

In the shelter of the great Keep of Renwath eight thousand people shelter from the Dark. The only hope for the besieged is to seek help from the hidden city of Quo. Ingold and Rudy set out to cross two thousand miles of desert. Beyond it they have to penetrate the walls of illusion that separate Quo from the world.

Book 3

## The Armies of Daylight

The survivors of the once-great Realm of Darwath shelter, squabble and struggle for power. Meanwhile the monstrous Dark threaten their great Keep. Is there a reason for the re-awakening of the Dark? The final volume of *The Darwath Trilogy* builds to a shattering and unexpected climax.

**DRAGONSBANE**
Barbara Hambly

It was said to be impossible to slay a dragon. But Lord John Aversin had earned himself the name of Dragonsbane once in his life and had become the subject of ballad and legend. Fired by the romance of his tale, young Gareth travelled far and wide across the Winterlands from the King's court to persuade the hero to rid the Deep of Ylferdun of the great Black Dragon, Morkeleb, oldest and mightiest of the dragon race. But Morkeleb was not the greatest danger that awaited John Aversin and his witch-woman. Just as Morkeleb posed the hardest test of skill and courage for the Dragonsbane, so Jenny Waynest would find her powers pitted against an adversary as deadly as the Black Dragon, and infinitely more evil.

'This is literary alchemy of a high order, and it confirms Hambly's place as one of the best new fantasists.'

*Locus*

'. . . a writer of unusual proficiency.'

*SF Chronicle*

'*Dragonsbane* is an enjoyable fantasy. Barbara Hambly takes a familiar opening, with witches and heroes and dragons, and gives the story unusual twists and vivid, believable characters. A good read.'

*Everywoman*

'. . . an excellent, beautifully written and thrilling story, and one of the most enjoyable I've read in a long time.'

*Johannesburg Star*

**THE SILENT TOWER**
Barbara Hambly

Another thrilling fantasy from best-selling author Barbara
Hambly.

Antryg Windrose, dog wizard student of the Dark Mage, has
been imprisoned in the Silent Tower for seven long, lonely
years.

But have his powers been limited by the spell-bound tower
walls, or is the life-sapping Void and the appearance of
appalling abominations throughout the countryside somehow
connected to him?

And is he linked to the strange occurrences noticed by young
computer programmer Joanna Sheraton at the San Serano
Aerospace Complex? Joanna has the feeling that someone is
following her, but who, and why? At a party thrown by her
boyfriend Gary, she is soon to find out: whirled through the
Void into an unfamiliar world, accompanied by a mad wizard
and a beautiful sasenna swordsman, she is about to discover
depths within herself she had never dreamed of, and horrors
worse than any nightmare . . .

**THE SILICON MAGE**
Barbara Hambly

Concluding the nail-biting story that began with THE SILENT TOWER . . .

The corrupt Archmage Suraklin has taken over the body, brain and computer of Gary, Joanna's ex-boyfriend. Through magic he is already able to leech the life-force out of two worlds to fuel his lust for eternal power and life: now he will harness science as well.

His main adversary, Antryg Windrose, dog-wizard and Joanna's lover, is imprisoned again in the Silent Tower, his mind and body broken. Joanna is on her own. Somewhere, in this strange medieval world full of superstition and corruption, where worship of the Dead God, lord of entropy, has emerged once more, where human sacrifice is practised and abominations abound, Suraklin has hidden his computer. Armed with a backpack full of software, a worm disc and a .38, Joanna Sheraton is all that stands between the Dark Mage and the death of the universe.

**THE LADIES OF MANDRIGYN**
Barbara Hambly

Determined to win back their men from the cruel fate assigned to them by the evil Wizard King Altiokis, the Ladies of Mandrigyn set out to hire the services of the mercenary leader Sun Wolf to destroy him. But not even a fortune of gold would tempt Sun Wolf to be fool enough to match his sword against the wizard's sorcery . . .

Sun Wolf awoke, some hours later, on a ship bound for far-flung Mandrigyn, lethal anzid coursing through his veins. The ladies held the only antidote, and Sun Wolf found himself an unwilling participant in a very dangerous game . . .

Following *The Ladies of Mandrigyn*
a new story featuring Sun Wolf and Star Hawk:

**THE WITCHES OF WENSHAR**
Barbara Hambly

Every female of the ancient House of Wenshar was possessed of a powerful magic: but their line is long dead, their desert city in ruins.

Yet there is still magic in Wenshar: the lady Kaletha has some gift for it and will train her neophytes to free their own talents. After his adventures in Mandrigyn, Sun Wolf, the mercenary, seeks her out to train his own newfound magic.

Shortly after his arrival a series of horrific supernatural killings turns Wenshar into a snakepit of superstitious fear and loathing. Sun Wolf finds himself in deadly danger as vicious tongues begin to wag . . .